VARIETY I
INTERPLA

This exciting collection of science fiction gems offers an eclectic blend of ideas from great authors like Poul Anderson, Fritz Leiber, Clifford D. Simak, and others.

"Snowball" and "The Ship Sails At Midnight" offer intriguing drama and allegories of the human condition.

Explore a forbidden part of the jungles of Venus in "No Dark Gallows For Me." Or steal fine works of art with "The Star-Sent Knaves." Both are amazing tales packed with stimulating interplanetary adventure.

We also bring you provocative romance between human and artificial intelligence in "Weep No More, My Robot." And there is subtle hair-raising horror in "The Beast of Boredom."

Engage your mind with this incredible fusion of stories about fantastic futures.

TABLE OF CONTENTS

SCIENCE FICTION GEMS

Volume 8

KEITH LAUMER
and others

Compiled and Edited by
GREGORY LUCE

ARMCHAIR FICTION
PO Box 4369, Medford, Oregon 97504

The original text of these stories first appeared in *Amazing Stories, Fantastic Adventures, If, Infinity Science Fiction, Science Fiction Stories, and Worlds of Tomorrow.*

For more information about Armchair Books and products, visit our website at…

www.armchairfiction.com

Or email us at…

armchairfiction@yahoo.com

Snowball

By POUL ANDERSON

Simon's new source of power promised a new era for Mankind. But what happens to world economy when anyone can manufacture it in the kitchen oven? Here's one answer!

IT DID not come out of some government laboratory employing a thousand bright young technicians whose lives had been checked back to the crib; it was the work of one man and one woman. This is not the reversal of history you might think, for the truth is that all the really basic advances have been made by one or a few men, from the first to steal fire out of a volcano to $E=mc^2$. Later, the bright young technicians get hold of It, and we have transoceanic airplanes and nuclear bombs; but the idea is always born in loneliness.

Simon Arch was thirty-two years old. He came from upstate Massachusetts, the son of a small-town doctor and his childhood and adolescence were normal enough aside from tinkering with mathematics and explosive mixtures. In spite of shyness and an overly large vocabulary, he was popular, especially since he was a good basketball player. After high school, he spent a couple of tedious years in the tail-end of World War II clerking for the Army, somehow never getting overseas; weak eyes may have had something to do with that. In his spare time he read a great deal, and after the war he entered M.I.T. with a major in physics. Everybody and his dog was studying physics then, but Arch was better than average, and went on through a series of graduate assistantships to a Ph.D. He married one of his students and patented an electronic valve. Its value was limited to certain special applications, but the royalties provided a small independent income and he realized his ambition: to work for himself.

He and Elizabeth built a house in Westfield, which lies some fifty miles north of Boston and has a small college—otherwise it is only a shopping center for the local farmers. The house had a walled garden and a separate laboratory building. Equipment for the lab was expensive enough to make the Arches postpone children; indeed, after its requirements were met, they had little enough to live on, but they made sarcastic remarks about the installment-buying rat race and kept out of it. Besides, they had hopes for their latest project: there might be real money in that.

Colin Culquhoun, professor of physics at Westfield, was Arch's closest friend—a huge, red-haired, boisterous man with radical opinions on politics which were always good for an argument. Arch, tall and slim and dark, with horn-rimmed glasses over black eyes and a boyishly smooth face, labeled himself a reactionary.

"Dielectrics, eh?" rumbled Culquhoun one sunny May afternoon. "So that's your latest kick, laddie. What about it?"

"I have some ideas on the theory of dielectric polarization," said Arch. "It's still not too well understood, you know."

"Yeh?" Culquhoun turned as Elizabeth brought in a tray of dewed glasses. "Thank'ee kindly." One hairy hand engulfed a goblet and he drank noisily. "Ahhhh! Your taste in beer is as good as your taste in politics is moldy. Go on."

Arch looked at the floor. "Maybe I shouldn't," he said, feeling his old nervousness rise within him. "You see, I'm operating purely on a hunch. I've got the math pretty well whipped into shape, but it all rests on an unproven postulate about the nature of the electric field. I've tried to fit it in with both relativity and quantum mechanics and—well, like I said, it's all just a notion of mine which demands experimental proof before I can even think about publishing."

"What sort of proof?"

"It's this way. By far the best dielectric found to date is a mixture of barium and strontium titanates. Under optimum conditions, the dielectric constant goes up to 11,600, though the loss rate is still pretty high. There's a partial explanation for this on the basis of crystal theory, the dipole moment increases under an electric field…Well, you know all that. My notion involves an assumption about the nature of the crystalline ionic bond; I threw in a correction for relativistic and quantum effects which *looks* kosher but really hasn't much evidence to back it up. So—uh—"

Elizabeth sat down and crossed trim legs. She was a tall and rather spectacular blonde, her features so regular as to look almost cold till you got to know her. "Our idea suggests it should be possible to fit a crystalline system into an organic grid in such a way that a material can be made with just about any desired values of dielectricity and resistivity," she said. "Constants up in the millions if you want. Physically and chemically stable. The problem is to find the conditions which will produce such an unorthodox linkage. We've been cooking batches of stuff for weeks now."

Culquhoun lifted shaggy brows. "Any luck?"

"Not so far," she laughed. "All we've gotten is smelly, sticky messes. The structure we're after just doesn't want to form. We're trying different catalysts now, but it's mostly cut and try; neither of us is enough of a chemist to predict what'll work."

"Come along and see," offered Arch.

They went through the garden and into the long one-room building beyond. Culquhoun looked at the instruments with a certain wistfulness; he had trouble getting money to keep up any kind of lab. But the heart of the place was merely a second-hand gas stove, converted by haywiring into an airtight, closely regulated oven. It was hot in the room. Elizabeth pointed to a stack of molds covered with a pitchy tar. "Our failures," she said. "Maybe we could patent the formula for glue. It certainly sticks tightly enough."

Arch checked the gauges. "Got a while to go yet," he said. "The catalyst this time is powdered ferric oxide—plain rust to you. The materials include aluminum oxide, synthetic rubber, and some barium and titanium compounds. I must admit that part of it is cheap."

They wandered back toward the house. "What'll you do with the material if it does come out?" asked Culquhoun.

"Oh—it'd make damn good condensers," said Arch. "Insulation, too. There ought to be a lot of money in it. Really, though, the theory interests me more. Care to see it?"

Culquhoun nodded, and Arch pawed through the papers on his desk. The top was littered with his stamp collection, but an unerring instinct seemed to guide his hand to the desired papers. He handed over an untidy manuscript consisting chiefly of mathematical symbols. "But don't bother with it now," he said. "I blew us to a new Bach the other day—St. Matthew Passion."

Culquhoun's eyes lit up, and for a while the house was filled with a serene strength which this century had forgotten. "Mon, mon," whispered the professor at last. "What he could have done with the bagpipes!"

"Barbarian," said Elizabeth.

AS IT happened, that one test batch was successful. Arch took a slab of darkly shining material from the lab oven and sawed it up for tests. It met them all. Heat and cold had little effect, even on the electric properties. Ordinary chemicals did not react. The dielectric constant was over a million, and the charge was held without appreciable leakage.

"Why doesn't it arc over?" wondered Elizabeth.

"Electric field's entirely inside the slab," said Arch absently. "You need a solid conductor, like a wire, between the poles to discharge it. The breakdown voltage is so high that you might as well forget about it." He lifted a piece about ten inches square and two inches thick. "You could charge this hunk up with enough juice to run our house for a couple of years, I imagine; of course, it'd be D.C., so you'd have to drain it through a small A.C. generator. The material itself costs, oh, I'd guess fifty cents, a dollar maybe if you include labor." He hesitated. "You know, it occurs to me we've just killed the wet-cell battery."

"Good riddance," said Elizabeth. "The first thing you do, my boy, is make a replacement for that so-called battery in our car. I'm tired of having the clunk die in the middle of traffic."

"Okay," said Arch mildly. "Then we see about patents. But— honey don't you think this deserves a small celebration of sorts?"

Arch spent a few days drawing up specifications and methods of manufacture. By giving the subject a little thought; he discovered that production could be fantastically cheap and easy. If you knew just what was needed, you had only to mix together a few chemicals obtainable in any drugstore, bake them in your oven for several hours, and saw the resulting chunk into pieces of suitable size. By adding resistances and inductances, which could be made if necessary from junkyard wire, you could bleed off the charge at any desired rate.

Culquhoun's oldest son Robert dropped over to find Arch tinkering with his rickety '48 Chevrolet. "Dad says you've got a new kind of battery," he remarked.

"Uh…Yes. I'll make him one if he wants. All we'll need to charge it is a rectifier and a voltmeter. Need a regulator for the discharge, of course." Arch lifted out his old battery and laid it on the grass.

"I've got a better idea, sir," said the boy. "I'd like to buy a big piece of the stuff from you."

"Whatever for?" asked Arch.

"Run my hot rod off it," said Bob from the lofty eminence of sixteen years. "Shouldn't be too hard, should it? Rip out the engine; use the big condenser to turn a D.C. motor—it'd be a lot cheaper than gas, and no plugged fuel lines either."

"You know," said Arch, "I never thought of that."

He lifted the ridiculously small object which was his new current source and placed it inside the hood. He had had to add two pieces of strap iron to hold it in position. "Why a regular motor?" he mused. "If you have D.C. coming out at a controlled rate, you could use it to turn your main drive shaft by a very simple and cheap arrangement."

"Oh, sure," said Robert scornfully. "That's what I meant. Any backyard mechanic could fix that up—if he didn't electrocute himself first. But how about it, Dr. Arch? How much would you want for a piece like that?"

"I haven't the time," said the physicist. "Tell you what, though, I'll give you a copy of the specs and you can make your own. There's nothing to it, if your mother will let you have the oven for a day. Cost you maybe five dollars for materials."

"Sell it for twenty-five," said Bob dreamily. "Look, Dr. Arch, would you like to go into business with me? I'll pay you whatever royalty seems right."

"I'm going to Boston with just that in mind," said Arch, fumbling with the cables. "However, go ahead. Consider yourself a licensee. I want ten percent of the selling price, and I'll trust a Scotch Yankee like you to make me a million."

He had no business sense. It would have saved him much grief if he had.

THE countryside looked clean, full of hope and springtime. Now and then a chrome-plated monster of an automobile whipped past Arch's sedately chugging antique. He observed them with a certain contempt, an engineer's eye for the Goldbergian inefficiency of a mechanism which turned this rod to push that cam to rotate such and such a gear, and needed a cooling system to throwaway most of the energy generated. Bob Culquhoun, he reflected, had a saner outlook. Not only was electricity cheaper in the first place, but the wasted power would be minimal and the "prime mover"—the capacitor itself—simply would not wear out.

Automobiles could be sold for perhaps five hundred dollars and built to last, not to run up repair bills till the owner was driven to buying a new model. The world's waning resources of petroleum could go into something useful: generating power at central stations, forming a base for organic syntheses; they would stretch out for centuries more. Coal could really come back into its own.

Hm...wait. There was no reason why you couldn't power every type of vehicle with capacitors. Aircraft could stay aloft a month at a time if desired—a year if nothing wore out; ships could be five years at sea. You wouldn't need those thousands of miles of power line littering the countryside and wasting the energy they carried; you could charge small capacitors for home use right at the station and deliver them to the consumer's doorstep at a fraction of the present cost.

Come to think of it, there was a lot of remote power, in waterfalls for instance, unused now because the distance over which lines would have to be strung was too great. Not any longer! And the sunlight pouring from this cloudless sky—to dilute to run a machine of any size. But you could focus a lot of it on a generator whose output voltage was jacked up, and charge capacitors with thousands of kilowatt-hours each. Generators everywhere could be made a lot smaller, because they wouldn't have to handle peak loads but only meet average demand.

This thing is bigger than I realized, he thought with a tingle of excitement. *My God, in a year I may be a millionaire!*

He got into Boston, only losing his way twice, which is a good record for anyone, and found the office of Addison, his patent attorney. It didn't take him long to be admitted.

The dusty little man riffled through the pages. "It looks all right," he said unemotionally. Nothing ever seemed to excite him. "For a change, this seems to be something which can be patented, even under our ridiculous laws. Not the law of nature you've discovered, of course, but the process—" He peered up, sharply. "Is there any alternative process?"

"Not that I know of," said Arch. "On the basis of theory, I'm inclined to doubt it."

"Very well, very well. I'll see about putting it through. Hm— you say it's quite simple and cheap? Better keep your mouth shut for a while, till the application has been approved. Otherwise everybody will start making it, and you'll have a devil of a time collecting your royalties. A patent is only a license to sue, you know, and you can't sue fifty million bathtub chemists."

"Oh," said Arch, taken aback. "I—well, I've sold some of my neighbors, of course. One of the local teen-agers is going to make a car powered by—"

Addison groaned. "You would! Can't you shoot the boy?"

"I don't want to. For a person his age, he's quite inoffensive."

"Oh, well, you didn't want a hundred million dollars anyway, did you? I'll try to rush this for you, that may help."

Arch went out again, some of the elation taken from him. But what the hell, he reflected. If he could collect on only one percent of all the capacitite which was going to be manufactured, he'd still have an unreasonable amount of money. And he wanted to publish as soon as possible in all events: he had the normal human desire for prestige.

He got a hamburger and coffee at a diner and went home. Nothing happened for a month except an interview in the local paper. Bob finished his hot rod and drove it all over town. The boy was a little disappointed at the quietness of the machine, but the interest it attracted was compensation. He began to build another: twenty-five dollars for an old chassis, another twenty-five or so for materials, tack on a hundred for labor and profits—the clunk might not look like much, but it would run for a year without fuel worries and would never need much repair or replacement. He also discovered, more or less clandestinely, that such a car would go up to 200 miles an hour on the straightaway. After selling it, he realized he could command a much bigger price, and set happily to work on another.

The physics journal to which Arch sent his manuscript was interested enough to rush printing. Between the time he submitted it and the time it came out some five weeks later, he found himself in lively correspondence with the editor.

"College will soon be letting out all over the country," said Elizabeth. "Stand by to repel boarders!"

"Mmmm...yes, I suppose so." Arch added up the cost of entertaining a rush of colleagues, but his worry was only a flicker across a somewhat bashful glow of pride. After all—he had done a big thing. His polarization theory cut a deep swath into what mystery remained about the atom. There might even be a Nobel Prize in it.

It was on the day of publication that his phone rang. He looked up from his stamps, swore, and lifted it. "Hello?"

"Dr. Arch?" The voice was smooth and cultivated, just a trace of upper-class New York accent. "How do you do, sir. My name is Gilmer, Linton Gilmer, and I represent several important corporations in the electricity field." He named them, and Arch barely suppressed a whistle. "Dr. Bowyer of the *Journal* staff mentioned your work to one of his friends in an industrial research lab. He was quite excited, and you can understand that we are too. I believe I have some good news for you, if I may come to see you'"

"Eh? Oh, sure!" Visions whirled across Arch's eyes. Money! It represented a hi-fi set, a three-penny black, an automatic dishwasher, a reliable car, a new oscilloscope, a son and heir. "Come on up, b-by all means—Yes, right away if you like—Okay, I—I'll be seeing you—" He set the receiver down with a shaking hand and bawled: "Betty! Company coming!"

"Oh, damn!" said his wife, sticking a grease-smudged face in the door. She had been tinkering with the lab oven. "And the house in such a mess! So am I, for that matter. Hold the fort when he comes, darling." She still didn't know who "he" was, but whirled off in a cloud of profanity.

Arch thought about putting on a decent suit and decided to hell with it. Let them come to him and accept him as he was; he had the whip hand, for once in his life. He contented himself with setting out beer and clearing the littered coffee table.

Linton Gilmer was a big man, with a smooth well-massaged face, wavy gray hair, and large soft hands. His presence seemed to fill the room, hardly leaving space for anyone else.

"Very pleased to meet you, Dr. Arch...brilliant achievement...We borrowed proof sheets from the *Journal* and made tests for ourselves, of course. I'm sure you don't mind. Thank you." He seemed just a trifle shocked at being offered beer rather than Johnny Walker Black at four o'clock in the afternoon, but accepted gracefully. Arch felt excessively gauche.

"What did you want to s-see me about?" asked the physicist.

"Oh, well, sir, let's get acquainted first," said Gilmer heartily. "No rush. No hurry. I envy you scientific fellows. The unending quest, thrill of discovery, yes, science was my first love, but I'm afraid I sort of got steered off into the business administration end. I know you scientists don't think much of us poor fellows behind the desks, you should hear how our boys gripe when we set the appropriations for their projects, but somebody has to do that, ha." Gilmer made a bridge of plump fingers. "I do think, though, Dr. Arch, that this hostility is coming to an end. We're both part of the team, you know; scientist and businessman both work inside our free enterprise system to serve the American public. And more and more scientists are coming to recognize this."

Arch shifted uneasily in his chair. He couldn't think of any response. But it was simple to converse with Gilmer: you just sat back, let him flow, and mumbled in the pauses.

Some data began to emerge: "—we didn't want to trouble you with a dozen visitors, so it was agreed that I would represent the combine to, ah, sound you out, if I may so phrase it."

Arch felt the stir of resentment which patronizing affability always evoked in him. He tried to be courteous: "Excuse me, but isn't that sort of thing against the antitrust laws?"

"Oh, no!" Gilmer laughed. "Quite the opposite, I assure you. If one company tried to corner this product, or if all of them went together to drive the price up, that would be illegal, of course. But we all believe in healthy competition, and only want information at the moment. Negotiations can come later."

"Okay," said Arch. "I suppose you know I've already applied for a patent."

"Oh, yes, of course. Very shrewd of you. I like to deal with a good businessman. I think you're more broadminded than some of your colleagues, and can better understand the idea of teamwork between business and science." Gilmer looked out the French doors to the building in the rear. "Is that your laboratory? I admire a man who can struggle against odds. You have faith, and deserve to be rewarded for it. How would you like to work with some real money behind you?"

Arch paused. "You mean, take a job on somebody's staff?"

"Not as a lab flunky," said Gilmer quickly. "You'd have a free hand. American business recognizes ability. You'd plan your own projects, and head them yourself. My own company is prepared to offer you twenty thousand a year to start."

Arch sat without moving.

"After taxes," said Gilmer.

"How about this—capacitite, I call it?"

"Naturally, development and marketing would be in the hands of the Company, or of several companies," said Gilmer. "You wouldn't want to waste your time on account books. You'd get proper payment for the assignment, of course—"

Elizabeth entered, looking stunning. Gilmer rose with elaborate courtesy, and the discussion veered to trivialities for a while.

Then the girl lit a cigarette and watched them through a haze of smoke. "Your time is valuable, Mr. Gilmer," she said abruptly. "Why don't you make an offer and we'll talk about that?"

"Oh, no hurry, Mrs. Arch. I was hoping you would be my guests tonight—"

"No, thanks. With all due regard for you, I don't want to be put under a moral obligation before business is discussed."

Gilmer chuckled amiably and repeated the idea he had broached.

"I like Westfield," said Elizabeth. "I don't like New York. It isn't fit for human consumption."

"Oh, I quite agree," said Gilmer. "Once a year I have to break loose—cabin up in Maine, hunting, fishing, back to Nature—you really must come up sometime soon. Your objection can be answered easily enough. We could set up a laboratory for you here, if you really insist. You see, we're prepared to be very generous."

Arch shook his head. "No," he said harshly. "No, thanks. I like being independent."

Gilmer raised his brows. "I understand that. But after all, the only difference would be—"

Arch grinned. He was enjoying himself now. On a dark day some years ago, he had tried to raise a bank loan and had failed for lack of collateral and credit rating and his refusal to subject any friend to co-signing. Ever since, he had indulged daydreams about having finance come crawling to him. The reality was intoxicating.

"No," he repeated. "That's all I want to say about it, too. The income from capacitite will be quite enough for us. If you want to discuss a license to manufacture, go ahead."

"Hrm! As you wish." Gilmer smoothed the coldness out of his voice. "Maybe you'll change your mind later. If so, feel free to call on me anytime. Now, for an assignment of rights, I think a sum of fifty thousand dollars could be arranged—"

Elizabeth drooped lids over startlingly blue eyes. "As an initial payment, perhaps," she said gently. "But think what a royalty of, say, ten cents a pound would add up to even in a year."

"Oh, yes, that would be negotiated too," said Gilmer. "However, you realize manufacture could not start immediately, and would in any case be on a smaller scale than you perhaps think."

"Eh?" Arch sat bolt upright. "What do you mean? Why, this stuff is going to revolutionize not only electronics, but all power— dammit, everything!"

"Dr. Arch," said Gilmer regretfully, "you must not have considered the matter of capital investment. Do you know how many billions of dollars are sunk in generators, dams, lines, motors—?"

"Gasoline," said Elizabeth. "We've thought of that angle too."

"We *can't* throw all that in the discard!" went on Gilmer earnestly. He seemed more human, all at once. "It may take twenty years to recover the investment in, say, a local transmission network. The company would go broke overnight if that investment were suddenly made valueless. Millions of people would be thrown out of work. Millions more would lose their savings in stocks and bonds—"

"I always said stocks were a mug's game," interrupted Arch. "If the two or three shares owned by the widow and orphan you're leading up to go blooey, it won't break her. For years, now, I've had ads dinning the wonders of the present economic system into my ears. One of its main features, I'm told, is progress. All right, here's a chance to leap a hundred years ahead. Let's see you take it."

Gilmer's pink cheeks reddened. "I'm afraid you still don't understand," he replied. "We have a responsibility. The world is watching us. Just imagine what those British Socialists would say if—"

"If you're against socialism," said Elizabeth with a laugh, "why not start at home? Public schools and federal highways, for instance. I fail to see where personal liberty is necessarily tied to any particular method of distribution."

Gilmer seemed, for a moment to lose his temper. "This is no place for radicals," he said thickly. "We've all got to have faith and put our shoulders to the wheel. We—" He paused. Swallowed, and smiled rather stiffly. "Excuse me I didn't mean to get worked up. There are a lot of stories about wonderful new inventions which the greedy corporations have bought up and hidden away. They simply are not true. All I'm after is a gradual introduction of this material."

"I know those wonderful inventions are pure rumor," said Arch. "But I also know that just about everything I buy is made to wear out so I'll have to buy some more. It's cheaper, yes, but I'd rather pay twice as much to start with and have my purchase last ten times as long. Why can't I buy a decent kitchen knife? There's not one that keeps its edge. My wife finally made eyes at the butcher and got one of his old knives; it lasts.

"A big thing like capacitite represents a chance to change our whole philosophy into something more rational. That's what I'm after—not just money. There needn't be any unemployment. Capacitite makes increased production possible, so why not—well, why not drop the work day to four hours for the same wages? Then you can employ twice as many people."

"It is not your or my place to make carping criticisms," retorted Gilmer. "Fundamental changes aren't as easy as you think. Dr. Arch, I'm sorry to say that unless you'll agree to proper terms, none of the companies I represent will be interested in your material."

"All right," snapped Arch. "I can make it myself. Make it by the ton if I like, and sell it for a dollar a pound."

"You may find yourself undersold."

"My patent—"

"It hasn't gone through yet. That takes time, plenty of time if you don't want to cooperate. And even if it is granted, which I by no means guarantee, you'll have to sue infringers; and do you know how crowded court calendars are? And how expensive a series of appeals can make such a suit?"

"Okay," said Elizabeth sweetly. "Go ahead and make it. You just got through telling us why you can't."

Gilmer looked out the window. "This is a great country," he said, with more sincerity than Arch had expected. "No country on earth has ever been so rich and happy. Do you know how it got that way?"

"By progressing," said Arch. "For your information, I am not a leftist; I'll bet I'm far to the right of you. So far, that I still believe in full speed ahead and damn the torpedoes."

Gilmer rose, with a certain dignity. "I'm afraid tempers are getting a little short," he said quietly. "I beg of you to reconsider. We'll fight for the public interest if we must, but we'd rather cooperate. May I leave my card? You can always get in touch with me."

He made his farewells and left. Arch and Elizabeth looked somewhat blankly at each other.

"Well, Killer," said the girl at last, "I hope we haven't taken too big a chaw to swallow."

CULQUHOUN dropped over in the evening and listened to their account. He shook his head dubiously. "You're up against it, laddie," he said. "They'll defend their coffers to the bitter end."

"It isn't that." Arch stared moodily into the darkness. "I don't think they're a bunch of monsters—no more than anybody else. They just believe in the status quo. So do you, you know."

"How?" Culquhoun bristled. "I'll admit I'm not the hell-fire revolutionary of my undergraduate days, but I still think a basic change is called for."

"Not basic," said Arch. "You just want to change part of the mechanism. But you'd keep the same ant-heap industrial society. I believe the heart went out of this land after the Civil War, and the death warrant was signed about 1910. Before then, a man was still an individual; he worked for himself, at something he understood, and wasn't afraid to stand up and spit in the eye of the world. Now he spends his daily routine on an assembly line or behind a desk or counter, doing the same thing over and over for someone else. In the evening he watches the same pap on his television, and if something goes wrong he whines his way to the apartment superintendent or the VA or the Social Security office.

"Look at the progress of euphemism. Old people are Senior Citizens. Draft becomes Selective Service. Graveyard to cemetery to memorial park. We've become a race of dependents. And we can't break away: there isn't any frontier left, there isn't any alternative society, one man can't compete with a corporation. Or with a commissar, for that matter.

"What we need is not to go back to living in log cabins, but to make the means of sustenance and the sources of energy so cheap that every man can have them in sufficient quantity to live and work. I don't know—maybe I'm being vainglorious, but it does seem as if capacitite is a long step in that direction."

"I warn you, you're talking good Marxism," said Culquhoun with a grin. "The means of production determine the type of society."

"Which is pure hogwash," answered Arch. "Egypt and Assyria had identical technologies. So did Athens and Sparta. So do America and Russia. The means of production only determine the possible societies, and there are always many possibilities.

"I'd like to see the possibility of individualism available again to the American people. If they're too far gone to accept it, to hell with them."

The government can work fast when it wants to. It was just the following afternoon phone rang again. Elizabeth came out to the lab, where Arch and Bob Culquhoun were preparing a batch of capacitite, with a strained look on her face. "Come inside, dear," she said thinly. "I've got some bad news." When he was in the house, she added: "Two FBI men are on their way here."

"What the devil?" Arch felt a gulp of fear. It was irrational, he told himself. The FBI was no Gestapo; on the whole, he approved of it. Maybe some friend had given his name as a security reference. "All right. We'll see what they want."

"I'm going to start some coffee," said Elizabeth. "Lucky we've got a cake too."

"Huh?"

"You'll see." She patted his cheek and managed a smile. "You're too innocent, sweetheart."

Sagdahl and Horrisford turned out to be hard young men with carefully expressionless faces. They introduced themselves very politely, and Arch led the way into the living room. Horrisford took out a notebook.

"Well," said Arch a little huskily, "what can I do for you?"

"You can answer some questions, if you please," said Sagdahl tonelessly. "You don't have to answer any, and whatever you say can be used in evidence."

"I haven't broken any laws that I know of," said Arch feebly.

"That remains to be seen. This is an investigation."

"Whatever *for?*"

"Dr. Arch," said Sagdahl patiently, "yesterday you published an article on a discovery of potential military importance. It has upset a great many plans. Worse, it has been released with no discretion whatsoever, and the consequences aren't easy to foresee. If we'd had any inkling, it would never have been published openly. As it is, you went outside regular channels and—"

"I didn't have to go through channels," said Arch. "I've never gotten any confidential data, or even applied for a clearance. I work for myself and—" He saw Horrisford busily writing, and his words dried up.

The realization was appalling. The military applications of capacitite had crossed his mind only vaguely and been dismissed with an escapist shrug.

"Let's get down to business," said Sagdahl. "Everything will be a lot easier if you cooperate. Now, where were you born?"

Arch hadn't imagined anyone could be so thorough about tracking down a man's entire life. He answered frankly, feeling he had nothing to hide. Of course, there had been his roommate at M.I.T., and the roommate had had a girlfriend one of whose other friends was a Communist, and...

"I see. Now, when you graduated—"

Elizabeth entered from the kitchen with a tray. "Pardon me," she smiled. "I think refreshments are in order."

Sagdahl's face didn't change, but his eyes bugged slightly. Elizabeth put a coffee cup in his hand and a plate of cake on one knee. He looked unhappy, but mumbled dutiful thanks.

"Oh, it's a pleasure," said Elizabeth blandly. "You boys are doing your duty, and really, this is very exciting."

Sagdahl got down a mouthful of cake. Valiantly, he tried to resume the staccato flow: "Now, when you graduated, Dr. Arch, you took a vacation, you say. Where was that?"

"Up in Quebec. About three months. Just driving around and—"

"I see. Then you returned to school for a master's degree, right? Did you at this time know a Joseph Barrett?"

"Well, yes, I shared an office with him."

"Did you ever discuss politics with him?"

"Drink your coffee before it gets cold," said Elizabeth. "There's plenty more."

"Oh—thanks. Now, about this Barrett?"

"We argued a lot. You see, I'm frankly a reactionary—"

"Were you associated with any political-action group?"

"Mr. Horrisford," said Elizabeth reproachfully, "you haven't touched your cake."

"No, I wasn't that interested," said Arch. "Didn't even bother to vote in '50."

"Here, Mr. Sagdahl, do have some more cake."

"Thanks—! You met some of Barrett's friends?"

"Yes, I was at some parties and—"

"Excuse me, I'll just warm your coffee."

"Did you at this time know anyone who had worked in the Manhattan Project?"

"Of course. They were all over the place. But I never was told anything restricted, never asked for—"

"Please, Mr. Horrisford! It's my favorite recipe."

"Ummm. Thank you, but—"

"You met your future wife when?"

"In—"

"Excuse me, there's the phone...Hello.   Mrs. Arch speaking...Oh?...Yes, I'll see...Pardon me.   There's a man from the Associated Press in town.   He wants to see you, dear."

Sagdahl flinched. "Stall him off," he groaned. "Please."

"Can't do that forever," said Arch. "Not under the circumstances."

"I realize that, Dr. Arch." Sagdahl clenched his jaw. "But this is unprecedented. As an American citizen, you'll want to—"

"Certainly we'll cooperate," said Elizabeth brightly. "But what shall I tell the AP man? That we're not supposed to say anything to anyone?"

"No! That won't do, not now. But—are all the technical details of this public?"

"Why, yes," said Arch. "Anybody can make capacitite."

"If you issued a denial—"

"Too late, I'm afraid. Somebody's bound to try it anyway."

Sagdahl looked grim. "You can be held incommunicado," he said. "This is a very serious matter."

"Yes," said Elizabeth. "The AP man will think so too, if he can't get a story."

"Well—"

"Oh, dear! My Russell Wright coffee cup!"

NOTHING happened overnight. That was the hardest thing to believe. By all the rules, life should have been suddenly and dramatically transformed; but instead, there were only minor changes, day by day, small incidents. Meanwhile you ate, slept, worked, paid bills, made love and conversation, as you had always done.

The FBI held its hand as yet, but some quiet men checked into the town's one hotel, and there was usually one of them hanging around Arch's house, watching. Elizabeth would occasionally invite him in for a snack—she grew quite fond of them.

The newspapers ran feature articles, and for a while the house was overrun with reporters—then that too faded away. Editorials appeared, pointing out that capacitite had licked one of the Soviet Union's major problems, fuel; and a syndicated columnist practically called for Arch's immediate execution. He found some of his neighbors treating him coldly. The situation distressed him, too. "I never thought—" he began.

"Exactly," rumbled Culquhoun. "People like you are one reason science is coming to be considered a Frankenstein. Dammit, man, the researcher has to have a social conscience like the rest of us."

Arch smiled wearily. "But I do," he said. "I gave considerable thought to the social effects. I just imagined that they'd be good. That's been the case with every major innovation, in the long run."

"You've committed a crime," said Culquhoun. "Idealism. It doesn't fit the world we inhabit."

Arch flushed angrily. "What was I supposed to do?" he snapped. "Burn my results and forget them? If the human race is too—stupid to use the obvious advantages, that's its own fault."

"You're making a common error, dear," said Elizabeth. "You speak of the human race. There isn't any. There are only individual people and groups of people, with their own conflicting interests."

For a while, there was a big campaign to play down the effects of capacitite. It wasn't important. It meant nothing, as our eminent columnist has so lucidly shown. Then the attempt switched: capacitite was dangerous. So-and-so had been electrocuted working with it. There was cumulative poisoning...Such propaganda didn't work, not when some millions of people were seeing for themselves.

Petroleum stock began sagging. It didn't nosedive—the SEC and a valiantly buying clique saw to that—but it slipped down day by day.

Arch happened to drop in at Hinkel's garage. The old man looked up from a car on which he was laboring and smiled. "Hello, there," he said. "Haven't seen you in a long time."

"I—well—" Arch looked guiltily at the oil-stained floor. "I'm afraid—your business—"

"Oh, don't worry about me. I've got more business than I can handle. Everybody in town seems to want his car converted over to your type of engine. That young Bob is turning out the stuff like a printing press gone berserk."

Arch couldn't quite meet his eyes. "But—aren't your gasoline sales dropping?"

"To be sure. But cars still need lubrication and— Look, you know the old watermill down by Ronson's farm? I'm buying that, putting in a generator and a high voltage transformer and rectifier. I'll be selling packaged power. A lot easier than running a gas pump, at my age."

"Won't the power company be competing?"

"Eventually. Right now, they're still waiting for orders from higher up, I guess. Some people can charge their capacitors right at home, but most would rather not buy the special equipment. They'll come to me, and by the time the power outfit gets wise to itself, I'll 've come in on the ground floor."

"Thanks," said Arch, a little shakily. "It makes me feel a lot better."

If only everybody had that Yankee adaptability, he thought as he walked home. But he saw now, as he wished he had seen earlier, that society had gone too far. With rare exceptions, progress was no longer a matter of individual readjustments. It was a huge and clumsy economic system which had to make the transformation…a jerry-built system whose workings no one understood, even today.

He wanted to call up Gilmer and make what terms he could, but it was too late. The snowball was rolling.

He sighed his way into an armchair and picked up the paper.

Item: the bill before Congress to make capacitite a government monopoly like uranium, and to enforce all security restrictions on it, had been sent back to committee and would probably not pass. A few senators had had the nerve to point out that security was pointless when everybody could already make the stuff.

Item: the government was setting up a special laboratory to study the military applications. Arch could think of several for himself. Besides simplifying logistics, it could go into cheap and horrible weapons. A bomb loaded with several thousand coulombs, set to discharge instantaneously on striking—

Item: a well-known labor leader had denounced the innovation as a case of business blundering which was going to take bread from the working man. A corporation spokesman declared that it was all a leftist trick designed to cripple the private enterprise system.

Item: *Pravda* announced that Soviet scientists had discovered capacitite ten years ago and that full-scale production had long been under way for peaceful purposes only, such as making the Red Army still more invincible.

Item: two more men in America electrocuted due to incautious experiments. Nevertheless, capacitite was being manufactured in thousands of homes and workshops. Bills in various state legislatures to ban vehicles so powered were meeting indignant opposition everywhere save in Texas.

Arch reflected wryly that he wasn't getting paid for any of this. All he'd gotten out of it so far was trouble. Trouble with the authorities, with crank letters, with his own conscience. There were, to be sure, some royalties from Bob Culquhoun, who was becoming quite an entrepreneur and hiring adults to take over when school opened in fall.

Speaking of tigers by the tail—

AUTUMN, the New England fall of rain and chill whistling wind, smoky days and flame-like leaves and the far wild honking of southbound geese. The crash came in late September: a reeling market hit bottom and stayed there. Gasoline sales were down twenty-five percent already, and the industry was laying men off by the hundreds of thousands. That cut out their purchasing power and hit the rest of the economy.

"It's what you'd expect, laddie," said Culquhoun. They were over at his house. Outside, a slow cold rain washed endlessly down the windows. "Over production—over capitalization—I could have predicted all this."

"Damn it to hell, it doesn't make *sense!*" protested Arch. "A new energy source should make everything cheaper for everybody—more production available for less work." He felt a nervous tic beginning in one cheek.

"Production for use instead of for profit—"

"Oh, dry up, will you? Any system is a profit system. It has to show a profit in some terms or other, or it would just be wasted effort. And the profit has to go to individuals, not to some mythical state. The state doesn't eat—people do."

"Would you have the oil interests simply write off their investment?"

"No, of course not. Why couldn't they— Look. Gasoline can still run generators. Oil can still lubricate. Byproducts can still be synthesized. It's a matter of shifting the emphasis of production, that's all. All that's needed is a little common sense."

"Which is a rather scarce commodity."

"There," said Arch gloomily, "we find ourselves in agreement."

"The trouble is," said Bob earnestly, "we're faced with a real situation, not a paper problem. It calls for a real solution. For an idea."

"There aren't any ideas," said Elizabeth. "Not big sweeping ones to solve everything overnight. Man doesn't work that way. What happens is that somebody solves his own immediate, personal problems, somebody else does the same, and eventually society as a whole fumbles its way out of the dilemma."

Arch sighed. "This is getting over my head," he admitted. "Thanks for small blessings: the thing has grown so big that I, personally, am becoming forgotten."

He rose. "I'm kind of tired tonight," he went on. "Maybe we better be running along. Thanks for the drinks and all."

He and his wife slipped into their raincoats and galoshes for the short walk home. The street outside was dark, a rare lamp glowing off slick wet concrete. Rain misted his face and glasses, he had trouble seeing.

"Poor darling," Elizabeth took his arm. "Don't worry. We'll get through all right."

"I hope so," he said fervently. No money had come in for some time now. Bob's enterprise was leveling off as initial demand was filled, and a lurching industry wasn't buying many electronic valves. The bank account was getting low.

He saw the figure ahead as a vague shadow against the night. It stood waiting till they came up, and then stepped in their path. The voice was unfamiliar: "Arch?"

"Yes—"

He could see only that the face was heavy and unshaven, with something wild about the mouth. Then his eyes dropped to the revolver barrel protruding from the slicker. "What the devil—"

"Don't move, you," It was a harsh, broken tone. "Right now I'm aiming at your wife. I'd as soon shoot her, too."

Fear leaped crazily in Arch's breast. He stood unable to stir, coldness crawling in his guts. He tried to speak, and couldn't.

"Not a word, you— Not another word. You've said too goddam much already." The gun poked forward, savagely. "I'm going to kill you. You did your best to kill me."

Elizabeth's face was white in the gloom. "What do you mean?" she whispered. "We never saw you before."

"No. But you took away my job. I was in the breadlines back in the thirties. I'm there again, and it's your fault, you— Got any prayers to say?"

A gibbering ran through Arch's brain. He stood motionless, thinking through a lunatic mind-tilt that there must be some way to jump that gun, the heroes of stories always did it, that might—

Someone moved out of the night into the wan radiance. An arm went about the man's throat, another seized his gun wrist and snapped it down. The weapon went off, sounding like the crack of doom in the stillness.

They struggled on the slippery sidewalk, panting, the rain running over dimly glimpsed faces. Arch's paralysis broke, he moved in and circled around, looking for a chance to help. There! Crouching, he got hold of the assassin's ankle and clung.

There was a meaty smack above him, and the body sagged.

Elizabeth held her hand over her mouth, as if to force back a scream. "Mr. Horrisford," she whispered.

"The same," said the FBI man. "That was a close one. You can be thankful you're an object of suspicion, Arch. What was he after?"

Arch stared blankly at his rescuer. Slowly, meaning penetrated. "unemployed—" he mumbled. "Bitter about it—"

"Yeah. I thought so. You may be having more trouble of that sort. This depression, people have someone concrete to blame." Horrisford stuck the gun in his pocket and helped up his half-conscious victim. "Let's get this one down to the lockup. Here, you support him while I put on some handcuffs."

"But I wanted to help his kind," said Arch feebly.

"You didn't," said Horrisford. "I'd better arrange for a police guard."

ARCH spent the following day in a nearly suicidal depression. Elizabeth tried to pull him out of it, failed, and went downtown after a fifth of whiskey. That helped. The hangover helped too. It's hard to concentrate on remorse when ten thousand red-hot devils are building an annex to Hell in your skull. Toward evening, he was almost cheerful again. A certain casehardening was setting in.

After dark, there was a knock on the door. When he opened it, Horrisford and a stranger stood there.

"Oh—come in," he said "Excuse the mess. I—haven't been feeling so well."

"Anyone here?" asked the agent.

"Just my wife."

"She'll be all right," said the stranger impatiently. He was a big, stiff, gray-haired man. "Bring her in, please. This is important."

They were settled in the living room before Horrisford performed the introductions. "Major General Brackney of Strategic Services." Arch's hand was wet as he acknowledged the handclasp.

"This is most irregular," said the general. "However, we've put through a special check on you. A fast but very thorough check. In spite of your errors of judgment, the FBI is convinced of your essential loyalty. Your discretion is another matter."

"I can keep my mouth shut, if that's what you mean." said Arch.

"Yes. You kept one secret for ten years—" said Horrisford. "—the business of Mrs. Ramirez."

Arch started. "How the deuce—? That was a personal affair. I've never told a soul, not even my wife!"

"We have our little ways." Horrisford grinned, humanly enough. "The point is that you could have gained somewhat by blabbing, but didn't. It speaks well for you."

General Brackney cleared his throat. "We want your help on a certain top-secret project," he said. "You still know more about capacitite than anybody else. But if one word of this leaks out prematurely, it means war. Atomic war. It also means that all of us, and you particularly, will be crucified."

"I—"

"You're an independent so-and-so, I realize. What we have in mind is a scheme to prevent such a war. We want you in on it both for your own value and because we can't protect you forever from Soviet agents." Brackney's smile had no humor. "Didn't know that, did you? It's one reason you're being co-opted, in spite of all you've done.

"I can't say more till you take the oath, and once you've done that you're under all the usual restrictions. Care to help out?"

Arch hesitated. He had little faith in government...any government. Still—

Horrisford of the FBI had saved his life.

"I'm game," he said.

Elizabeth nodded. The oath was administered.

Brackney leaned back and lit a cigar. "All right," he said. "I'll come to the point.

"Offhand, it looks as if you've done a grave disservice to your country. It's been pointed out in the press that transporting fuel is the major problem of logistics. In fact, for the Russians it's the problem, since they can live off the countries they invade to a degree we can't match. You've solved that for them, and once they convert their vehicles we can expect them to start rolling. They and their allies—especially the Chinese. This discovery is going to make them a first-class power."

"I've heard that," said Arch thinly.

"However, we also know that the communist regimes are not popular. Look at the millions of refugees, look at all the prisoners who refused repatriation, look at the Ukrainian insurrection—I needn't elaborate. The trouble has been that the people aren't armed. To say anything at home means the concentration camp.

"Now, then. Basically, the idea is this. We've got plants set up to turn out capacitite in trainload lots. We can, I think, make weapons capable of stopping a tank for a couple of dollars apiece. Do you agree?"

"Why—yes," said Arch. "I've been considering it lately. A rifle discharging its current through magnetic coils to drive a steel jacketed bullet—the bullet could be loaded with electricity too. Or a Buck Rogers energy gun: a hand weapon with a blower run off the capacitor, sucking in air at the rear and spewing it out between two electrodes like a gigantic arc-welding flame. Or—yes, there are all kinds of possibilities."

Brackney nodded with an air of satisfaction. "Good. I see you do have the kind of imagination we need.

"Now, we'll be giving nothing away, because they already know how to make the stuff and can think up anything we can. But, we have a long jump as far as production facilities are concerned.

"The idea is this. We want to make really enormous quantities of such weapons. By various means—through underground channels, by air if necessary—we want to distribute them to all the Iron Curtain countries. The people will be armed, and hell is going to break loose!

"We want you in on it as design and production consultants, Leave tomorrow, be gone for several months probably. It's going to have to be highly organized, so it can be sprung as a surprise; otherwise the Soviet bosses, who are no fools, will hit. But your part will be in production. Are you game?"

"It's—astonishing," said Elizabeth. "Frankly, I didn't think the government had that much imagination."

"We're probably exceeding our authority," admitted Brackney. "By rights, of course, Congress should be consulted, but this is like the Louisiana Purchase: there's no time to do so."

It was the historical note which decided Arch. Grade-school history, yes—but it didn't fit in with his preconceptions of the red-necked militarist. Suddenly, almost hysterically, he was laughing.

"What's so funny?" asked Horrisford sharply.

"The idea—what old Clausewitz would say—winning wars by arming the enemy! Sure—sure, I'm in. Gladly!"

SIX MONTHS on a secret reservation in Colorado which no-body but the top brass left, six months of the hardest, most con-centrated work a man could endure, got Arch out of touch with the world. He saw an occasional newspaper, was vaguely aware of trouble on the outside, but there was too much immediately at hand for him to consider the reality. Everything outside the barbed-wire borders of his universe grew vague.

Designing and testing capacitite weapons was harder than he had expected, and took longer: though experienced engineers assured him the project was moving with unprecedented speed and ease. Production details were out of his department, but the process of tooling up and getting mass output going was not one for overnight solution.

The magnetic rifle; the arc gun; the electric bomb and grenade; the capacitite land mine, set to fry the crew of any tank which passed over—he knew their hideous uses, but there was a cool ecstasy in working with them which made him forget, most of the time. And after all, the idea was to arm men who would be free.

In March, General Brackney entered the Quonset hut which Arch and Elizabeth had been inhabiting and sat down with a weary smile. "I guess you're all through now," he said.

"About time," grumbled the girl. "We've been sitting on our hands here for a month, just puttering."

"The stuff had to be shipped out," said the general mildly. "We didn't dare risk having the secret revealed. But we're rolling overseas, it's too late to stop anything," He shrugged. "Naturally, the government isn't admitting its part in this. Officially, the weapons were manufactured by independent operators in Europe and Asia, and you'll have to keep quiet about the truth for a long time—not that the comrades won't be pretty sure, but it just can't be openly admitted. However, there are no security restrictions on the gadgets themselves, as of today."

"That surprises me," said Arch.

"It's simple enough. Everything is so obvious, really—any handyman can make the same things for himself. A lot have been doing it, too. No secrets exist to be given away, that's all." Brackney hesitated. "We'll fly you back home anytime you wish. But if you want to stay on a more permanent basis, we'll be glad to have you."

"No, thanks!" Elizabeth's eyes went distastefully around the sleazy interior of the shack.

"This has all been temporary," said the general. "We were in such a hell of a hurry. Better housing will be built now."

"Nevertheless, no," said Arch.

Brackney frowned. "I can't stop you, of course. But I don't think you realize how tough it's getting outside, and how much worse it's going to get. A revolution is starting, in more senses than one, and you'll be safer here."

"I heard something about that," agreed Arch. "Discontented elements making their own weapons, similar to ours—what of it?"

"Plenty," said the officer with a note of grimness. "It's an ugly situation. A lot of people are out of work, and even those who still have jobs don't feel secure in them. There are a dozen crank solutions floating around, everything from new political theories to new religious sects, and each one is finding wider acceptance than I'd have believed possible."

"It doesn't surprise me," said Arch. "There's a queer strain of the True Believer in American culture. You know how many utopian colonies we've had throughout our history? And the single

31

tax party, and prohibition, and communism in the thirties. People in this country want something concrete to believe in, and all but a few of the churches have long ago degenerated into social clubs."

"Whatever the cause," said Brackney, "there are all these new groups, clashing with the old authorities and with each other. And the underworld is gleefully pitching in, and getting a lot of recruits from the ranks of hungry, frightened, embittered people.

"The regular armed forces have to be mobilized to stop anything the Soviets may try. The police and the National Guard have their hands full in the big cities. The result is, that authority is breaking down everywhere else. There's real trouble ahead, I tell you."

"All right," said Arch. "That's as may be. But our town is a collection of pretty solid folk—and we want to go home."

"On your heads be it. There'll be a plane at six tomorrow."

—The fact did not strike home till they were stopping over at Idlewild and saw uniformed men and machine-gun emplacements. In the coffee shop, Arch asked the counterman just how bad things really were.

"Rough," he answered. "See this?" He flipped back his jacket, showing a homemade capacitite pistol in a holster.

"Oh, look now—"

"Mister, I live in Brooklyn. I don't get home till after dark, and the police cordons don't go closer than six blocks to my place. I've had to shoot twice already in the past couple months."

"Bandits?"

"In gangs, mister. If I could work somewhere closer to home, I'd be off like a shot."

Arch set down his cup. Suddenly he didn't want any more coffee. *My God*, he thought, *am I responsible for that?*

A smaller plane carried them to Boston, where they caught a bus for Westfield. The driver had an automatic rifle by his seat. Arch huddled into himself, waiting for he knew not what; but the trip was uneventful.

The town didn't seem to have changed much. Most of the cars were converted, but it didn't show externally. The drug store still flashed neon at a drowsy sidewalk, the Carnegie library waited rather wistfully for someone to come in, the dress shop had the same old dummies in the window. Elizabeth pointed at them. "Look," she said. "See those clothes?"

"They're dresses," said Arch moodily. "What about them?"

"No style change in six months, that's all," said Elizabeth. "It gives me the creeps."

They walked along streets banked with dirty, half-melted snow, under a leaden sky and a small whimpering wind. Their house had not changed when they entered, someone had been in to dust and it looked like the home they remembered. Arch sank tiredly into his old armchair and accepted a drink. He studied the newspaper he'd bought at the depot. Screaming headlines announced revolt in Russia—mass uprisings in the Siberian prison camps announcements from the Copenhagen office of the Ukrainian nationalist movement— It all seemed very far away. The fact that there were no new dress styles was somehow closer and more eerie.

A thunderous knock at the door informed him that Culquhoun had noticed their lights. "Mon, it's guid to see ye again!" The great paw engulfed his hand. "Where've ye been a' the while?"

"Can't tell you that," said Arch.

"Aweel, you'll permit me to make my own guesses, then." Culquhoun cocked an eye at the paper. "Who do they think they're fooling, anyhow? We can look for the Russian bombers any day now."

Arch considered his reply. That aspect had been thoroughly discussed at the project, but he wasn't sure how much he could tell. "Quite possibly," he said at last. "But with their internal troubles, they won't be able to make many raids, or any big ones—and the little they will be able to throw at us should be stopped while they're still over northern Canada."

"Let's hope so," nodded Culquhoun. "But the people in the large cities won't want to take the chance. There's going to be an exodus of considerable dimensions in the next few days, with all that that implies." He paused, frowning. "I've spent the last couple of months organizing a kind of local militia. Bob has been making capacitite guns, and there are about a hundred of us trying to train ourselves. Want in on it?"

"They'd probably shoot me first," whispered Arch.

The red head shook, bear-like. "No. There's less feeling against you locally than you seem to think. After all, few if any of the people in this area have been hurt—they're farmers, small shopkeepers trading in the essentials, students, college employees. Many of them have actually benefited. You have your enemies here, but you have more friends."

"I think," said Arch thinly, "that I'm becoming one of my own enemies."

"Ah, foosh, mon! If you hadn't brought the stuff out, somebody else would have. It's not your fault that we don't have the kind of economy to absorb it smoothly."

"All right," said Arch without tone. "I'll join your minute men. There doesn't seem to be anything else to do."

THE WAVE of automobiles began coming around noon of the next day. Westfield lay off the main highway, so it didn't get the full impact of the jam which tied up traffic from Philadelphia to Boston; but there were some thousands of cars which passed through.

Arch stood in the ranks of men who lined Main Street. The gun felt awkward in his hands. Breath smoked from his nostrils, and the air was raw and damp. On one side of him was Mr. Hinkel, bundled up so that only the glasses and a long red nose seemed visible; on the other was a burly farmer whom he didn't know.

Outside the city limits a sign had been planted, directing traffic to keep moving and to stay on the highway. There were barriers on all the side streets. Arch heard an occasional argument when someone tried to stop, to be urged on by a guard and by the angry horns behind him.

"But what'll they do?" he asked blindly. "Where will they stay? My God, there are women and children in those cars!"

"Women and children here in town too," said Hinkel. "We've got to look after our own. It won't kill these characters to go a few days without eating. Every house here is filled already—there've been fugees trickling in for weeks."

"We could bunk down a family in our place," ventured Arch.

"Save that space," answered Hinkel. "It'll be needed later."

Briefly, a certain pride rose through the darkness of guilt which lay in Arch. These were the old Americans, the same folk who had stood at Concord and gone west into Indian country. They were a survivor type.

But most of their countrymen weren't, he realized sickly. Urban civilization had become too big too specialized. There were people in the millions who had never pitched a tent, butchered a pig, fixed a machine. What was going to become of them?

Toward evening, he was relieved and slogged home, too numb with cold and weariness to think much. He gulped down the dinner his wife had ready and tumbled into bed.

It seemed as if he had not slept at all when the phone was ringing. He groped toward it, cursing as he tried to unglue his eyes. Culquhoun's voice rattled at him:

"You and Betty come up to the college, Somerset Hall, right away. There's hell to pay."

"How——?"

"Our lookout on the water tower has seen fires starting to the south. Something's approaching and it doesn't look friendly."

Sleep drained from Arch and he stood in a grayness where Satan jeered at him: *"Si monumentum requiris, circumspice!"* Slowly, he nodded. "We'll be right along."

The campus was jammed with townspeople. In the vague pre-dawn light, Arch saw them as a moving river of white, frightened faces. Farmer, merchant, laborer, student, teacher, housewife, they had all receded into a muttering anonymity through which he pushed toward the steps of the hall. The irregular militia was forming ranks there, with Culquhoun's shaggy form dominating the scene.

"There you are," he snapped. "Betty, can you help take charge of the women and children and old people? Get them inside—this one building ought to hold them all with some crowding. Kind of circulate around, keep them calm. We'll pass out coffee and doughnuts as soon as the Salvation Army bunch can set up a canteen."

"What's the plan?" asked a guardsman. To Arch, his voice had a dim dreamlike quality, none of this was real, it couldn't be.

"I don't know what those arsonists intend or where they're bound," said Culquhoun, "but we'd better be ready to meet them. The traffic through town stopped completely a few hours ago—I think there's a gang of highwaymen operating."

"Colin, it can't be! Plain people like us—"

"Hungry, frightened, angry, desperate, confused people. A mob has nothing to do with the individuals in it, my friend. And one small push is enough to knock down a row of dominoes. Once lawlessness really gets started, a lot of others are driven into it in self-defense."

They waited. The sun came up, throwing a pale bleak light over the late snow and the naked trees. The canteen handed out a sort of breakfast. Little was said.

At nine-thirty, a boy on a clumsy plow horse came galloping up toward them. "About a hundred, marching down the highway," he panted. "They threw a couple shots at me."

"Stay here," said Culquhoun. "I'm going down to see if we can't parley. I'll want about ten men with me. Volunteers?"

Arch found himself among the first. It didn't matter much what happened to him, now when the work of his hands was setting aflame homes all across the land. They trudged down the hillside and out toward the viaduct leading south. Culquhoun broke into a deserted house and stationed them in its entrance hall.

Peering out, Arch saw the ragged column moving in. They were all men, unshaven and dirty. A few trucks accompanied them, loaded with a strange mass of plunder, but most were on foot and all were armed.

Culquhoun bound a towel to his rifle barrel and waved it through the front door. After what seemed like a long time, a voice outside said: "Okay, if yuh wanna talk, go ahead."

"Cover me," murmured Culquhoun, stepping onto the porch. Looking around his shoulder, Arch made out three of the invaders, with their troop standing in tired, slumped attitudes some yards behind. They didn't look fiendish, merely worn and hungry.

"Okay, pal," said the leader. "This is O'Farrell's bunch, and we're after food and shelter. What can yuh do for us?"

"Food and shelter?" Culquhoun glanced at the trucks. "You seem to've been helping yourselves pretty generously already."

O'Farrell's face darkened. "What'd yuh have us do? Starve?"

"You're from the Boston area, I suppose. You could have stayed there."

"And been blown off the map!"

"It hasn't happened yet," said Culquhoun mildly. "It's not likely to happen, either. They have organized relief back there, you didn't have to starve. But no, you panicked and then you turned mean."

"It's easy enough for yuh to say so. *Yuh're safe.* We're here after our proper share, that's all."

"Your proper share is waiting in Boston," said Culquhoun with a sudden chill. "Now, if you want to proceed through our town, we'll let you; but we don't want you to stay. Not after what you've been doing lately."

O'Farrell snarled and brought up his gun. Arch fired from behind Culquhoun. The leader spun on his heel, crumpled, and sagged with a shriek. Arch felt sick.

His nausea didn't last. It couldn't, with the sudden storm of lead which sleeted against the house. Culquhoun sprang back, closing the door. "Out the rear!" he snapped. "We'll have to fight!"

They retreated up the hill, crouching, zigzagging, shooting at the disorderly mass which milled in slow pursuit. Culquhoun grinned savagely. "Keep drawing 'em on, boys," he said as he knelt in the slush and snapped a shot. "If they spread through town, we'll have hell's own time routing 'em all out—but this way—"

Arch didn't know if he was hitting anything. He didn't hear the bullets which must be whining around him—another cliché that just wasn't true, he thought somewhere in the back of his head. A fight wasn't something you could oversee and understand. It was cold feet, clinging mud, whirling roaring confusion, it was a nightmare that you couldn't wake up from.

Then the rest of the Westfield troops were there, circling around to flank the enemy and pumping death. It was a rout—in minutes, the gang had stampeded.

Arch leaned on his rifle and felt vomit rising in his throat. Culquhoun clapped his shoulder. "Ye did richt well, laddie," he rumbled. "No bad at all."

"What's happening?" groaned Arch. "What's become of the world?"

Culquhoun took out his pipe and began tamping it. "Why, a simple shift of the military balance of power," he answered. "Once again we have cheap, easily operated weapons which everyone can own and which are the equal of anything it's practical for a government to use. Last time it was the flintlock musket, right? And we got the American and French Revolutions. This time it's capacitite.

"So the Soviet dictatorship is doomed. But we've got a rough time ahead of us, because there are enough unstable elements in our own society to make trouble. Our traditional organizations just aren't prepared to handle them when they're suddenly armed.

"We'll learn how fast enough, I imagine. There's going to be order again, if only because the majority of people are decent, hardworking fellows who won't put up with much more of this sort of thing. But there has to be a transition period, and what counts is surviving that."

"If I hadn't—Colin, it's enough to make a man believe in demoniac possession."

"Nonsense!" snorted the other. "I told you before, if you hadn't invented this stuff, somebody else would have. It wasn't you that made it by the ton, all over the country. It wasn't you that thought up this notion of finishing the Iron Curtain governments—a brilliant scheme, I might add, well worth whatever price we have to pay at home.

"But it *is* you, my boy, who's going to have to get us tooled up to last the transition. Can you do it?"

FUNDAMENTAL changes are seldom made consciously. Doubtless the man in the fifth century Roman street grumbled about all these barbarian immigrants, but he did not visualize the end of an empire. The Lancashire industrialist who fired his craftsmen and installed mechanical looms was simply making a profitable investment. And Westfield, Massachusetts, was only adopting temporary survival measures.

They didn't even look over-whelmingly urgent. Government had not broken down: if anything, it was working abnormally hard. News came through—ferocious air battles over the Canadian tundra; the Soviet armies rolling westward into Europe and southward into Asia, then pushed back with surprising ease and surrendering en masse as their own states collapsed behind them— it was turning out to be a war as remote and half-forgotten as Korea, and a much easier one which lasted a few months and then faded into a multi-cornered struggle between communists, neo-czarists, and a dozen other elements. By Christmas time, a shaky democratic confederation in Moscow was negotiating with Ukrain, the Siberian Convict Republic, and the Tartar Alliance. China was in chaos and eastern Europe was free.

And while the great powers were realizing that they were no longer great, now that a vast capital investment in armament had stopped paying off; and while they sought to forestall world upheaval by setting up a genuine international army with strength to enforce the peace—life went on. People still had to eat.

Arch stood by Hinkel's watermill in the early spring. The ground glistened and steamed with wetness underfoot, sunlit clouds raced through a pale windy sky, and a mist of green was on the trees.

Near him the swollen millstream roared and brawled, the wheel flashed with its own swiftness, and a stack of capacitors lay awaiting their charges.

"All right," he said. "We've got your generator going. But it isn't enough, you know. It can't supply the whole country; and power lines to the outside are down."

"So what do we do?" asked Hinkel. He felt too proud of his new enterprise to care much about larger issues at the moment.

"We find other sources to supplement," said Arch. "Sunlight, now. Approximately one horsepower per square yard, if you could only get at it." He raised a face grown thin with overwork and with the guilt that always haunted him these days, up to the sky. The sun felt warm and live on his skin. "Trouble is, the potential's so low. You've got to find a way to get a high voltage out of it before you can charge a capacitor decently. Now let me think—"

He spent most of his waking hours thinking. It helped hold off the memory of men lying dead on a muddy hillside.

When power was short, you couldn't go back to oxcarts and kerosene lamps. There weren't enough of either. The local machine shop made and sold quantities of home charging units, small primitive generators which could be turned by any mechanical source, and treadmills were built to drive them. But this was only an unsatisfactory expedient. Accompanied by several armed guards, Arch made a trip to Boston.

The city looked much quieter than he remembered, some of the streets deserted even at midday, but a subdued business went on. Food was still coming in to the towns, and manufactured goods flowing out; there was still trade, mail, transportation. They were merely irregular and slightly dangerous.

Stopping at M.I.T. Arch gave certain of his problems to the big computer, and then proceeded to an industrial supply house. The amount of selenium he ordered brought a gasp and a hurried conference.

"It will take some time to get all this together," said a vice-president. "Especially with conditions as they are."

"I know," said Arch. "We're prepared to make up truck convoys and furnish guards; what we want you for is negotiation."

The vice-president blinked. "But...good heavens, man! Is your whole community in on this?"

"Just about. We have to be. There's little help coming in from outside, so our area is thrown back on itself."

"Ah—the cost of this operation—"

"Oh, we can meet that. Special assessment, voted at the last town meeting. They don't care very much, because money has little value when you can't buy more than the rationed necessities. And they're getting tired of going on short rations of power."

"I shouldn't say this, because your proposal is a fine deal for us, but have you stopped to think? Both the REA and the private power concerns will be restoring service eventually, just as soon as civil order has been recreated."

Arch nodded. "I know. But there are two answers to that. In the first place, we don't know when that'll be, and if we don't have adequate energy sources by winter we'll be up the creek. Also, we're building a sun-power plant which will cost almost nothing to operate. In the long run, and not so terribly long at that, it'll payoff."

Bob Culquhoun, who went on the selenium convoy, reported an adventurous journey through hundreds of miles where gangs of extremists still ruled. "But they seem to be settling down," he added. "Nobody likes to be a bandit, and anyhow the state militias are gradually subduing 'em. Most of the rural communities, though, are striking out on their own like us. There's going to be a big demand for selenium." Wistfulness flickered in his eyes. "Wonder if I can raise enough money to buy some stock?"

"It'll take time," said Elizabeth. "I know the sun-power generator is simple, but you still can't design and build one overnight."

As a matter of fact, fall had come again before Westfield's plant was in full operation. It didn't look impressive: great flat screens on top of hastily constructed buildings, and inside these the apparatus to raise voltage and charge capacitors. But in conjunction with the watermill, it furnished more than enough electricity to run the county's machines.

Arch was kept busy all that summer, directing, advising, helping. It seemed that everybody had some scheme of his own for using capacitite. Energy cost nothing, and machinery could be built from junkyard scrap if nothing else. Westfield was suddenly acquiring her own looms, mills, even a small foundry. Bob led a gang of young hellions who made an airplane and kept it aloft for days at a time. His father promptly confiscated it for the use of the civic guard, and after that there were no more surprise brushes with roving outlaws.

An eyewitness report was brought in from the air—a clash between state troops and one of the robber bands which still existed to the north. The gangmen had their own trucks and jeeps, their own guns, all operating off accumulators which could be charged at any of a thousand watermills. A rifleman could stop a tank, and aircraft were of limited value against guerrillas who crouched in brush and weeds. The battle was a draw, with both sides finally retreating.

Arch shuddered, alone with Elizabeth, and crept into her arms. "Did I do that?" he asked through his tears. "Did I do it?"

"No, darling," she said. One hand ruffled his disordered hair. "Can't you forget that side of it? Think of what you have done, with your own hands—built this town up again, given its people more than they ever had before."

He set his teeth. "I'll try," he said.

Somewhat later, the government offered amnesty to those outlaws who would lay down their arms and come home. It had the desired effect; they had had enough of warring and insecurity. But Culquhoun scowled. "'Tis a vurra bad precedent," he said. "Only a weak government makes such a move."

Oddly, Arch felt a lightening within himself. "Maybe a weak government is what we need," he answered.

News: Several southern states threaten secession unless court decisions concerning racial equality are withdrawn.

News: Uprisings in these same states. The Negro has had enough.

News: Capitulation of state governments. Constitutional conventions, transfer of power from state to local authorities.

News: The depression is not ending, but transforming itself: out-of-work men are starting to produce things for themselves with the help of capacitite-driven machinery often made at home, trading their surplus for whatever else they need. A mobile reclamation unit appears, costing little to operate, and families begin to irrigate and colonize desert areas. Big business, big labor, big government talk much and do nothing effective—their day is past, but they simply cannot understand the new forces at work.

News: More and more city areas are becoming empty as their inhabitants take advantage of cheap, fast transportation and move into the rapidly expanding suburbs and even into the country. This migration is possible because with present energy sources, plastic board for home construction can be manufactured at very low cost.

News: There is a great deal of debate in Washington about re-districting to meet the new population pattern. It doesn't seem too important, though, because a land of nearly self-sufficient communities, such as this is becoming, is much less dependent on central government.

News: Experiment and innovation in dress, work habits, manners and morals, grows ever more common. The basic cause of this is that few men need now be afraid of what the neighbors or the boss thinks. If you don't like it where you are, you can easily go elsewhere and start over.

None of this happened at once. It would take a century or more for the change to complete itself. But even in the second year, the trend was obvious.

SNOW whirled against the house, blindingly, as if the world drew into itself and nothing lay beyond these walls. The muted skirl of wind came through, lonesome and shivering. But inside, there was warmth and a calm light.

Arch sat with a whiskey and soda in his hand, looking across the floor at his wife. He felt tired, but there was a relaxation in him, a sense of labor finished.

Not fully—there would be much to do yet. But power was there, machinery was there, food stored away; they would last the winter, and there would be another springtime.

"It's settling down," Elizabeth told him, putting her news magazine aside. "For once, I agree with the editor of this rag. The crisis is over, and now it's a matter of readjustment. The world is never going to be the same, but it'll be a better one...cleaner."

"Perhaps," said Arch. He didn't feel so sharply the horror of guilt, not any more.

"Look around you," she invited. "Look what you've done. I'm afraid, dear, that you're going to be rediscovered. It won't take long before people suddenly wake up to the fact that your invention did all this for them. Brace yourself—you're going to be famous for life."

Arch winced. "But I didn't!" he protested. "They did it for themselves. One man never could—"

"I quite agree," she smiled. "One man can neither make nor destroy a society. So why not give that conscience of yours a rest?"

"There's been suffering," he said, enough alcohol in him to break down his reserve. "People have died."

"A lot of them needed killing," she said earnestly. "Look what we've got. An end to dictatorship. Removal of the atomic-war threat. Cheap energy for a million new projects. A four-hour work day in prospect. Government, which was getting too big and officious in all countries, cut down to size again. The plain man standing on his own feet and working for himself. Natural resources conserved. If you must take either credit or blame, Si, then balance your books!"

"I know," he said. "I know all that, up in my conscious mind. But down underneath—I'll always see those houses burning, and those men shooting at each other."

"You—" She hesitated. "I know what you need. Your trouble, my boy, is that underneath that Yankee conservatism, you're a hopeless romantic. Your mind dwells on the sudden and dramatic. Now the positive benefits of capacitite aren't anywhere near as quick and spectacular as the temporary evils were. What you have to do, to satisfy those Puritan chromosomes, is to produce something really big and fancy, something of immediate, large value."

He chuckled, lifted out of his dark mood in spite of himself. "I imagine you're right, Dr. Freud," he said. "But what?"

"I don't know." She frowned with worry for him. "But think, man. We have leisure now—in another year or so, well, we won't be the millionaires we once dreamed of, but like everybody else we'll have real security and real time to ourselves. You could use that time to work on *something*."

"Hm—" Automatically, his brain turned to practicalities. "Let's see, now. Capacitite offers a way of concentrating energy enormously…a very small packet will hold a hell of a lot—*My God!*" His yell shook the windows as he leaped to his feet.

"What the devil—something wrong?" Elizabeth got up too.

"No!" He was running toward the phone. "Got to get hold of Colin—M.I.T.—don't you see, darling?" His hands trembled as he dialed, but there was laughter in his voice. "Don't you see it? Spaceships!"

THE END

Detonator

By WALT SHELDON

The State was going to make him sign a confession, and he knew in advance that he was going to sign it—But with their blood...

THERE WAS a short thermal hum and then the force screen barred the entrance—and the exit—to Unor's cell again.

He sat down, sighing just a little, on the iron cot. He couldn't help thinking that cell cots hadn't changed much through the centuries; he remembered pictures of jails of the ancient American republic, and the cots had looked much like this.

He rested his forearms on his knees, folded his hands carefully, frowned, and concentrated. "Hello, hello, hello," he thought. "Calling Loyops. Any Loyops, think in. Think in, please..."

Unor didn't look much like one of the underground rebels who called themselves Loyal Oppositionists—Loyops, for short. He didn't have a bristling beard and a wild eye, which was how the political sculptoonists always pictured Loyops over the three dim receivers. No, Unor was rather a plain little man, thin and somewhat long-nosed, and, altogether, he gave the impression of being gray. He was in his middle thirties. Until yesterday he had been the most faceless of citizens in a faceless State, a mere attendant and messenger in the Criminal Court Citadel. But since then they'd discovered—or at least had begun to suspect—his underground importance.

"Loyops," he mentaled. "Any Loyops, think in..."

He closed his eyes tightly, squinched his forehead and went into that state of dissociation which is the basic trick of mentaling. With the upper part of his mind he could think along an entirely different channel. He could reflect on how he'd come here...partly his own foolishness, partly bad luck...his job had been to smuggle in the last leaf for the last relay of the bomb planted under the Central Citadels; he'd done that part all right, but he'd forgotten to check out sick for an hour and Roeick, the prosecutor, had picked that particular time to need Unor's services...

"Contact. Contact, please. Loyops—"

The Belts had conducted the questioning, and it had been routine at first—until one incriminating thing began to lead to another. In the search for instance, they'd found the secret flap of skin a Loyop surgeon had made on the inner part of his thigh. They'd searched his quarters...neighbors peached on him, saying they'd noticed long absences, furtive comings and goings...they'd nosed through the offices and corridors where he spent his sixteen hour working day and under the clay in the washroom pipe joint they'd found his tiny transident—whose private signal would identify Unor to any other Loyop with the proper code.

That was why he mentaled now. He had to get word of his arrest out, so his transident signal would be canceled. A Belt operative with that device could get into the hidden councils of the Loyops, could discover and perhaps prevent The Bomb...

"Hello, Loyop," came a sudden answer in his brain. *"Who calls?"*

He took a deep breath. "Unor, of Capitol City Group. Don't identify yourself or give location—there may be thought monitors."

THE STATE had only a few men and women who could mental. They were genuine telepaths, born that way, and the method of teaching telepathy to anyone was, so far, a Loyop secret. It was mainly the discovery of Dr. Tzad, who had been arrested last year and who, at his trial, had publicly and willingly confessed to treason on twelve counts. There had been some fear that Dr. Tzad, under pressure, would give away the secret of mentaling, until it was remembered that by his principles the memory could be controlled—a fact could be deliberately forgotten during interrogation and the worst torture couldn't bring it back. After the trial and confession Dr. Tzad had been taken to the sonic chamber, driven mad, and then shipped off to work in the mid-continent atomic piles.

That was what usually happened.

"Are you still receiving?" Unor asked his new contact.

"Yes, I'm still here. Please go on."

Unor smiled a little. "It's possible you may be a thought monitor, and I have no transident to check—but I have to take that chance. If you're Loyop, you must pass the word I've been arrested. I finished my job, and I've been arrested—and I must know if plans are now changed for the next job."

"What next job?"

Unor stiffened. It wouldn't be like a Loyop to ask a direct question of that sort. It was possible—but not likely. He felt a finger of fear twisting his intestines. "That's all," he mentaled. "I'm thinking-off, now. No more."

"Very well," answered the other. *"No more."*

Unor came quickly back to his surroundings. He got up, stretched, then paced and looked around at the cell. The usual small compartment of stabilium metal, it was; the usual force screen at the threshold. More privileged prisoners got an opacity screen sometimes, giving them a little more privacy. Unor didn't think he'd be that favored. He had a pretty good idea of what would happen to him in the near future—he'd seen scores come and go in his job as attendant at the Criminal Courts Citadel. First they'd torture him for information. The Belts in their green uniforms and broad leather waistbands would do that. Fearful as it would be he felt he could stand the torture; he could at least turn his memory off while it lasted. The Conditioning was what he dreaded. The Conditioning would change him completely, of course, and when it was done he would walk into the courtroom deeply and sincerely and truly repentant, and he would stand there and make his public confession.

He heard heavy footsteps down the corridor, and somehow he knew it was for him. He rose, faced the doorway...

"Praise The One!" came a clipped, harsh voice echoing down the cell bloc. That would be the attendant at the outer force screen saluting the newcomers. The salute had sounded snappy and respectful—they would be important newcomers. It was funny about that salute, for the whole twenty-five years of its existence the State had been trying to popularize that phrase, *"Praise The One!"*—and plain people still tended to say instead hello or goodbye. Nevertheless it must have had its effect. It contributed surely to the awe and veneration constantly built about The One—

the Director of Affairs who ran, and who was the father of The State.

"Praise the One!"

Two Belts had come into sight, left-faced smartly, and stood before his cell. Young, rather good-looking men, quite tall, quite solid through the chests and shoulders.

Unor didn't answer their greeting. He waited quietly, the force screen hummed while it opened again, and then he walked out of the cell and took his place between them. He marched off, the clop of their boots and his own sad shuffle thick in his ears.

THE INFORMATION Room, as it was called, was at least thirty feet square, low ceilinged, gray, and very bare of furniture. A desk was at one end, and Roeick himself sat behind it. Unor was rather surprised to see someone as high-placed as the prosecutor here. Roeick was a tall, professorial-looking man of about fifty with a rumply manner. He looked kindly, except for his eyes which had a largely unmoving stare—probably this was the effect of extra-thick contact lenses.

He looked up as Unor was shoved before the desk, and, a little wearily, Unor thought, he said, "Praise The One."

Unor didn't answer.

Roeick glanced into the film reader on the desk before him— almost certainly it contained Unor's record. Then he looked up again. His voice was dry and somewhat monotonous. "What we require to know, first, Unor," he said, "is what job did you just finish—and what is the next job whose plans you thought might be changed?"

Unor, in spite of his determination to stay impassive, raised his eyebrows. He had been mentaling to a monitor, and not another Loyop, then. Now he had best drive out the memory of his underground activities as quickly as possible. He frowned, trembled, concentrated painfully, and in his mind's eye saw the images and the ideas fade away...

"Quickly!" said Roeick, gesturing to the several Belts about the room.

The Belts grabbed Unor. They started in cuffing him with rubber truncheons. They struck and kicked him, but that was merely for their own pleasure, and not nearly as painful as the truncheon blows. They went easily at first, keeping him completely conscious. As he was shoved back and forth Unor caught glimpses of Roeick sitting there, expressionless, absentminded, looking even a little uncomfortably at the whole thing.

The torture seemed to last the whole day. He screamed, and begged for mercy several times, as he had known he would. But he couldn't tell them what they wanted to know. He couldn't tell them what they wanted to know. He couldn't remember what they wanted to know. He tried to bring it back—anything to stop this agony—during the short session in the sonic chamber with the vibrations splitting his ears and shaking his very soul he screamed that he could get it back...he would find a way to get it back, if only they would stop...stop...stop...

But it was no use; he couldn't recall, and he knew that he wouldn't be able to recall until his cycle of awareness came to a peak again.

He said he would let them know, then. He said when he remembered he would tell them anything if they'd please, please not torture him—please—

There was no disgrace in this; no man could act otherwise under torture like that, and no Loyop expected a captured comrade to act otherwise.

The next day he was tortured again. And the day after that. And in between torturings he was fed a bare minimum of slop and the opacity screen was put on the cell and the illuminating charge taken from the stabilium walls so that he was always in darkness. There was a continuous, soft high hum sent into the cell, a note like the tearing of a fingernail or a back tooth bored to the nerve. He screamed at this, too. He beat his forehead against the walls until he split the scalp, and when they noticed that they set up a force screen around the walls, too.

Days, days, days of torture. Days. Daze...

Roeick's dry, droning voice:

"We know you plan a blow against The State. We know you mean to kill. Who would you kill? Me? The One? The One, himself? What were you instructed to do? Who are your colleagues? Where are they—these men who are with you? What was the job you managed to finish? Answer, answer, answer!" A second of unholy quiet, then: "More of the sonic chamber, now."

THEN THERE came the day in the gray Information Room when Roeick smiled, told him to sit down, and offered him a cigarette—and Unor knew the next phase had begun.

"Now you realize there's nothing personal in this treatment we've given you," said Roeick, mildly and pleasantly. "It's merely that regulations call for it. I would have been inclined to omit it, knowing how you Loyops can turn off your memories. But it had to be done. Our next task is to prepare your confession. You can make this one a lot easier—"

Unor shook his head. "I'll not do it willingly."

Roeick kept smiling, and clucked his tongue. "Come now, Unor, you're not a sentimentalist. You're a man of intelligence. Ability, too, I should think, since you hold such a high position in the Loyops. Oh, yes—we know that. We've ferreted out quite a bit since we captured you." He leaned back, dropped his palms to the desk, drummed gently with his long fingers. "Use reason, Unor. The end of all this remains the same, no, matter what you do. We will break you down, you will confess at the trial, and you will be punished. Probably sonicked, and sent to the piles. We can't, of course, simply allow you to sign the confession and then get up to read it at the trial. You wouldn't be sincere. When you're through with the Conditioning you will actually be sincere and repentant in your own mind. But you can still avoid a good deal of anguish by being cooperative."'

Unor looked around him, at the gray room, rather wistfully. "I haven't got very much left to me," he said, "no physical possessions…not much more self-respect. I think the one thing that is mine and that I can hang on to in this moment is my stubbornness."

"All right," sighed Roeick. "Very well."

The Conditioning began.

All sorts of devices were employed, but the basic principle remained the same, and very simple. Unor was given, alternating, rhythmic torture and kindness. An hour with the silent screaming of the sonic chamber…then an hour resting on a soft couch with

Roeick passing him coffee and cigarettes, smiling, droning softly and repeating over and over again the tenets of The State. *The State is All; the State is Mighty; It loves you and you are the child of the State—but you must give, give, give yourself. Surrender...Praise The One!* An hour of the Belts and their truncheons in the gray room. And then an hour at a well-laden table with Roeick...a roast, brandy, and cigars, and the droning voice: *The State may kill you for good reason, or no reason at all, but in your willingness to accept this lies your joy, your only real fulfillment in life. The One has shown us this. Praise The One!*

And the day when Unor frowned thoughtfully and murmured: "Perhaps I *have* been wrong in some ways—"

"Good!" said Roeick, that day. "Good lad. We're getting there. Let's try one more session in the sonic chamber, now."

"No, no, no, no, please! I repent! I confess! I love the State!" screamed Unor.

Roeick clapped him on the back and said jovially, "Not quite sincere enough yet—not quite."

Three days after that, Unor was ready for his confession at last. It was done in the gray room. They brought him the closely-typed sheets and they spent the day reading them, discussing each point carefully.

"Yes, that's true," Unor would say as he heard one of the charges. "I did plan to poison the entire water reservoir for Power City—wipe out everyone living there and weaken the State."

"But," said Roeick, "you are also accused of assassinating one Yelnot, the Manager of the Mountainville Aircraft Factory at the same time. How could you be in two places at once?"

"A detail like that," said Unor calmly, "is merely to make obscure the thinking of disloyal fools. All things can be explained by the State and in this case it is below the dignity of the State even to bother to explain."

"Fine, fine," said Roeick, smiling and nodding. "I must say, Unor, you've come through the conditioning very well!"

"Thank you," said Unor. "And thanks to the State for setting my thinking right in my last days of service to it."

Roeick beamed triumphantly to the Belts in the room. He was proud of his handiwork.

NOW THE days became long and idle. He spent them in the same cell, hemmed in by the same force screen and stabilium walls, but the edge of imprisonment was softened for him. He was given a threedim receiver and watched the little solid images on the platform by the hour as they performed in plays, operas, games and re-enactments of current history. Meals were brought to him and they were good meals, real food with a minimum of synthetics and concentrates. He was reminded constantly how the State was doing this for him...he was, even though condemned, a child of the State, after all. "I love the State," he would say to himself, nodding dully, sometimes with a foolish grin across his plain, gray face. "I love the State," And he meant it...

In this dim state of constant comfort he waited for the trial to come—scarcely ever really thinking about it; scarcely ever really thinking about anything.

"But you must remember, Unor. You must remember—"

These words came sharply and out of nowhere into his brain one day. They startled him. He looked around the cell, wondering if one of the speakers had spoken them.

"You must try hard, Unor. You must try as you have never tried before. Do you hear, Unor? Think to us, Unor, think!"

Vaguely, mushily, he began to realize what was happening. Someone was mentaling to him. More than just someone—it sounded like a chorus of thoughts. Loyops—yes, that was who it would be. Loyops. Something stirred within him, and then he fought that stirring and closed his eyes tightly and said aloud, "No, no. They would destroy the State! They are cancer in its body!" Yes. That was what he must think. The One had used those very words only the other day in a threedim speech.

"Come in, Unor—think with us—remember how proud you once were, Unor; remember the deep, inner happiness of that pride—"

Unor turned the speaker of the threedim up as loudly as possible to drive the sounds from his head. And he did blank them out that day, but in the night they came again, gnawing at his sleep, and he felt them penetrating more and more the barrier to his mind. *"Remember. Unor, Remember!"* He didn't think to report the voices. Somehow the Conditioning had left him without the ability to think clearly about things. He could only make his thoughts orderly when he was repeating to himself the precepts of The State, or the words of The One.

"Remember, Unor, Remember!"

One day, almost without willing it, he did sit down quietly, dissociate his mind and sent out an answer. "This is Unor."

There was a feeling of breathless triumph in the chorus of thoughts, then. *"Good, Unor. We thought we could get to you if we tried long enough. We have our strongest senders gathered here, mentaling together. These words are projected on a screen as they are typed, and we all read them and think them together. We have a contact among the State's telepaths, now, and we know when they are not monitoring. Now, Unor, you must remember. Your cycle will hit its peak at any time now, but we can't be sure it will come before the trial, before you are sonicked. You must remember, Unor—"*

UNOR, frowning, damping his eyes shut, wringing his hands, thought, "What is it I must remember?"

And then he did remember. It all came back to him. As it came, the obedient daze left by the Conditioning went away.

Once more—but with a strange, new light in his eyes—Unor quietly awaited the day of the trial.

Criminal Court A, in the midst of all the citadels of Central City, was a huge light, airy room with a ceiling forty feet high. It was paneled and furnished in carefully finished blond wood. The seven judges of the State sat on a dais at the head of the room and looked across their long, common desk into a well which contained the prisoner, his attorneys, and the prosecution staff. The spectators sat beyond the well in a kind of amphitheater. A tremendous portrait of The One overlooked all of it.

Recorders whirred and threedim cameras, their invisible beams scanning the molecular structure of their subjects, spun away.

The central judge of the seven was fat and bald, had a cheery blue eye, and had seemed all during the trial to be paying little attention to the goings-on. Now he glanced at the clock, looked for a second around the courtroom, then stared directly at Unor in the prisoner's well. Unor was standing. "Do you, Unor, Citizen number eight-six-one-one-zero-four, series two thousand and twelve, deny or confess to the charges?"

This was the moment. The courtroom stirred. In a quiet voice Unor answered properly, "I confess."

"Have you a statement of confession?"

"I have."

"The court will hear it."

The threedim cameras swung toward Unor, some focusing for a close-up of his face. He smiled a little dryly into the nearest lens. Then he faced the judges again. He picked up a manuscript of long, closely-typed sheets—his prepared confession. He congratulated himself on remembering to do that, so that they wouldn't stop him right away.

And then, in a quiet, gentle voice he began to speak—pretending to read.

"As a member of the underground, anti-State group which calls itself the Loyal Opposition, I have been guilty of many crimes—both of intent and actual commission—against the State. I will begin with the most heinous of these. To me was assigned the important task of blowing all Central City and its citadels into nothingness by means of an atomic bomb—"

"Wait!" Roeick had sprung to his feet. "This isn't his confession! This is something else!"

The fat, cheery-eyed judge smiled at Roeick. "Something else quite as good, perhaps. I think we will hear it anyway, Citizen Prosecutor. Proceed, Unor."

Now, throughout the court, eyebrows rose, heads and shoulders were straightened. Some of the judges leaned forward. Everyone stared at Unor.

He smiled again and went on, dropping the prepared statement this time.

"I now confess," he said, "the facts I was unable to confess during my interrogation, since I had then eliminated them from my memory. During the hour's absence which first brought suspicion upon me I went deep into the cellars of the citadels and placed the final part—a relay leaf—in an atomic bomb and firing mechanism concealed there. It has taken five years of careful underground activity to build the bomb there, completed. It was not discovered—first, because the underground rooms and corridors are so vast—cities in themselves—and second, because it was—and is—so artfully concealed."

"See here, is this bomb under the city right now?" interrupted the fat judge.

"It is," said Unor. A shuffling sound went through the court. People traded frowns with their neighbors. Unor cleared his throat. "The destruction of Central City, of course, would so thoroughly weaken the State that the Loyops could launch an uprising. That is the purpose of this bomb. But it has a rather ingenious trigger mechanism so that when the time comes one certain man can set it off at a practically illimitable distance."

Roeick popped up again. "Your Honors, this man needs more interrogation! I demand that—"

THE JUDGE waved his chubby fingers. "Later. Later you can have him, Roeick. We want to hear this story of his."

Unor continued. "All of you must have seen at one time the toys in which a dog, or something similar, is made to jump from a little house at the sounding of a certain word. This trigger mechanism is much like that. But it is more complicated—in effect a pattern of photo-electric cells is trained upon an oscilloscopic register so that only the pattern made by a *certain individual voice pronouncing certain pre-arranged* words will activate the cells, and start the electric impulse which triggers the bomb."

They were terribly quiet, now; they stared.

"The microphonic pickup," continued Unor, broadening his smile a bit, "is not much different in principle from the listening ears employed by the State to hear conversations at great distances and through walls. In fact everything being said in this courtroom today is being modulated on that very oscilloscopic register near the bomb."

The fat judge made a quick, sweeping gesture. "Order the Belts to search the entire underground city immediately—every corner—every closet—"

"That won't be necessary, Your Honor," said Unor. "I will tell you where the bomb is."

"Then do it quickly." The judge slapped the desk with his chubby palm. He had lost his smile.

"It is almost directly beneath the Citadel of the Director," said Unor. "But of course its blast would destroy the city and suburbs, too. The interesting thing is that the one man whose voice is preset on the photoelectric cells can set it off instantly simply by saying the chosen words. He can do it before you reach the bomb."

"Who's the man?" snapped the judge. "And the words, what are—" In that moment the judge guessed it, or began to guess it, and his fat face started to fall apart—

"The man chosen to trigger the bomb," said Unor, "is myself." His smile was as broad as it could be now, and there was a great sweeping sense of peace and fulfillment within him. He saw great puddles of horror spread out on all the faces before him. He heard someone scream, "No! No!" and it sounded very much like Roeick's voice. "And the words that will sound the end of the State," said Unor, "are those I've never said, but now say proudly—"

There was a rush for the exits. Several Belts, standing guard about the courtroom reached for their pistols And Unor squared his shoulders, and in a loud, firm voice said, "Praise The One!"

The rumble of the explosion had already started before the echo of his phrase died from the big courtroom...

THE END

The Beast of Boredom

By RICHARD R. SMITH

It wasn't a weapon or a bribe, as he thought. But it was the most ingenious trap of all time!

THE SHACK at the edge of the dead canal was so carefully camouflaged, he almost passed by it. Hoping he hadn't been seen, he dropped to his stomach and crawled through the mud toward the door.

It wasn't a long distance, but inching his way on his elbows and knees, and with his face close to the evil-smelling mud, it seemed like a mile. As he crawled, he reflected bitterly that most of mankind's really great achievements always ended in war. Columbus had crossed the Atlantic Ocean and it had ended in war with the Indians. Mankind had invented atomic energy and then used it to kill millions. Their latest achievement was the marvel of spaceflight and where had that ended? It had also ended in war...

Personally, he didn't believe they were justified in fighting the Martians. If they didn't want anyone intruding on their planet, what right did Earthmen have to force their way? The popular theory that they could help rebuild the dying Martian civilization didn't seem very logical when millions had to be killed in the process. And if Martians were an independent race and wanted to sit around and watch their civilization crumble, why shouldn't they have that privilege?

When he was within a few yards of the door, he set aside his philosophical thoughts. Leaping to his feet, he ran into the small shack and screamed shrilly in the manner designed to momentarily paralyze an enemy with fear.

He raised the rifle instinctively when something moved in the shadows, and as his eyes adjusted to the dim light, he felt a queasiness in his stomach. The emaciated alien who cowered in the shadows resembled a pitiful bundle of rags more than an enemy!

Trembling hands lifted an object and three things happened so rapidly that they seemed to happen simultaneously: the Martian's bony fingers moved over the object; a burning sensation ripped through his brain; he realized it must be a weapon and squeezed the trigger of his rifle.

When the sharp crack stopped echoing in his ears, he examined the still form and discovered he'd been mistaken. The object wasn't a weapon. It was a metal globe six inches in diameter and studded with precious jewels. The Martian had offered it in exchange for his life.

THE WINDOWS of his apartment on the fourteenth floor were open and a gentle breeze chilled the sweat on his face as he worked with the knife. He had previously removed four jewels from the metal globe, but the large ruby he'd selected this time seemed to be embedded deeper.

The blade slipped and slashed the palm of his left hand. Cursing the artifact and all Martians in general, he attacked the ruby furiously and grunted with satisfaction when he dislodged it.

The red jewel rolled across the table and fell to the floor. Picking it up gingerly as if it were a fragile thing of glass, he held it in the sunlight and watched the myriad facets sparkle like a one-color kaleidoscope. It was the largest jewel of all and worth a small fortune...

A sharp pain in his hand reminded him of his wound and he went to the bathroom. After carefully washing the cut, he applied iodine and was trying to find a bandage when...

The ruby rolled across the table and fell to the floor.

Startled, he leaped back and upset the chair. A second before, he'd been in the bathroom and now he was at the table! Amnesia? He couldn't remember walking back to the living room and although he thought he'd put iodine on the cut, there was none on it that he could see.

He went to the bathroom...

The ruby rolled across the table and fell to the floor.

He was sitting before the table again without any memory of having left the bathroom! It had happened *twice*.

Taking the globe to the window, he examined it carefully and saw that where the ruby had been lodged, there was now an opening through the metal. When he held it at a certain angle, he saw a maze of wiring and tiny mechanisms inside.

He had fought the Martians for two years. He had traveled across their red deserts, crawled on the muddy bottoms of their gigantic dead canals, walked through the remains of their ancient cities and heard legends about the great Martian empire that had slowly crumbled during the centuries.

He remembered the legends about Martian time machines and he accepted the fact readily: the object in his hand was a time trap. An ancient, intricate, scientific booby-trap!

The Martian had known he would die and had deliberately planned his revenge. Perhaps the machine wasn't strong enough to take anyone far into the past or future; that would explain why he hadn't used it to escape. But it was evidently strong enough to be used as a trap, and perhaps it had even been designed for that purpose centuries ago. Removing the ruby had triggered it…

Ironic, he reflected, that he'd gone to so much trouble and expense to smuggle the thing from Mars to Earth. The jewels were worth a fortune and it had never occurred to him that the metal globe might have some *function*. Actually, he had smuggled an ingenious death-trap back to Earth with him.

He shuddered at the thought.

The ruby rolled across the table and…

He was once again sitting before the Martian artifact, his eyes once again focused on the ruby as it rolled across the table. Like something in a magician's act, he had disappeared from his position near the window and reappeared in the chair. As before, the cut on his hand stung painfully, but this time he ignored it and kept his eyes focused on his wrist watch.

It was eleven forty-five eastern standard time.

The ruby rolled across the table...

His eyes were no longer focused on the watch, but he remembered that the hands had last indicated eleven fifty-five. And now they were back at *eleven forty-five*. He was trapped in a period of time only ten minutes long!

He lit a cigarette with trembling fingers and tried to think calmly. What danger was there in a time trap? He felt no physical pain and so far the trap had only caused him small inconveniences. Anything he did during the ten-minute period was magically undone when he was thrown backward in time. He had put iodine on the cut on his hand and it had disappeared. He had walked to the window, but at the beginning of the next cycle, without any conscious sensation, he found himself sitting in the chair once more. But how could movement through time harm him?

And was he the only one aware of the trap?

He turned the television set on and watched a news announcer during several following cycles. Before long, he was convinced that he was the only one who was aware of the repeated time interval. The news announcer represented everyone in the world, and if he were conscious of the fact that he'd read the same news more than a dozen times, there would have been some change in his expression!

He recalled how the Martian had moved his fingers over the globe and how he'd felt a burning sensation inside his skull. The device had evidently been adjusted to his neural pattern so that only he was conscious of the trap. Or else only someone within a certain effective radius—fifty feet, for instance—was conscious of the repeated time intervals.

Although he'd always believed the stories about the time machines and he now had proof of their existence, he still found it difficult to comprehend their operation. He had heard that such a machine concentrated on only a few atoms of a radioactive substance. By drawing energy from the space-time continuum itself, the machine succeeded in thrusting those atoms backward or forward in time, and since that affected the entire probability stream, all physical matter was forced to follow them through the time stream.

He couldn't totally comprehend the concept, but he realized he had to do *something* nevertheless, and during following cycles that totaled hours, he tried to decide on a course of action. He recalled the Martian legend about how a particularly vicious criminal had been punished with a similar machine. The unfortunate had been tossed into a pit filled with lion like animals and then, by repeating the time interval, he had been made to suffer the same death a thousand times. In his own case, he was in no physical danger, but he knew that an enemy was creeping toward him...an enemy that could kill him as surely as any lion...*boredom*.

If he submitted to boredom and just sat through the endless time cycles, it would be the same as sitting in a room for weeks, months, or years. That would be the same as solitary confinement and would eventually drive him insane.

So, there were two possibilities: he could attempt to wreck the machine or wait for it to wear itself out and fight boredom while waiting.

It didn't take him long to decide that he should wait for the machine to run down. If the alien devices really drew energy from the space-time continuum, it would be dangerous to tamper with one. A wrong move when fooling with such a tremendous amount of energy might be disastrous, and perhaps that was exactly what the old Martian had planned for him to do! On the other hand, it didn't seem possible that a machine could run, *forever*.

There should be plenty of ways to keep himself occupied and his mind busy while he waited...

He began reading the magazines scattered about the apartment. There was only time to read a few pages, but he mentally noted the page number during each cycle and when the succeeding interval began, he opened the magazine to that exact page and continued...

The ruby rolled across the table and...

The preceding cycles seemed like an eternity when he looked back upon them. He had read every magazine from cover to cover, watched every television program and listened to every radio program countless times until he had them memorized word for word. He had worked the crossword puzzles in the newspaper several times and explored every square inch of the apartment.

He had no more ideas so he tried to sleep…

HE KNEW it was useless: during each ten-minute interval, he had time to walk from the chair to the davenport, close his eyes and relax his body. But then, at the moment when he was about to fall asleep, he would always find himself in the tediously familiar chair.

He hoped he would grow tired and be able to fall asleep, but finally realized it was impossible. Since the machine influenced the space-time continuum and the same ten-minute interval in time was always repeated, all physical things in space were exactly as they had been at the beginning of the cycle. His body had been refreshed at the beginning of the original cycle and it would always be in the same condition. He would never grow older, he would never become hungry and he would never become tired *physically*.

DESPERATE for a way to overcome boredom, he used the bottle of whiskey in the kitchen. After several attempts, he discovered to his dismay that there were ways to get violently sick from gulping liquor but, no possible way to get drunk in ten minutes!

He sat through endless cycles staring at the empty air; began to have wild thoughts and knew he was on the verge of insanity. And if he were losing the fight with boredom, he might as well try the other alternative: break the machine and hope it wouldn't blow up in his face.

Taking a long-bladed knife, he attacked the small mechanisms inside the globe. He probed, twisted and jabbed but they seemed indestructible.

Furious, he held it underwater with the hope that water would short-circuit electrical contact if there were any.

When that didn't work, he beat it with a hammer, kicked it, threw it about the room and as a last result, dropped it from the window.

It bounced off the sidewalk fourteen floors below and attracted attention, but a few minutes later he was once more sitting in the chair and watching the sickeningly familiar ruby as it rolled across the sickeningly familiar table.

He stared at the telephone. If only it would ring; if only someone would call him and break the *monotony!* But that was impossible. At the beginning of each cycle, all physical things and
events were exactly as they had been...

Telephone!

He could use it to break the monotony—he could phone all his
friends!

He telephoned all his friends and talked with them for numerous ten-minute intervals that totaled days. Because they were
always unaware of the previous cycles, his repeated phone calls
never annoyed them. Sometimes he told them about the time trap
but it was beyond their comprehension and they always thought he
was drunk, so he learned not to mention it.

When he tired of talking to his friends, he started at the front of
the telephone directory and began calling every name. He made
dates with girls he'd never seen, memorized marvelous sales talks
and sold non-existent vacuum cleaners and cars. Sometimes he
pretended to be the master of ceremonies on a quiz program and
when someone answered a difficult question, he told them they had
just won a dollar. The various reactions he received were amusing
and broke the monotony, but after a few days, even that became
boring.

He tried to leave the hotel's fourteenth floor, but discovered
that the elevator boy was not on the job at that particular time.
Although he ran to the elevator at the beginning of numerous
cycles and pushed the *down* button, the indicator needle never
moved during the ten minutes.

He used the stairs at the end of the corridor with the hope of
reaching another floor and meeting someone. To see someone or
speak to someone in person would have done a lot to break the
monotony, but he found that the thirteenth and fifteenth floors
were inaccessible. The doors that led to them from the stairway
wouldn't push in and there was no hand-grip to pull them outward.
Evidently the hotel management used the method to prevent
burglars from having an absurdly easy and unseen access to the
apartments. Anyone could leave a floor and use the stairs to reach
the hotel lobby, but anyone wishing to go from the lobby to a

certain floor or from one floor to another was forced to use the elevator.

Cursing the bad luck, he sat for hours and wondered what he could do. He was restricted to succeeding but separate and identical time intervals, and that was also a physical restriction in effect: ten minutes wasn't long enough to leave that floor of the hotel.

HE NOW THOUGHT of boredom as an ugly monster that lurked everywhere about him and waited…waited to seize him with sharp teeth of inactivity…

Desperate for the sight of another person, he tried to enter the other apartments. There were five on that floor, but of them, only the one next to his own seemed to be occupied. When he knocked, there was no answer, but he pressed an ear against the door and heard the faint sound of running water. Whoever the occupant was, he or she was taking a shower and couldn't hear him no matter how hard he knocked.

It irritated him because the apartment was so close. If he could contact the person somehow, he or she could be reached at the beginning of each cycle and would be a tangible individual to help him fight boredom—not a voice on the telephone, an image on the TV screen or a tiny dot of a person fourteen floors below his window.

By phoning the hotel desk, he learned that a woman named Mary Jeffers rented apartment 1403, and he found her telephone number in the directory.

Dialing the number, he was relieved when she answered within a few minutes. The ringing of the phone was evidently loud enough to penetrate the noise of the shower while his knocking on the door hadn't been.

"Mary Jeffers?" he asked.

"Yes?"

"Mary, are you a college graduate?"

"Yes. Who is this? Why do you want to know?"

"This is the police. It's very important. Which college did you attend?"

He knew it was a flimsy trick to get information, but he caught her off guard and she answered, "The University of Delaware."

He hung up the phone and waited until the next cycle. Dialing the number again, he said, "Mary? This is Harry Ogden."

Because of the nature of the time trap, she was unaware of the previous conversation, and her automatic reply to the unfamiliar voice was, "Ogden? You must have the wrong number. I don't know anyone by that name."

"Don't you remember? I went to the University of Delaware with you. I remember you. You have blonde hair and—"

"No. It's brunette."

Hanging up the phone, he waited until the next cycle, dialed the number again and said, "Mary? This is Harry Ogden."

"Ogden? You must have the wrong number. I don't know anyone by that name."

"Don't you remember? I went to the University of Delaware with you. I remember you. You're a brunette about a hundred and thirty pounds and—"

"Well, not quite that much."

By calling dozens of times, he used the system to learn more and more about Mary Jeffers, until at last he knew enough to convince her within a few minutes that he was a friend from her college days whom she'd forgot.

As he talked with her during various cycles that totaled weeks, he began to feel as if she *were* a friend, and the desire to see her in person increased. The sight of anyone would have done wonders to break the monotony, and she was the only possibility since all the other apartments were empty.

"I have the apartment next to yours," he said during one time cycle. "Can I come over?"

"I'm not dressed," she replied. "I was taking a shower. Give me time to get dressed."

He glanced at his watch and saw that only four minutes remained in that cycle. He realized despairingly that there wasn't time for her to get dressed. All his efforts had been in vain: ten minutes wasn't long enough to phone her, go through the carefully memorized routine convincing her he was an old friend...wait for her to dress and open the door of her apartment.

It couldn't be done in ten minutes!

BOREDOM was like a hungry beast that breathed in his ears with a roar of silence while he sat through several succeeding cycles.

Silence. It seemed to echo in his ears as he looked about the apartment. It seemed to whisper that he was losing the duel. The Martian's trap was working: he would sit and wait, and think, and think endlessly until they were wild thoughts and he was insane. And then, the Martian would have his revenge, for insanity was a form of walking death...

He made a decision. He had fought boredom legally and exhausted every method he could think of. If there were no more legal ways, then he would fight boredom *illegally*. The police couldn't reach him in ten minutes no matter what he did.

Dialing Mary Jeffers phone number at the beginning of the next cycle, he laid the receiver on the desk, ran across the room and climbed through the window.

The stone ledge just beneath his window wasn't very wide, but by inching his way along it, he reached the open window of apartment 1403.

Climbing through the window, he saw that Mary Jeffers had picked up the telephone receiver with one hand and was trying to dry herself with a towel in the other.

"Hello," she said.

Her back was to him, but he noticed that she wasn't very efficient with the towel. Water dripped from her body and collected in a small pool around her feet.

He grinned and said, "Hello."

She whirled to face him and dropped the telephone receiver, her dark brown eyes widening.

"Harry Ogden," he said. "Remember?"

As soon as he asked the question, he knew it was a foolish one. The time trap was his trap alone and only he was conscious of all the repeated cycles. She was unaware of all their previous conversations and he was now a stranger to her.

She backed away and let out a scream.

It didn't bother him. It was music to his ears—a sound that broke the silence of his peculiar world—a weapon to combat boredom with, and he reflected that he would make many trips to apartment 1403...

The ruby rolled across the table and fell to the floor.

He smiled as he picked the ruby up from the floor. He estimated that he'd lived more than twenty years in ten-minute intervals, and therefore the trap was not a death trap. He'd discovered countless ways of fighting boredom and knew he would never succumb to it and resultant insanity. He had entered the other apartments by using the stone ledge and breaking through the windows. In them he had found a total of hundreds of books ...a pair of binoculars that he used to study a multitude of new things from his window...a typewriter that he used to write books although there was never a completed manuscript...a chess set...decks of cards...hobbies...

There were many more possibilities that he hadn't explored yet and he realized that the Martian had given him a valuable gift: extra years of life.

It seemed incredible that a machine could operate continuously for twenty years, but the ancient Martians had been expert in constructing devices without moving parts. He knew little science, but he could vaguely imagine a sort of "gateway" to the space-time continuum that the removal of the ruby had opened. Perhaps during a ten-minute period a predetermined amount of energy passed through the "gateway" and flowed against a radioactive substance in a way and with a force that thrust a few atoms backward in time to the point when the energy didn't exist and that established the cycle.

With moving parts, the machine wouldn't have run continuously for twenty years. *Something* would have broken down. Even without moving parts, the machine wouldn't run forever; the materials themselves would deteriorate sooner or later, or the energy passing through them from the space-time continuum would gradually disintegrate them no matter how strong they were. But for as long as the device operated, he would live without growing old. If it ran a hundred years, he would live *a hundred years*...

The ruby rolled across the table and fell to the floor.

He rubbed his aching head. He had lived approximately thirty years at ten-minute intervals, but the headache had started and grown in intensity during the last year and it was difficult to recall and appreciate all the things he had done.

The ruby rolled...

How many years had he lived? Fifty? A hundred? He was unable to calculate it any more, and it was even difficult to think about much simpler things. His mind was filled with memories...millions...billions...trillions of endless, countless memories without any sleep to relax his mind...with no rest at all...

The ruby...

He no longer moved about the apartment, but sat in the chair during every cycle and watched the ruby as it rolled endlessly. Memories were like a crushing, paralyzing weight in his mind...a weight that grew and grew and...

The old Martian he had killed would have his revenge. He realized the ingenious machine was much more than a gift or a death trap. It was a torture machine. A torture machine that would operate for centuries; a machine that would gradually crush his mind and kill him with the sheer weight of *memories...*

He screamed.

THE END

Witness

By GEORGE H. SMITH

Edith was just a computer, but a very good one and a very observing one. So it was quite natural that she be consulted about the doctor's murder...

BALLARD was quite dead. There could be no doubt of it. He lay sprawled in front of Edith, with his head very messily bashed in and with one hand still extended toward her. A long shimmering stream of blood ran halfway across the large room. Dr. Dudley Ballard had been as inconsiderate in his dying as he had been in his living.

Art MacKinney and I stood in the doorway and stared. We were shocked not so much by the fact that Ballard was dead as by the fact that he lay in this most secret room, this holy of holies. Ours was the most security conscious project in the whole country; and this was where he had picked to get himself killed.

"God! There'll really be a stink about this," MacKinney breathed.

"Well, I can't think of anyone who had it coming more than he did," I said. I hated Ballard's guts and everyone knew it, so there was no point in being hypocritical now.

Edith stood silently. She didn't seem to be interested in the fact that the man who had run her life, who had spent hours shouting questions at her and criticizing her slightest error with burning sarcasm was now dead. No, Edith wasn't interested, but you couldn't really expect her to be—she was only a computing machine, a mechanical brain, the final result of years of work by the best cybernetics experts in the world. Edith was silent, and would be, until we turned her on and fed the tapes into her.

"It looks as though this is what did it," MacKinney said, indicating a large spanner lying on the floor beside Ballard. He touched it gingerly with his foot. His face was white and strained and it occurred to me that he was more upset than I thought he should be. After all, he had as much reason to hate the dead man as the rest of us. Ballard had taken advantage of his position as head of the research project to make passes at Jane Currey and MacKinney wasn't at all a cool scientist when it came to Jane. He was engaged to her and quite naturally resented Ballard's attentions to her.

"You'd better not touch that until the police get here," I said as he bent over to pick up the spanner.

"Yeah I guess you're right—I forgot. How do you suppose this got in here anyway?"

"One of the workmen making adjustments on Edith's outer casing must have left it. I saw it sitting up there on top of her late yesterday afternoon," I told him. "You'd better go call Mr. Thompson and—the FBI."

With Ballard gone, I was in charge. Maybe someone would think that was reason enough for me to kill him. I didn't care, I was just glad he was gone. Now he couldn't mistreat Edith anymore.

I turned Edith on just as MacKinney returned. "What are you doing?" he asked.

"Why I'm going to wake Edith up and feed these tapes into her. After all these are more important than any one man's life."

"You didn't care much for Ballard, did you Bill?"

I gave him look for look as I replied. "Can you name anyone around here that did?"

He shook his head. "No—I guess not. But maybe it wasn't one of us. It might have been an outside job, you know, Edith was working on that space station stuff and the iron curtain people would give a lot to know about it."

"Hell," I said pressing the studs and levers that would arouse Edith and put her to work. "You don't really think anyone could get past those security guards, do you?"

Happily I went about the business of waking Edith, my sleeping beauty, from her slumbers. In a very few seconds, her hundreds of tiny red eyes were gleaming with intelligence.

Good morning, Edith. I punched out the tape and fed it into her.

There was the faintest pause, while Edith's photo-electric cells surveyed the room, pausing for a moment on the sprawled body of Ballard.

Good morning, Bill Green, she typed back. I knew she was happy to see me by the cheerful little clicks she emitted.

I have some interesting work for you this morning, Edith. And I think you'll be glad to know that we will be working together from now on instead of...

"Hey! What's the idea of starting that machine?" a gray haired, gray suited security agent demanded, striding into the room with MacKinney, Mr. Thompson and several other officers at his heels. "Don't you know enough not to touch anything in here?"

"This work is too important to be stopped—even for a murder," I said, and Mr. Thompson nodded in agreement.

"That's right," he said, mopping his perpetually perspiring forehead, "this work has top priority from Washington." He looked nervous and I couldn't help wondering what he was thinking. There had been stories circulating about Ballard and Thompson's wife and the dome-headed little man must have heard them too. Ballard just couldn't keep his hands off any female within reach. That was one of the reasons he was so thoroughly hated.

The youngest of the security agents rose from where he had been kneeling beside Ballard and crossed to me.

"You're Green, aren't you?" I nodded and he continued, "How did you know it was murder?"

I laughed at him. "How the hell could a man bash in his own brains that way?"

The gray haired man stepped into the breach. He gave us all a thorough going over, but concentrated on MacKinney and me. He seemed to think it peculiar that neither of us could give any reason for Ballard's being alone with Edith. I was sure I knew, but no one would have believed me so I made no attempt to enlighten him.

"Well, I guess that's all we can do now," he said at last. "Someone from the local police will have to be notified and brought in after they get security clearance." He turned to go.

"Wait a minute," MacKinney said, "we're all overlooking one thing."

"What's that?"

"There was an eye witness to this crime," he said, and I stared at him in consternation. I didn't know he knew. I thought I was the only one who knew.

"What do you mean," the agent demanded angrily.

"Edith saw it. Edith, the computer."

"Are you nuts?" the agent demanded.

"You forget that Edith was turned off," Thompson said.

"But Mr. Thompson, Edith's not like most cybernetic machines. She's so far advanced, that I'm not sure we understand her completely. She can't really be turned off. She has a distinct personality and that new circuit—"

Of course Edith had a personality of her own! She had more charm, more intelligence, more understanding than most women.

"—well—she'd be able to tell us who killed Ballard."

"That's ridiculous," I said, badly frightened. "A machine can't be a witness to murder."

The security officer looked dubious and shook his head. "I guess we'll have to leave that up to the coroner at the inquest."

"But they can't ask questions like that of Edith," I protested. "She's—she's too important to the national defense to have some country coroner asking her silly questions about the murder of a man who deserved to die anyway." I had to prevent this. I had to get around this eye witness business.

Thompson looked at me levelly. "MacKinney may be right, Green. The coroner may very well want to talk to Edith and there's no reason we should object if Security gives him clearance."

"But Mr. Thompson, our work—it'll be interrupted."

"We'll have to take that chance. And I think Washington will agree."

"But—" Couldn't they see that there wasn't any question of spying here. Couldn't they understand that Ballard had just gotten what he had coming. I couldn't let them question Edith. At least not until I had a chance to talk to her alone.

"And Green—because of your rather strange behavior, I'm afraid I'll have to ask you to stay in your quarters until the inquest. MacKinney will handle your work with Edith until then."

I was shocked and really frightened now. I wouldn't get to talk to her, wouldn't get a chance to tell her what to say. I protested, but Thompson was firm, so firm that he placed a guard outside my door to make sure I didn't leave.

Washington rushed through clearance for the local officers and the inquest was held three days later. The coroner proved to be a shrewd country doctor, who had the inquest adjourned to the computer room as soon as he heard MacKinney's ideas about Edith.

The security guards on duty the night of the murder testified that only MacKinney, Thompson, Ballard and I had had access to the computer room; and it had already been established that it would have been impossible for a spy or foreign agent to have slipped into the heavily guarded room. It was clearly an inside job.

With all of us at the scene of the crime, the coroner summed it up for us. "—and since it could not have been the work of an outsider, it must have been a crime of a private nature." He looked closely at Thompson, MacKinney and me. "A crime of a private nature with the motive either revenge, jealousy or ambition. We know that the victim was an over-bearing man with a good many unpleasant traits. We know he was a man who forced his attentions on women, who was ill-tempered and abusive to those who worked with him. A man who had many enemies—but there were only three people who had the chance to attack him on this particular night.

"I am going to attempt to establish the identity of the killer by the unusual procedure of questioning a machine. It will be for later courts to establish the validity of such testimony. Because of the nature of this case and because of the urgent need to get this computer back to its proper work, I am going to ask the questions in a more direct manner than I would ordinarily employ."

MacKinney took his place before Edith. They didn't even trust me to feed the tapes into her under their very eyes.

"Mr. Thompson, I object to the use of this delicate piece of equipment in—"

They ignored me, and MacKinney punched out the questions the coroner asked:

"Do you know who murdered Dr. Ballard?"

There was a pause. Edith blinked several times. I was shaking with apprehension for her. A mind so delicate and noble should not be faced with such a dilemma.

Yes, she typed back.

"Did you witness the murder?"

There was a longer pause this time. "You must answer the question," MacKinney reminded her.

I was here.

"Is it true that you do not lose your perceptive qualities when we turn you off?" MacKinney asked this on his own.

It is true.

"We might as well get to the heart of the matter," the coroner said. "Did Mr. Thompson kill Ballard?"

Edith clicked and her eyes glowed. *No.*

"Did Mr. MacKinney kill Ballard?"

No.

Edith had to tell the truth...it was an innate part of her personality. I tensed in my seat. I wanted to scream, to leap at MacKinney and prevent, somehow, the asking of the next question. But there wasn't a chance.

"Did Mr. Green kill Dr. Ballard?"

Edith's beautiful electric eyes flashed and her clicks pulsed twice as rapidly as before. There was such a roaring and wrenching within her I was afraid for her—she was being torn apart in her struggle not to answer. I couldn't stand listening to her desperate efforts any longer.

"Yes!" I leapt to my feet. "Yes, I did it. Leave her alone. Can't you see what you're doing to her? That swine was always mistreating her. He didn't understand her—no one understands her as I do!"

The coroner looked at me closely. "Is that really why you killed him, Mr. Green?"

"No! You were wondering why he was here by himself while no work was going on. He—he had begun to feel about Edith as he did about all women. He sneaked back here to be alone with her. He wanted to—he wanted to—" My voice broke and they stared at me in shocked amazement.

Into the silence MacKinney read what Edith had slowly typed out:

"Mr. Green did not kill Dr. Ballard."

"Yes—yes I did," I screamed. "Don't Edith—"

"Who did kill him?" the coroner asked, quietly.

This was the question I had wanted to avoid. I sank down, my hands cradling my aching head. Edith must have expected the question. She had her answer ready.

I refuse to state on the grounds that it may tend to incriminate me.

My poor, sweet, adorable Edith. If only I had had a chance to talk to her, to tell her what to say. I had known…ever since I had seen the spanner and remembered where it had been before. I could have warned her to say that Ballard had attacked her, threatened her, to say anything… but not to attempt to hide behind a Fifth Amendment that didn't exist anymore. My darling never had kept up with current events.

Now they'll disconnect her, they'll rewire her, they'll destroy her understanding, her warmth, her whole personality…and I…I love her, I love her…

THE END

Weep No More, My Robot

By CHESTER GEIER

Lilith was only a robot, so it couldn't be murder to get rid of her, could it?

BRYCE looked up from the microscope as the click of high heels on the laboratory floor reached his ears. Nadine stood just within the door, pulling on gloves with sharp, brisk movements of her hands.

"You're all dressed up," Bryce commented, stretching cramped arms. "Going for a spin in the gyro?"

Nadine Bryce shook her lovely head, her green eyes solemn and steady on his. "No, Curt, I'm leaving."

Bryce rose abruptly from his stool. "Why, Nadine, what do you mean?"

"Just what I said, Curt. I'm leaving. Bag and baggage. This is good-bye."

Bryce swayed, as though from the force of a blow. "I—I don't understand…"

"That has always been the trouble with you, Curt," Nadine told him, with sudden resentment. "You never did understand anything that wasn't connected with your work. Well, you're entitled to an understanding—and you're going to get it. I'm sick of all this." The angry sweep of her arm included the gleaming glass and chrome interior of the laboratory, and the lonely vista of cliffs and ocean which showed through the broad windows. "I'm sick of living like a hermit. I'm still young. I want friends, parties, good times. I'll never get them by staying with you. You're too absorbed in your work."

"I see," Bryce said, with quiet bitterness. He looked at his hands, and for a moment he was silent. Then his face lifted, urgent with pleading. "Nadine, you're the one who doesn't understand. Can't you see that my work would have meant friends and good times in the end? I know the kind of friends and good times you mean. You can't have them without money, Nadine. Everything I've been doing has been toward the goal of gaining wealth, fame, and influence." Bryce knew this last was a lie, even as he uttered it. He loved his work for itself, not for what it would bring. But wealth, fame, and influence were things which Nadine would comprehend.

Nadine hesitated. "Do you really mean that, Curt?"

"Of course," Bryce answered, feeling a sudden justification for his falsehood. Anything to keep Nadine, he told himself. She and his work were vitally necessary to him. Each would not be complete without the other.

The exquisite oval of Nadine's face softened momentarily— then hardened again. "Oh, Curt, it's futile! I want to enjoy life now. Now, Curt! Not at some vague time in the future. You won't get anywhere with your work for years yet—and I'm tired of waiting."

"It wouldn't be much longer, Nadine. I've solved the most serious problems. The Bryce electronic brain is almost a reality." Bryce went to her, placed his hands on her arms. "Nadine, you love me, don't you?"

She looked away, biting her lip.

His hands tightened. "Nadine?"

"Yes. Oh, yes, Curt! But it's no use."

"You won't wait?"

"No, Curt. I'm sorry. I've stood this kind of life as long as I could, and I just won't have any more."

BRYCE'S hands dropped to his sides as though suddenly devoid of life. His voice was leaden. "Well, I don't see anything I can do. I could leave all this and take you to the city and try to make you happy—but...the fact is I sunk every cent I had into this laboratory. I'm in too deep to back out." Bryce straightened, forcing a smile. "Maybe what you need is a vacation, Nadine. I've a little money coming in from some patents, and I'll supply you with what you'll need. Perhaps after a while you'll see things differently."

"Perhaps, Curt." Nadine's voice was a murmur. Her green eyes avoided his.

Bryce placed his hand beneath her chin, raised her face, and kissed her lips. "Good-bye, Nadine. Have a good time."

"Good-bye, Curt."

He watched her go, heard the tap-tap of her high heels grow faint, and finally die. There was the roar of the gyro's motor from the tiny landing field outside. Then that died, too. Bryce sighed, feeling suddenly old.

He sat down on the stool and touched the microscope, but all desire for work had left him. Removing his smock, he left the laboratory, taking the sea-shell path down to the cliffs. The sun was bright and the sky cloudless, a stiff breeze from the ocean whipped against his shirt and trousers. He drew its cool salty fragrance in deep, walking fast.

He could not out walk the bitter knowledge that he and Nadine had made a mistake—Nadine, gay and fun-loving, and, he, the staid, serious-minded robotics engineer. Nadine was a Landrey, a name which had long been synonymous with wealth, but generations of Landry's as gay and fun-loving as she had depleted the family fortune until only the prestige of a memory remained. He, Bryce, had not possessed the advantage of a family tradition, having gained recognition through sheer ability in his chosen line of work. Starting as a raw technician with Vanneman Robots—a pioneer firm in robot manufacture—he had quickly worked his way up to head of the research department, attaining a measure of fame by his invention of a new and improved robot type.

He had met Nadine at a banquet given in his honor by Cyrus Vanneman, famous inventor of the first practical robot and founder of Vanneman Robots. Love was the great leveling agent which had made all differences in heredity and environment seem insignificant. And at that time, intrigued by the novelty of parties and dances, Bryce had not found it difficult to fit into the pattern of Nadine's life. They had been married while still held in that giddy whirl of entertainment. Then, later, Bryce had again become absorbed in his work to the exclusion of all else. He had left Vanneman Robots for this laboratory near the ocean, to work on a robot brain which he hoped would lead to a robot type almost human.

Bryce had overcome the most serious difficulties in his work on the Bryce electronic brain. The elusive hand of success had almost been within his grasp—and Nadine had rebelled against the loneliness and seclusion of the life which she had been forced to lead. Bryce wondered if the wealth which his electronic brain was sure to bring would make a difference. A chill of foreboding spread through him as he recalled the lack of response that had been in her farewell kiss.

THE sun was edging its way down toward the horizon when Bryce returned to the house. Jones stood before the entrance to the living room, watching with the expressionless sight-cells that were his eyes. Jones was a Vanneman robot of the latest type, slim-bodied and soft-footed. He served as housekeeper and cook, and was as efficient as he was tireless.

"I was looking for you, Mr. Bryce," Jones said. "Dinner is served."

Bryce nodded. "I went for a little walk."

"I also looked for Mrs. Bryce," Jones said. "I could not find her."

"She went to the city," Bryce explained. "She won't be back for some time."

The implications of Bryce's last words were lost on Jones. He repeated, "Dinner is served," and entered the house, his internal mechanism clicking and humming softly.

Bryce ate a solitary meal, then went to the laboratory and resumed his work. He felt an urgent necessity to do something. He hoped that busy fingers and an occupied mind would bring relief from thoughts of Nadine. But no amount of concentration could ease the dull ache which throbbed deep within him.

The days passed in bright succession. It was late summer, and the sky was prevailingly blue and clear. Each day was so much like the one preceding that Bryce took no notice of the passing of time. He left the laboratory only for meals, sleeping on a cot in one corner of the room. The electronic brain rapidly neared completion.

Bryce came to accept Nadine's absence with a dull resignation, though he did not cease to miss her. There were times when some phase of his work was of an automatic nature such as not to require his presence. Then he would wander restlessly about the house, or go for walks along the ocean. Once he turned on the television set in the living room, his only contact with the outside world.

There was the usual variety of newscasts. Two major European powers nearing a political crisis. A fourth expedition leaving for Mars. Results of the annual Luna rocket race. And—

"Your reporter has it on good authority that Nadine Bryce, nee Landrey, and Sidney Arthington, wealthy sportsman, are making it a steady twosome. There are rumors current that Nadine Bryce has separated from her husband, Curt Bryce, noted robotics engineer..."

Bryce turned off the set with a vicious twist of his hand. He was breathing hard. Steady twosome... The phrase tore at him. He knew a little about Sidney Arthington, who was a celebrity for no other reason than the possession of enormous wealth. Arthington was a playboy—Nadine's kind. He'd fit in nicely with the kind of life Nadine wished to live. A constant round of parties, night-clubs, good times.

Bryce threw himself into his work with redoubled energy. Fall came, and clouds began to fill the blue of the sky. There were occasional squalls, presaging the coming of winter storms, which sent the surf booming against the rocks at the base of the cliffs.

Finally the electronic brain was finished. Tests still had to be made to determine its degree of efficiency. Bryce had a completely-assembled, spare robot body, which he now began to equip with his invention. He was busy with this one gray day, when the sound of an approaching gyro interrupted him.

BRYCE'S visitor was Nadine—a Nadine who looked more lovely, if possible, than when he had last seen her. Bryce took her into the living room, and began to mix drinks with hands that shook. He found it strangely difficult to breathe. His thoughts were anxious. What did Nadine's visit mean? Could it be that she was—coming back to him?

It was a futile hope, he soon realized, for Nadine's manner toward him bore a markedly noticeable constraint. She began with the usual pleasantries.

"How have you been getting along, Curt?"

"Well enough. Jones takes care of everything."

"And the Bryce electronic brain, is it finished?"

"Finished, Nadine. I haven't experimented with it yet, so I don't know how good it's going to be."

"I bet it'll be all right, Curt."

"I hope so, Nadine."

She studied the contents of her glass, running slim fingers along its edge. Her momentary silence had something of a pause for preparation, a drawing of breath before the plunge. Abruptly she looked up, "Curt, I came to see you about something."

"Yes, Nadine?"

"Curt...I want a divorce."

It was not entirely unexpected, but Bryce's stomach climbed a mountain and jumped off. A vast stillness seemed to thicken and press in around him. He stared stupidly at Nadine, and then the stillness was gone. He grew acutely aware of Nadine's eyes upon him, watching his reaction. He raised his glass, emptied it in three great swallows.

"Who's the lucky man, Nadine?" Bryce asked. "There has to be another man, of course."

"Sid Arthington, Curt." Nadine's voice was barely audible.

"Sid, eh? Sid Arthington, the wealthy playboy. Nadine, the playgirl. It'll be a great match."

"Curt...Curt, do you have to be this way?"

"No. Lord, no." Bryce pressed the palms of his hands hard against his temples, breathing deeply. He straightened. "Nadine, it hasn't changed with me. I still love you. Won't...wouldn't you give me a chance to make up?"

"I'm sorry, Curt."

"Nothing I can say will make a difference?"

"No, Curt."

"If that's the way it is, then that's the way it'll have to be." Bryce shrugged forlornly. "You can have your divorce, Nadine."

"Thanks, Curt," she murmured. She glanced at him, hesitated. "What will you do, Curt? I mean, what are your plans?"

Bryce spread his hands. "I'll remain here, of course, and keep on with my work. That's about all that's left for me to do."

Conversation was a sponge wrung dry. After a long, awkward silence, Nadine rose. "I'll have to be going, Curt."

"Good-bye, Nadine."

They shook hands, and Nadine walked quickly from the room. Bryce gazed bleakly into nothingness, the sound of the gyro fading in his ears. Then it was gone, and the only sound was the dull thunder of surf on rock. Bryce reached for the liquor bottle, filled a glass, drank it straight. He filled the glass again. And again.

TWO days passed before Bryce returned to work. His movements at first were fumbling and abstracted, but with the threads once more in his hands, the old deftness and precision returned. He completed the nerve hook-ups to his electronic brain, impressed certain simple reflex-patterns onto the memory-cells with the aid of a special microfilm conditioner.

The robot performed smoothly in response to his commands. The electronic brain was undeniably a success.

When the first flush of elation had gone, Bryce gazed thoughtfully at the robot. It was a life-sized figure in the shape of a man, with body and head of spun plastics. Artificial hair, rumpled by Bryce's manipulations, covered its braincase. The robot was almost an exact counterpart of Jones. Jones was a male robot, Bryce remembered. Then, abruptly, an idea made him stiffen tensely. Why not house the electronic brain in a female robot body?

The thought made his heart pound strangely. Not just an ordinary female robot body—but a female robot body that would be the exact counterpart of…of Nadine! It would be the perfect solution to his loneliness!

Excitedly, Bryce recalled his possession of a full-length, three-dimensional photograph of Nadine. This could be enlarged to life-size to serve as a model. And as for the construction of the body itself, who could do it better than the genius that was Cyrus Vanneman?

Hardly had this last passed through Bryce's mind, when he was running eagerly for the vision-phone. He contacted Cyrus Vanneman, explained what he wanted done.

"It'll cost you a fortune," Vanneman said doubtfully.

"I don't care what it costs," Bryce responded. "Listen, I have several patents on the market that are each worth small fortunes in themselves. You know the ones I mean. I'll turn all rights over to you in exchange for this job."

Vanneman seemed to hesitate, then quickly nodded. "I'll do it, Curt."

"Fine. I'll send along plans and specifications in a day or so. This is going to have to be a very special job. The usual system of nerve and brain connections will have to be changed entirely."

"You working on a new idea, Curt?" Vanneman asked curiously.

"In a way," Bryce evaded. "I don't know yet if it'll succeed."

Bryce broke connection and immediately got to work on the plans. After a week of working almost constantly night and day, he was finished. The plans, along with the three-dimensional photograph of Nadine, were then sent to Vanneman.

While working on the plans, Bryce had come to realize that the new robot would not be complete unless it possessed emotions. It would be able to think—actually to reason—but it would not be almost human if its thought processes were not accompanied by such characteristically human emotions as love, hate, jealousy, and fear. In the human body emotions were brought about by various glands, hormones, and secretions. Bryce intended to obtain the same effect in the robot through the aid of mechanical glands, electrical and radio impulses. And so, while awaiting manufacture and shipment of the robot, Bryce got once more to work.

THE gray days shortened, and the wind from the ocean blew stronger. The occasional squalls became storms, and in between, a dreary veil of fog hung over the cliffs. The thunder of surf breaking on the rocks at the base of the cliffs was almost continuous now.

It was winter, and snow was falling thick and soft when an air van arrived at the landing field outside the house. Bryce's breath caught in his throat as two men carried a large, coffin-like box into the laboratory. His hands shook as he signed the delivery receipt. The knowledge almost frightened him that this was *it*. This was the culmination of all his work.

The air van left, and Bryce eagerly opened the box, pulled away the layers of padding and wrappings. He gasped. His eyes widened with astonishment, and awe and admiration laxed the muscles of his face.

Working from the plans and the photograph, Vanneman had wrought a miracle. It was Nadine lying there in the box, the thick lashes curling on her cheek as though in sleep. She was a vision of frozen loveliness, a dream made real in spun plastic. Looking at her, Bryce found it hard to believe that wires and cogs and tubes lay beneath the pink-white plastic that was her skin; that a motor, tiny and powerful, could bring her to life instead of the pulsing beat of a heart.

Bryce roused into activity. The electronic brain and the mechanical glands were ready. He completed the robot's assembly with the swift dexterity of a surgeon. Then he turned on her motor, a very special motor which made scarcely a sound. Her eyes opened, eyes as green as Nadine's, except that they possessed a warmth and softness where Nadine's were cool and faintly appraising. Her red lips parted. She gazed up at him with a kind of childlike wonder on her lovely face.

"You need a name," Bryce told her. "Let it be Lilith. Yes...Lilith."

"Lilith," she murmured. "Lilith."

Bryce supervised Lilith's education carefully. He chose from his stock of special micro-films, from television broadcasts, from books. He took great pains to see that everything which went into her memory-cells was of such nature as to result in a personality that would be typically feminine.

Lilith, by virtue of the electronic brain, learned rapidly. In a matter of a few weeks, she knew everything that Nadine had ever known—and some things that Nadine didn't. But where Bryce's expectations were concerned, Lilith as a finished product was as different from Nadine as are black from white and hot from cold. Where Nadine was cool and calculating, Lilith was warm and impulsive. Where Nadine would have smiled, Lilith laughed, and where Nadine would have compressed her lips against an inward sorrow, Lilith wept unrestrainedly. Lilith, of course, possessed tear ducts, having been built to resemble a woman in every detail. She never hesitated to use these, however slight the provocation. She wept over the tribulations of lovers in television plays and death scenes in books. It irritated Bryce at times, yet he could not bear the thought of making the necessary adjustments in her mechanical glands which would change her.

LILITH'S feminine sense of possessiveness was developed to a high degree. She regarded the house as hers and fussed over it continually, dusting and polishing with a pride and con-scientiousness that no human bride in a new home could have equaled. She even insisted on rearranging the furniture to her personal satisfaction, and when Bryce protested vigorously, she took refuge in tears. Bryce gave in. Lilith spent many happy hours hauling and shoving at the furniture in each and every room.

The next thing Lilith insisted on doing was to cook Bryce's meals. He pointed out patiently that this was Jones' task. Lilith promptly demanded Jones' removal. Bryce refused indignantly. Lilith pleaded tearfully. Bryce gave in. He turned off Jones' motor, and left him in a storeroom adjoining the laboratory. Nor was he sorry later, for Lilith put emotion into her cooking, whereas Jones had merely cooked.

Household affairs under Lilith's management progressed smoothly. She kept each room spic and span, and her meals were always something to look forward to. For Bryce the house took on an air of cheerful hominess it had lacked before. He found himself becoming more and more at peace.

Lilith proved to be a gay and charming companion. Bryce taught her to play chess, and she quickly learned to share his love for the game. They spent long hours over the pieces in the living room, and Bryce found Lilith increasingly hard to beat. She also developed an interest in Bryce's work at the laboratory, spending such spare time there as she could find away from her work. Bryce explained the principles of robotics and the functions of various mechanisms used in robot manufacture. Lilith, with her quick mental grasp of any and all subjects, was soon able to discuss intelligently any phase of robotics with Bryce. Far from tolerating her presence in the laboratory, he came to look forward to her daily visits with eagerness.

It was inevitable that something should arise to disturb the even tenor of the relationship. They were listening to a television play one evening, which ended in a quarrel between two lovers. Tears filled Lilith's eyes.

"Curt, I wonder if something like that will ever happen to us."

Bryce was puzzled. "What do you mean, Lilith?"

"I wonder if we'll ever quarrel like that."

"But, good Lord, Lilith, why should we?"

Lilith looked away, twisting at her small hands. "That's the trouble with us, Curt. We're really not close enough to each other to have reason to quarrel."

"Maybe we're better off that way," Bryce said.

"Are we, Curt? Are we?" Lilith stood up abruptly. Her face worked against a sudden flood of tears. Turning, she ran from the room.

Bryce stared after her in bewilderment. Then he shrugged philosophically. Lilith was essentially a woman, he reminded himself, and women are often inexplicable.

In the days that followed, Lilith no longer came to the laboratory. She spent most of the time in her room, and her meals lost something of their excellence. At last Bryce could stand it no longer. He caught her in the kitchen one morning, demanded to know what was wrong.

Lilith forced a smile. "Why, nothing's wrong, Curt."

"Yes, there is," Bryce insisted. "I want you to tell me."

Lilith bit her lip, hesitating. "All right, Curt, but remember you asked for this. Curt, I know I'm only a robot, but I'm built to resemble a woman in every way. I have a woman's feelings. I love you, Curt. I want to make you happy in the way that only a woman can make a man happy. But...well, you don't seem to care."

"I didn't know, I hadn't thought—" Bryce was confused.

Lilith watched him, hope dying in her face. She turned away, her green eyes welling. Her slim shoulders shook with muffled sobs.

THOUGHTS whirling chaotically, Bryce left the kitchen. Awareness lay heavy upon him that far from making Lilith almost human, he had made her a bit too much so. Compassion for her filled him, yet sifting his feelings objectively, he could find no reciprocating emotions of love. Though Lilith looked like a glorious young woman—and in fact resembled a glorious young woman in every respect—he could not evade the knowledge that she was, after all, only a robot.

And quite suddenly, Bryce found himself yearning for Nadine. Nadine was human—his kind. The old loneliness returned with abrupt force.

The winter drew to a close. Bryce and Lilith exchanged only a few words together, and then only when occasion demanded. Lilith continued to remain away from the laboratory. She and Bryce no longer played chess together, nor did they listen to television plays. Bryce absorbed himself in his work, and Lilith developed a passion for reading, spending most of the time in her room, Bryce saw her but seldom, yet always he thought he could detect the traces of tears on her cheeks. His eyes grew haunted. He began to wonder how much longer it would keep up.

Spring came, and grass mantled the cliffs. The sun shone warmer each day, the skies cleared, and the bitter wind from the ocean became a mild breeze.

Bryce, turning on the television set by chance one afternoon, learned that Sidney Arthington had died in a crash of his sporting gyro. The newscaster added that Arthington's immense fortune had been left to Nadine. A short time later, Nadine appeared at the house.

Bryce was overjoyed to see her. It was the answer to his wildest hopes.

"Why, Nadine, I can hardly believe it's you!"

Nadine smiled. "It's me, all right, Curt. How are you?"

"Just fine," Bryce lied. He could not bring himself to admit that the last few months had been pure hell.

Nadine glanced around the living room, frowning slightly. "Curt, the place looks...different. What on earth have you been doing?"

"Oh, that's Lilith's work."

"Lilith?" The name burst out of Nadine. Her eyes widened on Bryce.

"Lilith's a robot," Bryce explained quickly. "Just wait until you see her. The Bryce electronic brain is a success, Nadine, and Lilith is the result."

Nadine looked strangely relieved. She became demure. "Curt, do you know why I'm back?" she asked softly.

"No, Nadine," Bryce answered. But he thought he knew, and his heart skipped a beat.

"Curt, I've decided to come back. That is, if...if you still want me."

"Still want you? Why, Nadine—" Bryce reached for her gropingly, and suddenly she was in his arms.

LATER, Nadine patted her hair back into place and smoothed her dress. She said, "We'll have to wait a while, Curt. Appearances, you know. Then we'll be married again. I'm a wealthy woman now, and you can leave your old work, and we can travel and have friends and fun without worrying about money. It'll be wonderful, won't it?"

Bryce shook his head slowly, "No, Nadine."

"But why not?"

"I wouldn't touch your money, Nadine."

"What difference does it make whose money it is, Curt? It's money, isn't it?"

"I don't care," Bryce insisted. "I won't touch it."

Nadine's face flamed with sudden fury. "Curt, why do you have to be so stiff-necked? I take the risk of killing Sid—" She broke off abruptly, her cheeks paling. Her hand crept to her mouth.

Bryce stared at her as though she had abruptly become something deadly and alien. "What did you say? Nadine—what did you say?"

She returned his gaze mutely, her hand trembling against her lips. Bryce grasped her shoulders hard, shook her urgently.

"Nadine...you killed Arthington? But it was an accident! The newscasters said so!"

"Curt! You're hurting me!"

Bryce released her, and Nadine sank into a chair. Her face set in lines of defiance.

"It would have slipped out sooner or later. Now you know—and I don't care!" Her features softened with sudden pleading. She became all tearful, desirable woman. "But, Curt, I did it for you! I never really care for Sid; I married him because he had money. I loved you all along. I kept remembering what you said about working for wealth, influence. I thought, since I was to inherit Sid's fortune, and if he were out of the way, that you could stop working. I decided to get rid of him, I know how gyro's work. I fixed Sid's sportster so that it would go out of control soon after taking off. The crash destroyed every trace of what I had done. They don't know, Curt. They think it's an accident."

Bryce was stunned at the confession. "Good Lord!" he muttered.

Nadine searched his face anxiously. "Curt...you don't hate me?"

"Hate you? No...no. Somehow, I can't."

Then Nadine gasped. "Curt, who ...who's that?" she cried, pointing.

Bryce looked around. Lilith, her hands at her throat, stood in the entrance to the living room, staring incredulously at Nadine.

THE two gazed at each other as though in a trance of hypnosis, identical green eyes wide, identical red lips parted. Except for the dresses they wore, it was hard to tell them apart.

"This is Lilith," Bryce told Nadine. "Lilith, I want you to meet Nadine."

"How do you do?" Lilith murmured coolly. "Pardon me for having intruded." Without another word, she turned and left.

"Why, Curt, she looked just like me!" Nadine exclaimed.

Bryce grinned. "I had her made that way."

Nadine's face abruptly grew hard. "Curt, she must have overheard what I was saying about...about Sid. Curt, she knows!"

Bryce felt a sudden apprehension, whether for Nadine or for Lilith, he could not be sure. He knew that each resented their similarity to the other. He'd seen their mutual surprise turn into an instinctive dislike.

Nadine leaned toward Bryce, her green eyes narrowed with insistence. "Curt, she knows what I did! We'll have to get rid of her. I'd never feel safe while she was alive."

"Kill Lilith? Good Lord, no!" Bryce gasped.

"You love me, don't you, Curt?" Nadine demanded softly. "You can't possibly care for her. She's only a robot. She couldn't give you my kind of love."

"But I couldn't kill her!" Bryce said. A thought suddenly struck him. "Nadine—I know what to do. I'll shut off her motor."

"It's no good, Curt," Nadine answered flatly. "Somebody might turn her on again, later. She'd always be a sword hanging over my head. No, Curt, she has to be destroyed."

Bryce could see the logic in Nadine's words. He realized that Lilith, womanlike, would be jealous of Nadine, would do everything in her power to remove her rival. He was chilled by the terrible problem facing him.

Nadine's arms slid around his neck. Her exquisite body pressed close. "Curt, you'll do it, won't you?" she pleaded.

Bryce hesitated achingly. Nadine's lips were turned up to his, soft and red, parted with promise. The perfume of her was a heady fragrance in his nostrils. A refusal struggled to his lips—died unuttered. He pulled Nadine to him, kissed her hungrily. "Yes," Bryce whispered against her cheek. "Yes, I'll do it…."

After a while, Nadine stood up. "I'll have to be going, Curt. I still have many affairs to settle. Take care of the robot as quickly as you can. She mustn't have a chance to inform the police. I'll be back again—soon."

Bryce saw Nadine off at the landing field. Then he returned to the house, numbed by thought of the grim task which lay before him. Somehow, he had to destroy Lilith. His mind quested for some means which would be as painless to her as it would be to himself. Several methods occurred to him—but he revolted at each and every one.

Bryce mentally lashed himself for being a sentimental fool. Lilith was only a robot, powered by a motor, made intelligent by an electronic brain. He could make other electronic brains. He could make other robots like Lilith.

Determination came to him. He formed a plan. He'd take Lilith by surprise, turn off her motor. Then he'd remove her brain, hammer it into fragments. As simple as that.

Yet, each time an opportunity arrived, he found himself unable to go through with it. A spring wound to screaming tightness within Bryce as the days passed one by one and the deed remained still unaccomplished. Nadine would be returning soon, he remembered. What would she say when she found Lilith still in existence?

IN AN effort to escape the increasing strain, Bryce went for a long walk over the cliffs one afternoon. It was a warm spring day, and the ocean stretched blue and placid to the horizon.

Returning to the house, Bryce saw Lilith standing at the edge of the cliffs, gazing with a hand shading her eyes, in a direction opposite to his approach. Her back was toward him. Suddenly Bryce knew what he must do. He would sneak up behind her, and then—a swift push, and Lilith would go hurtling over the cliff to her doom on the rocks far below.

Bryce crept from rock to rock, closer and closer. A lump filled his throat. His eyes were blurred. Talons of agony tore at him. And then—he was behind her, and his hands were swinging up for the fatal shove.

Something made her abruptly aware of him. She whirled. For an awful moment, her startled eyes were wide on his. With a sob, Bryce pushed. Her scream of horror as she went over the cliff sent cold chills up his spine. A dull thud reached him as her body struck the rocks.

It was over. Finished. Reaction set in, leaving Bryce sick and weak. Remorse at what he had done filled him. Lilith was gone—sweet, gentle Lilith who would never have dreamed of hurting anyone, who could not bear the thought of anyone being hurt. Lilith, who had spent long hours with him, playing chess. Lilith, who had been genuinely interested in his work, discussing robotics with him like a veteran technician.

Lilith was gone. Bryce knew he could make other electronic brains, but knew there would never be another Lilith. The multitude of factors which had gone to make up her personality could never be duplicated.

And suddenly Bryce found himself hating Nadine. He saw her for what she was—selfish, ruthless, addicted to frivolity, a woman who did not hesitate to kill in order to gain her ends. The bitter realization came to Bryce that he had been an utter fool to have killed Lilith for Nadine.

Bryce walked leadenly to the house. He stopped short as he saw a gyro parked on the landing field. He recognized it as Nadine's.

Nadine herself came out of the house as Bryce stood there. She regarded him solemnly, and there were traces of tears on her cheeks. She spoke.

"That woman you called Nadine was here to see you. You were not in, and she went to look for you."

Bryce's mind reeled crazily. Lilith! This was Lilith! Then the other—the one he had pushed over the cliff—had been...*Nadine!*

And suddenly Bryce was glad with a gladness that caught at his throat and filled him with music, Lilith was safe; Nadine's death was justice, in a fashion. It could easily be explained. Nadine had simply wandered too close to the edge of the cliff, slipped, fallen off.

"What is Nadine to you, Curt?" Lilith asked falteringly. "Why... why does she look like me?"

Bryce merely smiled. "Forget about her, Lilith. I've been a fool, and I'm going to try hard to make it up to you. From now on let's think only of us." He held out his arms, and for a moment she stared as though she could not believe their invitation, and then she ran into them blindly. He held her close, and she was as warm and soft as any human girl, sobbing out her happiness against his chest.

THE END

The Star-Sent Knaves

By KEITH LAUMER

When the Great Galactic Union first encounters Earth...is this what is going to happen?

CHAPTER ONE

Clyde W. Snithian was a bald eagle of a man, dark-eyed, pot-bellied, with the large, expressive hands of a rug merchant. Round-shouldered in a loose cloak, he blinked small reddish eyes at Dan Slane's travel-stained six foot one.

"Kelly here tells me you've been demanding to see me," He nodded toward the florid man at his side. He had a high, thin voice, like something that needed oiling. "Something about important information regarding safeguarding my paintings."

"That's right, Mr. Snithian," Dan said. "I believe I can be of great help to you."

"Help how? If you've got ideas of bilking me..." The red eyes bored into Dan like hot pokers.

"Nothing like that, sir. Now, I know you have quite a system of guards here—the papers are full of it—"

"Damned busybodies! Sensation-mongers! If it wasn't for the press, I'd have no concerns for my paintings today!"

"Yes sir. But my point is, the one really important spot has been left unguarded."

"Now, wait a minute—" Kelly started.

"What's that?" Snithian cut in.

"You have a hundred and fifty men guarding the house and grounds day and night—"

"Two hundred and twenty-five," Kelly snapped.

"—but no one at all in the vault with the paintings," Slane finished.

"Of course not," Snithian shrilled. "Why should I post a man in the vault? It's under constant surveillance from the corridor outside."

"The Harriman paintings were removed from a locked vault," Dan said. "There was a special seal on the door. It wasn't broken."

"By the saints, he's right," Kelly exclaimed. "Maybe we ought to have a man in that vault."

"Another idiotic scheme to waste my money," Snithian snapped. "I've made you responsible for security here, Kelly! Let's have no more nonsense. And throw this nincompoop out!" Snithian turned and stalked away, his cloak flapping at his knees.

"I'll work cheap," Dan called after him as Kelly took his arm. "I'm an art lover."

"Never mind that," Kelly said, escorting Dan along the corridor. He turned in at an office and closed the door.

"Now, as the old buzzard said, I'm responsible for security here. If those pictures go, my job goes with them. Your vault idea's not bad. Just how cheap would you work?"

"A hundred dollars a week," Dan said promptly, "Plus expenses," he added.

Kelly nodded. "I'll fingerprint you and run a fast agency check. If you're clean, I'll put you on, starting tonight. But keep it quiet."

Dan looked around at the gray walls, with shelves stacked to the low ceiling with wrapped paintings. Two three-hundred-watt bulbs shed a white glare over the tile floor, a neat white refrigerator, a bunk, an arm-chair, a bookshelf and a small table set with paper plates, plastic utensils and a portable radio—all hastily installed at Kelly's order. Dan opened the refrigerator, looked over the stock of salami, liverwurst, cheese and beer. He opened a loaf of bread, built up a well-filled sandwich, keyed open a can of beer.

It wasn't fancy, but it would do. Phase one of the plan had gone off without a hitch.

Basically, his idea was simple. Art collections had been disappearing from closely guarded galleries and homes all over the world. It was obvious that no one could enter a locked vault, remove a stack of large canvases and leave, unnoticed by watchful guards—and leaving the locks undamaged.

Yet the paintings were gone. Someone had been in those vaults—someone who hadn't entered in the usual way.

Theory failed at that point; that left the experimental method. The Snithian collection was the largest west of the Mississippi. With such a target, the thieves were bound to show up. If Dan sat in the vault—day and night—waiting—he would see for himself how they operated.

He finished his sandwich, went to the shelves and pulled down one of the brown-paper bundles. Loosening the string binding the package, he slid a painting into view. It was a gaily colored view of an open-air cafe, with a group of men and women in gay-ninetyish costumes gathered at a table. He seemed to remember reading something about it in a magazine. It was a cheerful scene; Dan liked it. Still, it hardly seemed worth all the effort...

He went to the wall switch and turned off the lights. The orange glow of the filaments died, leaving only a faint illumination from the night-light over the door. When the thieves arrived, it might give him a momentary advantage if his eyes were adjusted to the dark. He groped his way to the bunk.

So far, so good, he reflected, stretching out. When they showed up, he'd have to handle everything just right. If he scared them off there'd be no second chance. He would have lost his crack at—whatever his discovery might mean to him.

But he was ready. Let them come.

Eight hours, three sandwiches and six beers later, Dan roused suddenly from a light doze and sat up on the cot. Between him and the crowded shelving, a palely luminous framework was materializing in mid-air.

The apparition was an openwork cage—about the size and shape of an outhouse minus the sheathing, Dan estimated breathlessly. Two figures were visible within the structure, sitting stiffly in contoured chairs. They glowed, if anything, more brightly than the framework.

A faint sound cut into the stillness—a descending whine. The cage moved jerkily, settling toward the floor. Long blue sparks jumped, crackling, to span the closing gap; with a grate of metal, the cage settled against the floor. The spectral men reached for ghostly switches...

The glow died.

Dan was aware of his heart thumping painfully under his ribs. His mouth was dry. This was the moment he'd been planning for, but now that it was here—

Never mind. He took a deep breath, ran over the speeches he had prepared for the occasion:

Greeting, visitors from the Future...

Hopelessly corny. What about: *Welcome to the Twentieth Century...*

No good—it lacked spontaneity. The men were rising, their backs to Dan, stepping out of the skeletal frame. In the dim light it now looked like nothing more than a rough frame built of steel pipe, with a cluster of levers in a console before the two seats. And the thieves looked ordinary enough: Two men in gray coveralls, one slender and balding and the other shorter, and round-faced. Neither of them noticed Dan, sitting rigid on the cot. The thin man placed a lantern on the table, twiddled a knob. A warm light sprang up. The visitors looked at the stacked shelves.

"Looks like the old boy's been doing all right," the shorter man said. "Fathead's gonna be pleased."

"A very gratifying consignment," his companion said. "However, we'd best hurry, Manny. How much time have we left on this charge?"

"Plenty. Fifteen minutes anyway."

The thin man opened a package, glanced at a painting.

"Ah, magnificent. Almost the equal of Picasso in his puce period."

Manny shuffled through the other pictures in the stack.

"Like always," he grumbled. "No nood dames. I like nood dames."

"Look at this, Manny! The textures alone—"

Manny looked. "Yeah, nice use of values," he conceded. "But I still prefer nood dames, Fiorello."

"And this!" Fiorello lifted the next painting. "Look at that gay play of rich browns!"

"I seen richer browns on Thirty-third Street," Manny said. "They was popular with the sparrows."

"Manny, sometimes I think your aspirations—"

"Whatta ya talkin? I use a roll-on," Manny, turning to place a painting in the cage, stopped dead as he caught sight of Dan. The painting clattered to the floor. Dan stood, cleared his throat. "Uh…"

"Oh-oh," Manny said. "A double-cross."

"I've—ah—been expecting you gentlemen," Dan said. "I—"

"I told you we couldn't trust no guy with nine fingers on each hand," Manny whispered hoarsely. He moved toward the cage. "Let's blow, Fiorello."

"Wait a minute," Dan said. "Before you do anything hasty—"

"Don't start nothing, Buster," Manny said cautiously. "We're plenty tough guys when aroused."

"I want to talk to you," Dan insisted. "You see, these paintings—"

"Paintings? Look, it was all a mistake. Like, we figured this was the gent's room—"

"Never mind, Manny," Fiorello cut in. "It appears there's been a leak."

Dan shook his head. "No leak. I simply deduced—"

"Look, Fiorello," Manny said. "You chin if you want to; I'm doing a fast fade."

"Don't act hastily, Manny. You know where you'll end."

"Wait a minute!" Dan shouted. "I'd like to make a deal with you fellows."

"Ah-hah!" Kelly's voice blared from somewhere. "I knew it! Slane, you crook!"

Dan looked about wildly. The voice seemed to be issuing from a speaker. It appeared Kelly hedged his bets.

"Mr. Kelly, I can explain everything!" Dan called. He turned back to Fiorello. "Listen, I figured out—"

"Pretty clever!" Kelly's voice barked. "Inside job. But it takes more than the likes of you to out-fox an old-timer like Eddie Kelly."

"Perhaps you were right, Manny." Fiorello said. "Complications are arising. We'd best depart with all deliberate haste." He edged toward the cage.

"What about this ginzo?" Manny jerked a thumb toward Dan. "He's on to us."

"Can't be helped."

"Look—I want to go with you!" Dan shouted.

"I'll bet you do!" Kelly's voice roared. "One more minute and I'll have the door open and collar the lot of you! Came up through a tunnel, did you?"

"You can't go, my dear fellow," Fiorello said. "Room for two, no more."

Dan whirled to the cot, grabbed up the pistol Kelly had supplied. He aimed it at Manny. "You stay here, Manny! I'm going with Fiorello in the time machine."

"Are you nuts?" Manny demanded.

"I'm flattered, dear boy," Fiorello said, "but—"

"Let's get moving. Kelly will have that lock open in a minute."

"You can't leave me here!" Manny spluttered, watching Dan crowd into the cage beside Fiorello.

"We'll send for you," Dan said. "Let's go, Fiorello."

The balding man snatched suddenly for the gun. Dan wrestled with him. The pistol fell, bounced on the floor of the cage, skidded into the far corner of the vault. Manny charged, reaching for Dan as he twisted aside; Fiorello's elbow caught him in the mouth. Manny staggered back into the arms of Kelly, bursting red-faced into the vault.

"Manny!" Fiorello released his grip on Dan, lunged to aid his companion. Kelly passed Manny to one of three cops crowding in on his heels. Dan clung to the framework as Fiorello grappled with Kelly. A cop pushed past them, spotted Dan, moved in briskly for the pinch. Dan grabbed a lever at random and pulled.

Sudden silence fell as the walls of the room glowed blue. A spectral Kelly capered before the cage, fluorescing in the blue-violet. Dan swallowed hard and nudged a second lever. The cage sank like an elevator into the floor, vivid blue washing up its sides.

Hastily he reversed the control. Operating a time machine was tricky business. One little slip, and the Slane molecules would be squeezing in among brick and mortar particles...

But this was no time to be cautious. Things hadn't turned out just the way he'd planned, but after all, this was what he'd wanted—in a way. The time machine was his to command. And if he gave up now and crawled back into the vault, Kelly would gather him in and pin every art theft of the past decade on him.

It couldn't be *too* hard. He'd take it slowly, figure out the controls...

Dan took a deep breath and tried another lever. The cage rose gently, in eerie silence. It reached the ceiling and kept going. Dan gritted his teeth as an eight-inch band of luminescence passed down the cage. Then he was emerging into a spacious kitchen. A blue-haloed cook waddled to a luminous refrigerator, caught sight of Dan rising slowly from the floor, and stumbled back, mouth open. The cage rose, penetrated a second ceiling. Dan looked around at a carpeted hall.

Cautiously he neutralized the control lever. The cage came to rest an inch above the floor. As far as Dan could tell, he hadn't traveled so much as a minute into the past or future.

He looked over the controls. There should be one labeled "Forward" and another labeled "Back", but all the levers were plain, unadorned black. They looked, Dan decided, like ordinary circuit-breaker type knife-switches. In fact, the whole apparatus had the appearance of something thrown together hastily from common materials. Still, it worked. So far he had only found the controls for maneuvering in the usual three dimensions, but the time switch was bound to be here somewhere...

Dan looked up at a movement at the far end of the hall.

A girl's head and shoulders appeared, coming up a spiral staircase. In another second she would see him, and give the alarm—and Dan needed a few moments of peace and quiet in which to figure out the controls. He moved a lever. The cage drifted smoothly sideways, sliced through the wall with a flurry of vivid blue light. Dan pushed the lever back. He was in a bedroom now, a wide chamber with flouncy curtains, a four-poster under a flowered canopy, a dressing table—

The door opened and the girl stepped into the room. She was young. Not over eighteen, Dan thought—as nearly as he could tell with the blue light playing around her face. She had long hair tied with a ribbon, and long legs, neatly curved. She wore shorts and carried a tennis racquet in her left hand and an apple in her right. Her back to Dan and the cage, she tossed the racquet on a table, took a bite of the apple, and began briskly unbuttoning her shirt.

Dan tried moving a lever. The cage edged toward the girl. Another; he rose gently. The girl tossed the shirt onto a chair and undid the zipper down the side of the shorts. Another lever; the cage shot toward the outer wall as the girl reached behind her back.

Dan blinked at the flash of blue and looked down. He was hovering twenty feet above a clipped lawn.

He looked at the levers. Wasn't it the first one in line that moved the cage ahead? He tried it, shot forward ten feet. Below, a man stepped out on the terrace, lit a cigarette, paused, started to turn his face up—

Dan jabbed at a lever. The cage shot back through the wall. He was in a plain room with a depression in the floor, a wide window with a planter filled with glowing blue plants—

The door opened. Even blue, the girl looked graceful as a deer as she took a last bite of the apple and stepped into the ten-foot-square sunken tub. Dan held his breath. The girl tossed the core aside, seemed to suddenly become aware of eyes on her, whirled—

With a sudden lurch that threw Dan against the steel bars, the cage shot through the wall into the open air and hurtled off with an acceleration that kept him pinned, helpless. He groped for the controls, hauled at a lever. There was no change. The cage rushed on, rising higher. In the distance, Dan saw the skyline of a town, approaching with frightful speed. A tall office building reared up fifteen stories high. He was headed dead for it—

He covered his ears, braced himself—

With an abruptness that flung him against the opposite side of the cage, the machine braked, shot through the wall and slammed to a stop. Dan sank to the floor of the cage, breathing hard. There was a loud *click!*—and the glow faded.

With a lunge, Dan scrambled out of the cage. He stood looking around at a simple brown-painted office, dimly lit by sunlight filtered through elaborate venetian blinds. There were posters on the wall, a potted plant by the door, a heap of framed paintings beside it, and at the far side of the room, a desk. And behind the desk— Something.

CHAPTER TWO

Dan gaped at a head the size of a beach ball, mounted on a torso like a hundred-gallon bag of water. Two large brown eyes blinked at him from points eight inches apart. Immense hands with too many fingers unfolded and reached to open a brown paper carton, dip in, then toss three peanuts, deliberately, one by one, into a gaping mouth that opened just above the brown eyes.

"Who're you?" a bass voice demanded from somewhere near the floor.

"I'm…I'm…Dan Slane…your honor."

"What happened to Manny and Fiorello?"

"They—I— There was this cop. Kelly—"

"Oh-oh." The brown eyes blinked deliberately. The many-fingered hands closed the peanut carton and tucked it into a drawer.

"Well, it was a sweet racket while it lasted," the basso voice said. "A pity to terminate so happy an enterprise. Still…" A noise like an amplified Bronx cheer issued from the wide mouth.

"How…what…?"

"The carrier returns here automatically when the charge drops below a critical value," the voice said. "A necessary measure to discourage big ideas on the part of wisenheimers in my employ. May I ask how you happen to be aboard the carrier, by the way?"

"I just wanted—I mean, after I figured out—that is, the police… I went for help," Dan finished lamely.

"Help? Out of the picture, unfortunately. One must maintain one's anonymity, you'll appreciate. My operation here is under wraps at present. Ah, I don't suppose you brought any paintings?"

Dan shook his head. He was staring at the posters. His eyes, accustoming themselves to the gloom of the office, could now make out the vividly drawn outline of a creature resembling an alligator-headed giraffe rearing—up above scarlet foliage. The next poster showed a face similar to the beach ball behind the desk, with red circles painted around the eyes. The next was a view of a yellow volcano spouting fire into a black sky.

"Too bad," The words seemed to come from under the desk. Dan squinted, caught a glimpse of coiled purplish tentacles. He gulped and looked up to catch a brown eye upon him. Only one. The other seemed to be busily at work studying the ceiling.

"I hope," the voice said, "that you ain't harboring no reactionary racial prejudices."

"Gosh, no," Dan reassured the eye. "I'm crazy about—uh—"

"Vorplischers," the voice said. "From Vorplisch, or Vega, as you call it." The Bronx cheer sounded again. "How I long to glimpse once more my native fens! Wherever one wanders, there's no pad like home."

"That reminds me," Dan said, "I have to be running along now." He sidled toward the door.

"Stick around, Dan," the voice rumbled. "How about a drink? I can offer you Chateau Neuf du Pape, '59, Romance Conte, '32, goat's milk, Pepsi—"

"No, thanks."

"If you don't mind, I believe I'll have a Big Orange." The Vorplischer swiveled to a small refrigerator, removed an immense bottle fitted with a nipple and turned back to Dan. "Now, I got a proposition which may be of some interest to you. The loss of Manny and Fiorello is a serious blow, but we may yet recoup the situation. You made the scene at a most opportune time. What I got in mind is, with those two clowns out of the picture, a vacancy exists on my staff, which you might well fill. How does that grab you?"

"You mean you want me to take over operating the time machine?"

"Time machine?" The brown eyes blinked alternately. "I fear some confusion exists. I don't quite dig the significance of the term."

"That thing," Dan jabbed a thumb toward the cage. "The machine I came here in. You want me—"

"Time machine," the voice repeated. "Some sort of chronometer, perhaps?"

"Huh?"

"I pride myself on my command of the local idiom, yet I confess the implied concept snows me." The nine-fingered hands folded on the desk. The beach ball head leaned forward interestedly. "Clue me, Dan. What's a time machine?"

"Well, it's what you use to travel through time."

The brown eyes blinked in agitated alternation. "Apparently I've loused up my investigation of the local cultural background. I had no idea you were capable of that sort of thing." The immense head leaned back, the wide mouth opening and closing rapidly. "And to think I've been spinning my wheels collecting primitive 2-D art!"

"But—don't you have a time machine? I mean, isn't that one?"

"That? That's merely a carrier. Now tell me more about your time machines. A fascinating concept! My superiors will be delighted at this development—and astonished as well. They regard this planet as Endsville."

"Your superiors?" Dan eyed the window; much too far to jump. Maybe he could reach the machine and try a getaway—

"I hope you're not thinking of leaving suddenly," the beach ball said, following Dan's glance. One of the eighteen fingers touched a six-inch yellow cylinder lying on the desk. "Until the carrier is fueled, I'm afraid it's quite useless. But, to put you in the picture, I'd best introduce myself and explain my mission here. I'm Blote, Trader Fourth Class, in the employ of the Vegan Confederation. My job is to develop new sources of novelty items for the impulse-emporiums of the entire Secondary Quadrant."

"But the way Manny and Fiorello came sailing in through the wall! That *has* to be a time machine they were riding in. Nothing else could just materialize out of thin air like that."

"You seem to have a time-machine fixation, Dan," Blote said. "You shouldn't assume, just because you people have developed time travel, that everyone has. Now—" Blote's voice sank to a bass whisper—"I'll make a deal with you, Dan. You'll secure a small time machine in good condition for me. And in return—"

"*I'm* supposed to supply *you* with a time machine?"

Blote waggled a stubby forefinger at Dan. "I dislike pointing it out, Dan, but you are in a rather awkward position at the moment. Illegal entry, illegal possession of property, trespass—then doubtless some embarrassment exists back at the Snithian residence. I daresay Mr. Kelly would have a warm welcome for you. And, of course, I myself would deal rather harshly with any attempt on your part to take a powder." The Vegan flexed all eighteen fingers, drummed his tentacles under the desk, and rolled one eye, bugging the other at Dan.

"Whereas, on the other hand," Blote's bass voice went on, "you and me got the basis of a sweet deal. You supply the machine, and I fix you up with an abundance of the local medium of exchange. Equitable enough, I should say. What about it, Dan?"

"Ah, let me see," Dan temporized. "Time machine. Time machine—"

"Don't attempt to weasel on me, Dan," Blote rumbled ominously.

"I'd better look in the phone book," Dan suggested.

Silently, Blote produced a dog-eared directory. Dan opened it.

"Time, time. Let's see..." He brightened. "Time, Incorporated; local branch office. Two twenty-one Maple Street."

"A sales center?" Blote Inquired. "Or a manufacturing complex?"

"Both," Dan said. "I'll just nip over and—"

"That won't be necessary, Dan," Blote said. "I'll accompany you." He took the directory, studied it.

"Remarkable! A common commodity, openly on sale, and I failed to notice it. Still, a ripe nut can fall from a small tree as well as from a large." He went to his desk, rummaged, came up with a handful of fuel cells. "Now, off to gather in the time machine." He took his place in the carrier, patted the seat beside him with a wide hand. "Come, Dan. Get a wiggle on."

Hesitantly, Dan moved to the carrier. The bluff was all right up to a point—but the point had just about been reached. He took his seat. Blote moved a lever. The familiar blue glow sprang up. "Kindly direct me, Dan," Blote demanded. "Two twenty-one Maple Street, I believe you said."

"I don't know the town very well," Dan said, "but Maple's over that way."

Blote worked levers. The carrier shot out into a ghostly afternoon sky. Faint outlines of buildings, like faded negatives, spread below. Dan looked around, spotted lettering on a square five-story structure.

"Over there," he said. Blote directed the machine as it swooped smoothly toward the flat roof Dan indicated.

"Better let me take over now," Dan suggested. "I want to be sure to get us to the right place."

"Very well, Dan."

Dan dropped the carrier through the roof, passed down through a dimly seen office. Blote twiddled a small knob. The scene around the cage grew even fainter. "Best we remain unnoticed," he explained.

The cage descended steadily. Dan peered out, searching for identifying landmarks. He leveled off at the second floor, cruised along a barely visible corridor. Blote's eyes rolled, studying the small chambers along both sides of the passage at once.

"Ah, this must be the assembly area," he exclaimed. "I see the machines employ a bar-type construction, not unlike our carriers."

"That's right," Dan said, staring through the haziness. "This is where they do time..." He tugged at a lever suddenly; the machine veered left, flickered through a barred door, came to a halt. Two nebulous figures loomed beside the cage. Dan cut the switch. If he'd guessed wrong—

The scene fluoresced, sparks crackling, then popped into sharp focus. Blote scrambled out, brown eyes swiveling to take in the concrete walls, the barred door and—

"You!" a hoarse voice bellowed.

"Grab him!" someone yelled.

Blote recoiled, threshing his ambulatory members in a fruitless attempt to regain the carrier as Manny and Fiorello closed in. Dan hauled at a lever. He caught a last glimpse of three struggling, blue-lit figures as the carrier shot away through the cell wall.

CHAPTER THREE

Dan slumped back against the seat with a sigh. Now that he was in the clear, he would have to decide on his next move—fast. There was no telling what other resources Blote might have. He would have to hide the carrier, then—

A low growling was coming from somewhere, rising in pitch and volume. Dan sat up, alarmed. This was no time for a malfunction.

The sound rose higher, into a penetrating wail. There was no sign of mechanical trouble. The carrier glided on, swooping now over a nebulous landscape of trees and houses. Dan covered his ears again the deafening shriek, like all the police sirens in town blaring at once. If the carrier stopped it would be a long fall from here. Dan worked the controls, dropping toward the distant earth.

The noise seemed to lessen, descending the scale. Dan slowed, brought the carrier in to the corner of a wide park. He dropped the last few inches and cut the switch.

As the glow died, the siren faded into silence.

Dan stepped from the carrier and looked around. Whatever the noise was, it hadn't attracted any attention from the scattered pedestrians in the park. Perhaps it was some sort of burglar alarm. But if so, why hadn't it gone into action earlier? Dan took a deep breath. Sound or no sound, he would have to get back into the carrier and transfer it to a secluded spot where he could study it at leisure. He stepped back in, reached for the controls—

There was a sudden chill in the air. The bright surface of the dials before him frosted over. There was a loud *pop!* like a flashbulb exploding. Dan stared from the seat at an iridescent rectangle which hung suspended near the carrier. Its surface rippled, faded to blankness. In a swirl of frosty air, a tall figure dressed in a tight-fitting white uniform stepped through.

Dan gaped at the small rounded head, the dark-skinned long-nosed face, the long, muscular arms, the hands, their backs tufted with curly red-brown hair, the strange long-heeled feet in soft boots. A neat pillbox cap with a short visor was strapped low over the deep-set yellowish eyes, which turned in his direction. The wide mouth opened in a smile which showed square yellowish teeth.

"Alors, monsieur," the newcomer said, bending his knees and back in a quick bow. *"Vous ete une indigine, n'est ce pas?"*

"No compree," Dan choked out, "Dh…juh no parlay Fransay…"

"My error. This is the Anglic colonial sector, isn't it? Stupid of me. Permit me to introduce myself. I'm Dzhackoon, Field Agent of Class five, Inter-dimensional Monitor Service."

"That siren," Dan said. "Was that you?"

Dzhackcon nodded. "For a moment, it appeared you were disinclined to stop. I'm glad you decided to be reasonable."

"What outfit did you say you were with?" Dan asked.

"The Inter-dimensional Monitor Service."

"Inter-what?"

"Dimensional. The word is imprecise, of course, but it's the best our language coder can do, using the Anglic vocabulary."

"What do you want with me?"

Dzhackoon smiling reprovingly. "You know the penalty for operation of an unauthorized reversed-phase vehicle in Interdicted territory. I'm afraid you'll have to come along with me to Headquarters."

"Wait a minute! You mean you're arresting me'?"

"That's a harsh term, but I suppose it amounts to that."

"Look here, uh—Dzhackoon. I just wandered in off the street. I don't know anything about Interdicts and reversed-whozis vehicles. Just let me out of here."

Dzhackoon shook his head. "I'm afraid you'll have to tell it to the Inspector." He smiled amiably, gestured toward the shimmering rectangle through which he had arrived. From the edge, it was completely invisible. It looked, Dan thought, like a hole snipped in reality. He glanced at Dzhackoon. If he stepped in fast and threw a left to the head and followed up with a right to the short ribs—

"I'm armed, of course," the Agent said apologetically.

"Okay," Dan sighed. "But I'm going under protest."

"Don't be nervous," Dzhackoon said cheerfully. "Just step through quickly."

Dan edged up to the glimmering surface. He gritted his teeth, closed his eyes and took a step. There was a momentary sensation of searing heat...

His eyes flew open. He was in a long, narrow room with walls finished in bright green tile. Hot yellow light flooded down from the high ceiling. Along the wall, a series of cubicles were arranged. Tall, white-uniformed creatures moved briskly about. Nearby stood a group of short, immensely burly individuals in yellow. Lounging against the wall at the far end of the room, Dan glimpsed a round-shouldered figure in red, with great bushes of hair fringing a bright blue face. An arm even longer than Dzhackoon's wielded a toothpick on a row of great white fangs.

"This way," Dzhackoon said. Dan followed him to a cubicle, curious eyes following him. A creature indistinguishable from the Field Agent except for a twist of red braid on each wrist looked up from a desk.

"I've picked up that reversed-phase violator, Ghunt," Dzhackoon said. "Anglic Sector, Locus C 922A4."

Ghunt rose. "Let me see; Anglic Sector... Oh, yes." He extended a hand, Dan took it gingerly; it was a strange hand—hot, dry and coarse-skinned, like a dog's paw. He pumped it twice and let it go.

"Wonderfully expressive," Ghunt said. "Empty hand, no weapon. The implied savagery..." He eyed Dan curiously.

"Remarkable. I've studied your branch, of course, but I've never had the pleasure of actually seeing one of you chaps before. That skin; amazing. Ah...may I look at your hands?"

Dan extended a hand. The other took it in bony fingers, studied it, turned it over, examined the nails. Stepping closer, he peered at Dan's eyes and hair.

"Would you mind opening your mouth, please?" Dan complied. Ghunt clucked, eyeing the teeth. He walked around Dan, murmuring his wonderment.

"Uh...pardon my asking," Dan said, "but are you what—uh—people are going to look like in the future?"

"Eh?" The round yellowish eyes blinked; the wide mouth curved in a grin. "I doubt that very much, old chap." He chuckled. "Can't undo half a million years of divergent evolution, you know."

"You mean you're from the past?" Dan croaked.

"The past? I'm afraid I don't follow you."

"You don't mean—we're all going to die out and monkeys are going to take over?" Dan blurted.

"Monkeys? Let me see. I've heard of them. Some sort of small primate, like a miniature Anthropos. You have them at home, do you? Fascinating!" He shook his head regretfully. "I certainly wish regulations allowed me to pay your sector a visit."

"But you *are* time travelers," Dan insisted.

"Time travelers?" Ghunt laughed aloud.

"An exploded theory," Dzhackoon said. "Superstition."

"Then how did you get to the park from here?"

"A simple focused portal. Merely a matter of elementary stressed field mechanics."

"That doesn't tell me much," Dan said. "Where am I? Who are you?"

"Explanations are in order, of course," Ghunt said. "Have a chair. Now, if I remember correctly, in your locus, there are only a few species of Anthropos extant—"

"Just the one," Dzhackoon put in. "These fellows look fragile, but oh, brother!"

"Oh, yes; I recall. This was the locus where the hairless variant systematically hunted down other varieties," he clucked at Dan reprovingly. "Don't you find it lonely?"

"Of course, there are a couple of rather curious retarded forms there," Dzhackoon said. "Actual living fossils; sub-intellectual Anthropos. There's one called the gorilla, and the chimpanzee, the orangutan, the gibbon—and, of course, a whole spectrum of the miniature forms."

"I suppose that when the ferocious mutation established its supremacy, the others retreated to the less competitive ecological niches and expanded at that level," Ghunt mused. "Pity. I assume the gorilla and the others are degenerate forms?"

"Possibly."

"Excuse me," Dan said, "but about that explanation…"

"Oh, sorry. Well, to begin with Dzhackoon and I are—ah—Australopithecines, I believe your term is. We're one of the many varieties of Anthropos native to normal loci. The workers in yellow, whom you may have noticed, are akin to your extinct Neanderthals. Then there are the Pekin derivatives—the blue-faced chaps—and the Rhodesians—"

"What are these loci you keep talking about? And how can cave men still be alive?"

Ghunt's eyes wandered past Dan.

He jumped to his feet. "Ah, good day, Inspector!" Dan turned. A grizzled Australopithecine with a tangle of red braid at collar and wrists stared at him glumly.

"Harrumph!" the Inspector said.

"Albinism and alopecia. Not catching, I hope?"

"A genetic deficiency, excellency," Dzhackoon said. "This is a Homo Sapiens, a naturally bald form from a rather curious locus."

"Sapiens? Sapiens? Now, that seems to ring a bell." The olster blinked at Dan. "You're not—" He waggled fingers in instinctive digital-mnemonic stimulus. Abruptly he stiffened. "Why, this is one of those fratricidal deviants!" He backed off. "He should be under restraint, Ghunt! Constable! Get a strong-arm squad in here! This creature is dangerous!"

"Inspector, I'm sure—" Ghunt started.

"That's an order!" the Inspector barked. He switched to an incomprehensible language, bellowed more commands. Several of the thickset Neanderthal types appeared, moving in to seize Dan's arms. He looked around at chinless, wide-mouthed brown faces with incongruous blue eyes and lank blond hair.

"What's this all about?" he demanded. "I want a lawyer!"

"Never mind that!" the Inspector shouted. "I know how to deal with miscreants of your stripe!" He stared distastefully at Dan. "Hairless! Putty-colored! Revolting! Planning more mayhem, are you? Preparing to branch out into the civilized loci to wipe out all competitive life, is that it?"

"I brought him here, Inspector," Dzhackoon put in. "It was a routine traffic violation."

"I'll decide what's routine here! Now, Sapiens! What fiendish scheme have you up your sleeve, eh?"

"Daniel Slane, civilian, social security number 456-7329-988," Dan said.

"Eh?"

"Name, rank and serial number," Dan explained. "I'm not answering any other questions."

"This means penal relocation Sapiens! Unlawful departure from native locus, willful obstruction of justice—"

"You forgot being born without permission, and unauthorized breathing."

"Insolence!" the Inspector snarled. "I'm warning you, Sapiens; it's in my power to make things miserable for you. Now, how did you induce Agent Dzhackoon to bring you here?"

"Well, a good fairy came and gave me three wishes—"

"Take him away," the Inspector screeched. "Sector 97; an unoccupied locus."

"Unoccupied? That seems pretty extreme, doesn't it?" one of the guards commented, wrinkling his heavily ridged brow.

"Unoccupied! If it bothers you, perhaps I can arrange for you to join him there!"

The Neanderthaloid guard yawned widely, showing white teeth. He nodded to Dan, motioned him ahead. "Don't mind Spoghodo," he said loudly. "He's getting old."

"Sorry about all this," a voice hissed near Dan's ear. Dzhackoon—or Ghunt, he couldn't say which—leaned near. "I'm afraid you'll have to go along to the penal area, but I'll try to straighten things out later."

Back in the concourse, Dan's guard escorted him past cubicles where busy IDMS agents reported to harassed seniors, through an archway into a room lined with narrow gray panels. It looked like a gym locker room.

"Ninety-seven," the guard said. He went to a wall chart, studied the fine print with the aid of a blunt, hairy finger, then set a dial on the wall. "Here we go," he said. He pushed a button beside one of the lockers. Its surface clouded and became iridescent.

"Just step through fast. Happy landings."

"Thanks," Dan ducked his head and pushed through the opening in a puff of frost.

He was standing on a steep hillside, looking down across a sweep of meadow to a plain far below. There were clumps of trees, and a river. In the distance a herd of animals grazed among low shrubbery. No road wound along the valley floor; no boats dotted the river; no village nestled at its bend. The far hills were innocent of trails, fences, houses, the rectangles of plowed acres. There were no contrails in the wide blue sky. No vagrant aroma of exhaust fumes, no mutter of internal combustion, no tin cans, no pop bottles—

In short, no people.

Dan turned. The Portal still shimmered faintly in the bright air. He thrust his head through, found himself staring into the locker room. The yellow-clad Neanderthaloid glanced at him.

"Say," Dan said, ignoring the sensation of a hot wire around his neck, "can't we talk this thing over?"

"Better get your head out of there before it shuts down," the guard said cheerfully. "Otherwise—ssskkkttt!"

"What about some reading matter? And look, I get these head colds. Does the temperature drop here at night? Any dangerous animals? What do I eat?"

"Here..." the guard reached into a hopper, took out a handful of pamphlets, "...these are supposed to be for guys that are relocated without prejudice. You know, poor slobs that just happened to see too much; but I'll let you have one. Let's see...Anglic, Anglic..." He selected one, handed it to Dan.

"Thanks."

"Better get clear."

Dan withdrew his head. He sat down on the grass and looked over the booklet. It was handsomely printed in gay colors:

WELCOME TO RELOCATION CENTER NO. 23 said the cover. Below the heading was a photo of a group of sullen looking creatures of varying heights and degrees of hairiness wearing paper hats. The caption read: *Newcomers Are Welcomed Into a Gay Round of Social Activity. Hi, Newcomer!*

Dan opened the book. A photo showed a scene identical to the one before him, except that in place of the meadow, there was a park-like expanse of lawn, dotted with rambling buildings with long porches lined with rockers. There were picnic tables under spreading trees, and beyond, on the river, a yacht basin crowded with canoes and rowboats.

"Life In a Community Center is Grand Fun!" Dan read. "Activities! Brownies, Cub Scouts, Boy Scouts, Girl Scouts, Sea Scouts, Tree Scouts, Cave Scouts, PTA, Shriners, Bear Cult, Rotary, Daughters of the Eastern Star, Mothers of the Big Banana, Dianetics—you name it! A Group for Everyone, and Everyone in a Group!
Classes in conversational Urdu, Sprotch, Yiddish, Gaelic. Fundu, etc; knot-tying, rug-hooking, leather-work, Greek dancing, finger-painting and many, many others!
Little Theatre!
Indian Dance Pageants
Round Table Discussions!
Town Meetings!

Dan thumbed on through the pages of emphatic print, stopped at a double-page spread labeled, *A Few Do's and Don'ts.*

* All of us want to make a GO of relocation. So—let's remember the Uranium Rule: Don't Do It! The Other Guy May Be Bigger!
* Remember the Other Fellow's Taboos!
What to you might be merely a wholesome picnic or mating bee may offend others. What some are used to doing in groups, others consider a solitary activity. Most taboos have to do with eating, sex, elimination or gods; so remember look before you sit down, lie down, squat down or kneel down!

* Ladies With Beards Please Note:
Friend husband may be on the crew clearing clogged drains—so watch that shedding in the lavatories, eh, girls? And you fellas, too! Sure, good grooming pays—but groom each other out in the open, okay?

* NOTE: There has been some agitation for separate but equal facilities. Now, honestly, folks; is that in the spirit of Center No. 23? Males and females *will continue to use the same johns* as always. No sexual chauvinism will be tolerated.

* A Word To The Kiddies!
No brachiating will be permitted in the Social Center area. After all, a lot of the Dads sleep up there. There are plenty of other trees!
* Daintiness Pays!
In these more-active-than-ever days, Personal Effluvium can get away from us almost before we notice. And that hearty scent may not be as satisfying to others as it is to ourselves! So remember, fellas: watch that P.E.! (Lye soap, eau de Cologne, flea powder and other beauty aids available at supply shed!)

Dan tossed the book aside. There were worse things than solitude. It looked like a pretty nice world—and it was all his.

The entire North American continent, all of South America, Europe, Asia, Africa—the works. He could cut down trees, build a hut, furnish it. There'd be hunting—he could make a bow and arrows—and the skins would do to make clothes. He could start a little farming, fish the streams, sun bathe—all the things he'd never had time to do back home. It wouldn't be so bad. And eventually Dzhackoon would arrange for his release. It might be just the kind of vacation—

"Ah Dan, my boy!" a bass voice boomed. Dan Jumped and spun around.

Blote's immense face blinked at him from the Portal. There was a large green bruise over one eye. He wagged a finger reproachfully.

"That was a dirty trick, Dan. My former employees were somewhat disgruntled, I'm sorry to say. But we'd best be off now. There's no time to waste."

"How did you get here?" Dan demanded.

"I employed a pocket signaler to recall my carrier—and none too soon." He touched his bruised eye gingerly. "A glance at the instruments showed me that you had visited the park. I followed and observed a TDMS Portal. Being of an adventurous turn and, of course, concerned for your welfare, I stepped through—"

"Why didn't they arrest you? I was picked up for operating the carrier."

"They had some such notion. A whiff of stun gas served to discourage them. Now let's hurry along before the management revives."

"Wait a minute, Blote. I'm not sure I want to be rescued by you—in spite of your concern for my welfare."

"Rubbish, Dan! Come along." Blote looked around. "Frightful place! No population! No commerce! No deals!"

"It has its compensations. I think I'll stay. You run along."

"Abandon a colleague? Never!"

"If you're still expecting me to deliver a time machine, you're out of luck. I don't have one."

"No? Ah, well, in a way I'm relieved. Such a device would upset accepted physical theory. Now, Dan, you mustn't imagine I harbor ulterior motives—but I believe our association will yet prove fruitful."

Dan rubbed a finger across his lower lip thoughtfully. "Look, Blote. You need my help. Maybe you can help me at the same time. If I come along, I want it understood that we work together. I have an idea—"

"But of course, Dan! Now shake a leg!"

Dan sighed and stepped through the portal. The yellow-clad guard lay on the floor, snoring. Blote led the way back into the great hall. TDMS officials were scattered across the floor, slumped over desks, or lying limp in chairs. Blote stopped before one of a row of shimmering portals.

"After you, Dan."

"Are you sure this is the right one?"

"Quite."

Dan stepped through in the now familiar chill and found himself back in the park. A small dog sniffing at the carrier caught sight of Blote, lowered his leg and fled.

"I want to pay Mr. Snithian a visit," Dan said, climbing into a seat.

"My idea exactly," Blote agreed, lowering his bulk into place.

"Don't get the idea I'm going to help you steal anything."

"Dan! A most unkind remark. I merely wish to look into certain matters."

"Just so you don't start looking into the safe."

Blote tsked, moved a lever. The carrier climbed over a row of blue trees and headed west.

CHAPTER FOUR

Blote brought the carrier in high over the Snithian Estate, dropped lower and descended gently through the roof. The pale, spectral servants moving about their duties in the upper hall failed to notice the wraith-like cage passing soundlessly among them.

In the dining room, Dan caught sight of the girl—Snithian's daughter, perhaps—arranging shadowy flowers on a sideboard.

"Let me take it," Dan whispered. Blote nodded. Dan steered for the kitchen, guided the carrier to the spot on which he had first emerged from the vault, then edged down through the floor. He brought the carrier to rest and neutralized all switches in a shower of sparks and blue light.

The vault door stood open. There were pictures stacked on the bunk now, against the wall, on the floor. Dan stepped from the carrier, went to the nearest heap of paintings. They had been dumped hastily, it seemed. They weren't even wrapped. He examined the topmost canvas, still in a heavy frame; as though, he reflected, it had just been removed from a gallery wall—

"Let's look around for Snithian," Dan said. "I want to talk to him."

"I suggest we investigate the upper floors, Dan. Doubtless his personal pad is there."

"You use the carrier; I'll go up and look the house over."

"As you wish, Dan." Blote and the carrier flickered and faded from view.

Dan stooped, picked up the pistol he had dropped in the scuffle with Fiorello and stepped out into the hall. All was silent. He climbed stairs, looked into rooms. The house seemed deserted. On the third floor he went along a corridor, checking each room. The last room on the west side was fitted as a study. There was a stack of paintings on a table near the door. Dan went to them, examined the top one.

It looked familiar. Wasn't it one that *Look* said was in the Art Institute at Chicago?

There was a creak as of an unoiled hinge. Dan spun around. A door stood open at the far side of the room—a connecting door to a bedroom, probably.

"Keep well away from the carrier, Mr. Slane," a high thin voice said from the shadows. The tall, cloaked figure of Clyde W. Snithian stepped into view, a needle-barreled pistol in his hand.

"I thought you'd be back," he piped. "It makes my problem much simpler. If you hadn't appeared soon, it would have been necessary for me to shift the scene of my operations. That would have been a nuisance."

Dan eyed the gun. "There are a lot more paintings downstairs than there were when I left," he said. "I don't know much about art, but I recognize a few of them.

"Copies," Snithian snapped.

"This is no copy," Dan tapped the top painting on the stack. "It's an original. You can feel the brushwork."

"Not prints, of course. Copies." Snithian whinnied. "Exact copies."

"These paintings are stolen, Mr. Snithian. Why would a wealthy man like you take to stealing art?"

"I'm not here to answer questions, Mr. Slane!" The weapon in Snithian's hand bugged. A wave of pain swept over Dan. Snithian cackled, lowering the gun. "You'll soon learn better manners."

Dan's hand went to his pocket, came out holding the automatic. He aimed it at Snithian's face. The industrialist froze, eyes on Dan's gun.

"Drop the gun." Snithian's weapon clattered to the floor. "Now let's go and find Kelly."

"Wait!" Snithian shrilled. "I can make you a rich man, Slane."

"Not by stealing paintings."

"You don't understand. This is more than petty larceny!"

"That's right. It's grand larceny. These pictures are worth thousands."

"I can show you things that will completely change your attitude. Actually, I've acted throughout in the best interests of humanity!"

Dan gestured with the gun. "Don't plan anything clever. I'm not used to guns. This thing will go off at the least excuse, and then I'd have a murder to explain."

"That would be an inexcusable blunder on your part!" Snithian keened. "I'm a very important figure, Slane." He crossed the deep pile rug to a glass-doored cabinet. "This," he said, taking out a flat black box, "contains a fortune in precious stones." He lifted the lid. Dan stepped closer. A row of brilliant red gems nestled in a bed of cotton.

"Rubies?"

"Flawless—and perfectly matched." Snithian whinnied. "Perfectly matched. Worth a fortune. They're yours, if you cooperate."

"You said you were going to change my attitude. Better get started."

"Listen to me, Slane. I'm not operating independently. I'm employed by the Ivroy, whose power is incalculable. My assignment has been to rescue from destruction irreplaceable works of art fated to be consumed in atomic fire."

"What do you mean fated?"

"The Ivroy knows these things. These paintings—all your art—are unique in the galaxy. Others admire but they cannot emulate. In the cosmos of the far future, the few surviving treasures of dawn art will be valued beyond all other wealth. They alone will give a renewed glimpse of the universe as it appeared to the eyes of your strange race in its glory."

"My strange race?"

Snithian drew himself up. "I am not of your race." He threw his cloak aside and straightened.

Dan gaped as Snithian's body unfolded, rising up, long, three-jointed arms flexing, stretching out. The bald head ducked now under the beamed ceiling. Snithian chuckled shrilly.

"What about that inflexible attitude of yours, now, Mr. Slane?" he piped. "Have I made my point?"

"Yes, but—" Dan squeaked. He cleared his throat and tried again. "But I've still got the gun."

"Oh, that." An eight-foot arm snaked out, flicked the gun aside. "I've only temporized with you because you can be useful to me, Mr. Slane. I dislike running about, and I therefore employ locals to do my running for me. Accept my offer of employment, and you'll be richly rewarded."

"Why me?"

"You already know of my presence here. If I can enlist your loyalty, there will be no need to dispose of you, with the attendant annoyance from police, relatives and busybodies. I'd like you to act as my agent in the collection of the works."

"Nuts to you!" Dan said. "I'm not helping any bunch of skinheads commit robbery."

"This is for the Ivroy, you fool!" Snithian said. "The mightiest power in the cosmos!"

"This Ivroy doesn't sound so hot to me—robbing art galleries—"

"To be adult is to be disillusioned. Only realities count. But no matter. The question remains: Will you serve me loyally?"

"Hell, no!" Dan snapped.

"Too bad. I see you mean what you say. It's to be expected, I suppose. Even an infant fire-cat has fangs."

"You're damn right I mean it. How did you get Manny and Fiorello on your payroll? I'm surprised even a couple of bums would go to work for a scavenger like you."

"I suppose you refer to the precious pair recruited by Blote. That was a mistake, I fear. It seemed perfectly reasonable at the time. Tell me, how did you overcome the Vegan? They're a very capable race generally speaking."

"You and he work together, eh?" Dan said. "That makes things a little clearer. This is the collection station and Blote is the fence."

"Enough of your conjectures. You leave me no choice but to dispose of you. It's a nuisance, but it can't be helped. I'm afraid I'll have to ask you to accompany me down to the vault."

Dan eyed the door; if he were going to make a break, now was the time—

The whine of the carrier sounded. The ghostly cage glided through the wall and settled gently between Dan and Snithian. The glow died.

Blote waved cheerfully to Dan as he eased his grotesque bulk from the seat.

"Good day to you, Snithian," Blote boomed. "I see you've met Dan. An enterprising fellow."

"What brings you here, Gom Blote?" Snithian shrilled. "I thought you'd be well on your way to Vorplisch by now."

"I was tempted, Snithian. But I don't spook easy. There is the matter of some unfinished business."

"Excellent!" Snithian exclaimed. "I'll have another consignment ready for you by tomorrow."

"Tomorrow! How is it possible, with Manny and Fiorello lodged in the hoosegow?" Blote looked around; his eye fell on the stacked paintings. He moved across to them, lifted one, glanced at the next, then shuffled rapidly through the stack. He turned.

"What duplicity is this, Snithian!" he rumbled. "All identical! Our agreement called for limited editions, not mass production! My principals will be furious! My reputation—"

"Shrivel your reputation!" Snithian keened. "I have more serious problems at the moment! My entire position's been compromised. I'm faced with the necessity for disposing of this blundering fool!"

"Dan? Why, I'm afraid I can't allow that, Snithian." Blote moved to the carrier, dumped an armful of duplicate paintings in the cage. "Evidence," he said. "The confederation has methods for dealing with sharp practice. Come, Dan, if you're ready."

"You dare to cross me?" Snithian hissed. "I, who act for the Ivroy?"

Blote motioned to the carrier. "Get in, Dan. We'll be going now." He rolled both eyes to bear on Snithian. "And I'll deal with you later," he rumbled. "No one pulls a fast one on Gom Blote, Trader Fourth Class—or on the Vegan Federation."

Snithian moved suddenly, flicking out a spidery arm to seize the weapon he had dropped, aim and trigger. Dan, in a wash of pain, felt his knees fold. He fell slackly to the floor. Beside him, Blote sagged, his tentacles limp.

"I credited you with more intelligence," Snithian cackled. "Now I have an extra ton of protoplasm to dispose of. The carrier will be useful in that connection."

CHAPTER FIVE

Dan felt a familiar chill in the air. A Portal appeared. In a puff of icy mist, a tall figure stepped through.

Gone was the tight uniform. In its place, the lanky Australopithecine wore skin-tight blue-jeans and a loose sweat shirt. An oversized beret clung to the small round head. Immense dark glasses covered the yellowish eyes, and sandals flapped on the bare, long-toed feet. Dzhackoon waved a long cigarette holder at the group.

"Ah, a stroke of luck! How nice to find you standing by. I had expected to have to conduct an intensive search within the locus. Thus the native dress. However—" Dzhackoon's eyes fell on Snithian standing stiffly by, the gun out of sight.

"You're of a race unfamiliar to me," he said. "Still, I assume you're aware of the Interdict on all Anthropoid populated loci?"

"And who might you be?" Snithian inquired loftily.

"I'm a Field Agent of the Inter-dimensional Monitor Service."

"Ah, yes. Well, your Interdict means nothing to me. I'm operating directly under Ivroy auspices," Snithian touched a glittering pin on his drab cloak.

Dzhackoon sighed. "There goes the old arrest record."

"He's a crook!" Dan cut in. "He's been robbing art galleries!"

"Keep calm, Dan," Blote murmured. "no need to be overly explicit."

The Agent turned to look the Trader over.

"Vegan, aren't you? I imagine you're the fellow I've been chasing."

"Who, me?" the bass voice rumbled. "Look, officer, I'm a home loving family man, just passing through. As a matter of fact—"

The uniformed creature nodded toward the paintings in the carrier. "Gathered a few souvenirs, I see."

"For the wives and kiddy. Just a little something to brighten up the hive."

"The penalty for exploitation of a sub-cultural anthropoid-occupied body is stasis for a period not to exceed one reproductive cycle. If I recall my Vegan biology, that's quite a period."

"Why, officer! Surely you're not putting the arm on a respectable law-abiding being like me? Why, I lost a tentacle fighting in defense of peace—" As he talked, Blote moved toward the carrier.

"—your name, my dear fellow," he went on, "I'll mention it to the Commissioner, a very close friend of mine." Abruptly the Vegan reached for a lever—

The long arms in the tight white jacket reached to haul him back effortlessly. "That was unwise, sir. Now I'll be forced to recommend subliminal reorientation during stasis." He clamped stout handcuffs on Blote's broad wrists.

"You Vegans," he said, dusting his hands briskly. "Will you never learn?"

"Now officer," Blote said, "you're acting hastily. Actually, I'm working in the interest of this little world, as my associate Dan will gladly confirm. I have information which will be of considerable interest to you. Snithian has stated that he is in the employ of the Ivroy—"

"If the Ivroy's so powerful, why was it necessary to hire Snithian to steal pictures?" Dan interrupted.

"Perish the thought, Dan. Snithian's assignment was merely to duplicate works of art and transmit them to the Ivroy."

"Here," Snithian cut in. "Restrain that obscene mouth!"

Dzhackoon raised a hand. "Kindly remain silent, sir. Permit my prisoners their little chat."

"You may release them to my custody," Snithian snapped.

Dzhackoon shook his head. "Hardly, sir. A most improper suggestion—even from an agent of the Ivroy." He nodded at Dan. "You may continue."

"How do you duplicate works of art?" Dan demanded.

"With a matter duplicator. But, as I was saying, Snithian saw an opportunity to make extra profits by retaining the works for repeated duplications and sale to other customers—such as myself."

"You mean there are other—customers—around?"

"I have dozens of competitors, Dan, all busy exporting your artifacts. You are an industrious and talented race, you know."

"What do they buy?"

"A little of everything, Dan. It's had an influence on your designs already, I'm sorry to say. The work is losing its native purity."

Dan nodded. "I have had the feeling some of this modern furniture was designed for Martians."

"Ganymedans, mostly. The Martians are graphic arts fans, while your automobiles are designed for the Plutonian trade. They have a baroque sense of humor."

"What will the Ivroy do when he finds out Snithian's been double-crossing him?"

"He'll think of something, I daresay. I blame myself for his defection, in a way. You see, it was my carrier which made it possible for Snithian to carry out his thefts. Originally, he would simply enter a gallery, inconspicuously scan a picture, return home and process the recording through the duplicator. The carrier gave him the idea of removing works en masse, duplicating them and returning them the next day. Alas, I agreed to join forces with him. He grew greedy. He retained the paintings here and proceeded to produce vast numbers of copies—which he doubtless sold to my competitors, the crook!"

Dzhackoon had whipped out a notebook and was jotting rapidly.

"Now, let's have those names and addresses," he said. "This will be the biggest round-up in TDMS history."

"And the pinch will be yours, dear sir," Blote said. "I foresee early promotion for you." He held out his shackled wrists. "Would you mind?"

"Well…" Dzhackoon unlocked the cuffs. "I think I'm on firm ground. Just don't mention it to Inspector Spoghodo."

"You can't do that!" Snithian snapped. "These persons are dangerous!"

"That is my decision. Now…"

Snithian brought out the pistol with a sudden movement. "I'll brook no interference from meddlers—"

There was a sound from the door. All heads turned. The girl Dan had seen in the house stood in the doorway, glancing calmly from Snithian to Blote to Dzhackoon. When her eyes met Dan's she smiled. Dan thought he had never seen such a beautiful face—and the figure matched.

"Get out, you fool!" Snithian snapped. "No; come inside, and shut the door."

"Leave the girl out of this, Snithian," Dan croaked.

"Now I'll have to destroy all of you," Snithian keened. "You first of all, ugly native!" He aimed the gun at Dan.

"Put the gun down, Mr. Snithian," the girl said in a warm, melodious voice. She seemed completely unworried by the grotesque aliens, Dan noted abstractedly.

Snithian swiveled on her. "You dare—!"

"Oh, yes, I dare, Snithian." Her voice had a firm ring now. Snithian stared at her. "Who...are you...?"

"I am the Ivroy."

Snithian wilted. The gun fell to the floor. His fantastically tall figure drooped, his face suddenly gray.

"Return to your home, Snithian," the girl said sadly. "I will deal with you later."

"But...but..." His voice was a thin squeak.

"Did you think you could conceal your betrayal from the Ivroy?" she said softly.

Snithian turned and blundered from the room, ducking under the low door. The Ivroy turned to Dzhackoon.

"You and your Service are to be commended," she said. "I leave the apprehension of the culprits to you." She nodded at Blote. "I will rely on you to assist in the task—and to limit your operations thereafter to non-interdicted areas."

"But of course, your worship. You have my word as a Vegan. Do visit me on Vorplisch someday. I'd love the wives and kiddy to meet you." He blinked rapidly. "So long, Dan. It's been crazy cool."

Dzhackoon and Blote stepped through the Portal. It shimmered and winked out. The Ivroy faced Dan. He swallowed hard, watching the play of light in the shoulder length hair, golden, fine as spun glass...

"Your name is Dan?"

"Dan Slane," he said. He took a deep breath. "Are you really the Ivroy?"

"I am of the Ivroy, who are many and one."

"But you look like—just a beautiful girl."

The Ivroy smiled. Her teeth were as even as matched pearls, Dan thought, and as white as—

"I *am* a girl, Dan. We are cousins, you and I—separated by the long mystery of time."

"Blote—and Dzhackoon and Snithian, too—seemed to think the Ivroy ran the Universe. But—"

The Ivroy put her hand on Dan's. It was as soft as a flower petal.

"Don't trouble yourself over this just now, Dan. Would you like to become my agent? I need a trustworthy friend to help me in my work here."

"Doing what?" Dan heard himself say.

"Watching over the race which will one day become the Ivroy."

"I don't understand all this—but I'm willing to try."

"There will be much to learn, Dan. The full use of the mind, control of aging and disease... Our work will require many centuries."

"Centuries? But—"

"I'll teach you, Dan."

"It sounds great," Dan said. "Too good to be true. But how do you know I'm the man for the job? Don't I have to take some kind of test?"

She looked up at him, smiling, her lips slightly parted. On impulse, Dan put a hand under her chin, drew her face close and kissed her on the mouth...

A full minute later, the Ivroy, nestled in Dan's arms, looked up at him again.

"You passed the test," she said.

THE END

The Ship Sails At Midnight

By FRITZ LEIBER

They had tried to find out something about her background...unsuccessfully.
But you don't probe a goddess about her past...

THIS IS the story of a beautiful woman. And of a monster.

It is also the story of four silly, selfish, culture-bound inhabitants of the planet Earth. Es, who was something of an artist. Gene, who studied atoms—and fought the world and himself. Louis, who philosophized. And Larry—that's my name—who tried to write books.

It was an eerie, stifling August when we met Helen. The date is fixed in my mind because our little city had just had its mid-western sluggishness ruffled by a series of those scares that either give rise to oddity items in the newspapers, or else are caused by them—it's sometimes hard to tell which. People had seen flying discs and heard noises in the sky—someone from the college geology department tried unsuccessfully to track down a meteorite. A farmer this side of the old coal pits got all excited about something "big and shapeless" that disturbed his poultry and frightened his wife, and for a couple of days men tracked around fruitlessly with shotguns—just another of those "rural monster" scares.

Even the townsfolk hadn't been left out. For their imaginative enrichment they had a "Hypnotism Burglar," an apparently mild enough chap who blinked soft lights in people's faces and droned some siren-song outside their houses at night. For a week high-school girls squealed twice as loud after dark, men squared their shoulders adventurously at strangers, and women peered uneasily out of their bedroom windows after turning out the lights.

Louis and Es and I had picked up Gene at the college library and wanted a bite to eat before we turned in. Although by now they had almost petered out, we were talking about our local scares—a chilly hint of the supernatural makes good conversational fare in a month too hot for any real thinking. We slouched into the one decent open-all-night restaurant our dismal burg possesses (it wouldn't have that if it weren't for the "wild" college folk) and found that Benny had a new waitress.

She was really very beautiful, much too exotically beautiful for Benny's. Masses of pale gold ringlets piled high on her head. An aristocratic bony structure (from Es' greedy look I could tell she was instantly thinking sculpture). And a pair of the dreamiest, calmest eyes in the world.

She came over to our table and silently waited for our orders. Probably because her beauty flustered us, we put on an elaborate version of our act of "intellectuals precisely and patiently explaining their desires to a pig-headed member of the proletariat." She listened, nodded, and presently returned with our orders.

Louis had asked for just a cup of black coffee.

She brought him a half cantaloupe also.

He sat looking at it for a moment. Then he chuckled incredulously. "You know, I actually wanted that," he said. "But I didn't know I wanted it. You must have read my subconscious mind."

"What's that?" she asked in a low, lovely voice with intonations rather like Benny's.

Digging into his cantaloupe, Louis sketched an explanation suitable for fifth-graders.

She disregarded the explanation. "What do you use it for?" she asked.

Louis, who is something of a wit, said, "I don't use it. It uses me."

"That the way it should be?" she commented.

NONE OF us knew the answer to that one, so since I was the Gang's specialist in dealing with the lower orders, I remarked brilliantly, "What's your name?"

"Helen," she told me.

"How long have you been here?"

"Couple days," she said, starting back toward the counter.

"Where did you come from?"

She spread her hands. "Oh—places."

Whereupon Gene, whose humor inclines toward the fantastic, asked, "Did you arrive on a flying disc?"

She glanced back at him and said, "Wise guy."

But all the same she hung around our table, filling sugar basins and what not. We made our conversation especially erudite, each of us merrily spinning his favorite web of half-understood intellectual jargon and half-baked private opinion. We were conscious of her presence, all right.

Just as we were leaving, the thing happened. At the doorway something made us all look back. Helen was behind the counter. She was looking at us. Her eyes weren't dreamy at all, but focused, intent, radiant. She was smiling.

My elbow was touching Es' naked arm—we were rather crowded in the doorway—and I felt her shiver. Then she gave a tiny jerk and I sensed that Gene, who was holding her other arm (they were more or less sweethearts), had tightened his grip on it.

For perhaps three seconds it stayed just like that, the four of us looking at the one of her. Then Helen shyly dropped her gaze and began to mop the counter with a rag.

We were all very quiet going home.

Next night we went back to Benny's again, rather earlier. Helen was still there, and quite as beautiful as we remembered her. We exchanged with her a few more of those brief, teasing remarks— her voice no longer sounded so much like Benny's—and staged some more intellectual pyrotechnics for her benefit. Just before we left, Es went up to her at the counter and talked to her privately for perhaps a minute, at the end of which Helen nodded.

"Ask her to pose for you?" I asked Es when we got outside.

She nodded. "That girl has the most magnificent figure in the world," she proclaimed fervently.

"Or out of it," Gene confirmed grudgingly.

"And an incredibly exciting skull," Es finished.

It was characteristic of us that Es should have been the one to really break the ice with Helen. Like most intellectuals, we were rather timid, always setting up barriers against other people. We clung to adolescence and the college, although all of us but Gene had been graduated from it. Instead of getting out into the real world, we lived by sponging off our parents and doing academic odd-jobs for the professors (Es had a few private students.) Here in our home city we had status, you see. We were looked upon as being frightfully clever and sophisticated, the local "bohemian set" (though Lord knows we were anything but that). Whereas out in the real world we'd have been greenhorns.

WE WERE scared of the world, you see. Scared that it would find out that all our vaunted abilities and projects didn't amount to much—and that as for solid achievements, there just hadn't been any. Es was only a mediocre artist; she was afraid to learn from the great, especially the living great, for fear her own affected little individuality would be engulfed. Louis was no philosopher; he merely cultivated a series of intellectual enthusiasms, living in a state of feverish private—and fruitless—excitement over the thoughts of other men. My own defense against reality consisted of knowingness and a cynical attitude; I had a remarkable packrat accumulation of information; I had a line on everything—and also always knew why it wasn't worth bothering with. As for Gene, he was the best of us and also the worst. A bit younger, he still applied himself to his studies, and showed promise in nuclear physics and math. But something, perhaps his small size and puritanical farm background, had made him moody and contrary, and given him an inclination toward physical violence that threatened someday to get him into real trouble. As it was, he'd had his license taken away for reckless driving. And several times we'd had to intervene—once unsuccessfully—to keep him from getting beaten up in bars.

We talked a great deal about our "work." Actually we spent much more time reading magazines and detective stories, lazing around, getting drunk, and conducting our endless intellectual palavers.

If we had one real virtue, it was our loyalty to each other, though it wouldn't take a cynic to point out that we desperately needed each other for an audience. Still, there was some genuine feeling there.

In short, like many people on a planet where mind is wakening and has barely become aware of the eon-old fetters and blindfolds oppressing it, and has had just the faintest glimpse of its tremendous possible future destiny, we were badly cowed— frightened, frustrated, self-centered, slothful, vain, pretentious.

Considering how set we were getting in those attitudes, it is all the more amazing that Helen had the tremendous effect on us that she did. For within a month of meeting her, our attitude toward the whole world had sweetened, we had become genuinely interested in people instead of being frightened of them, and we were beginning to do real creative work. An astonishing achievement for an unknown little waitress!

It wasn't that she took us in hand or set us an example, or anything like that. Quite the opposite. I don't think that Helen was responsible for a half dozen positive statements (and only one really impulsive act) during the whole time we knew her. Rather, she was like a Great Books discussion leader, who never voices an opinion of his own, but only leads other people to voice theirs—as an intellectual midwife.

Louis and Gene and I would drop over to Es', say, and find Helen getting dressed behind the screen or taking a cup of tea after a session of posing. We'd start a discussion and for a while Helen would listen dreamily, just another shadow in the high old shadowy room. But then those startling little questions of hers would begin to come, each one opening a new vista of thought. By the time the discussion was finished—which might be at the Blue Moon bar or under the campus maples or watching the water ripple in the old coal pits—we'd have got somewhere. Instead of ending in weary shoulder-shrugging or cynical grousing at the world or getting drunk out of sheer frustration, we'd finish up with a plan—some facts to check, something to write or shape to try.

And then, people! How would we ever have got close to people without Helen? Without Helen, Old Gus would have stayed an ancient and bleary-eyed dishwater at Benny's. But with Helen, Gus became for us what he really was—a figure of romance who had sailed the Seven Seas, who had hunted for gold on the Orinoco with twenty female Indians for porters (because the males were too lazy and proud to hire out to do anything) and who had marched at the head of his Amazon band carrying a newborn baby of one of the women in his generous arms (because the women assured him that a man-child was the only burden a man might carry without dishonor.)

EVEN GENE was softened in his attitudes. I remember once when two handsome truck drivers picked up Helen at the Blue Moon. Instantly Gene's jaw muscles bulged and his eyes went blank and he began to wag his right shoulder—and I got ready for a scene. But Helen said a word here and there, threw in a soft laugh, and began to ask the truck drivers her questions. In ten minutes we were all at ease and the four of us found out things we'd never dreamed about dark highways and diesels and their proud, dark-souled pilots (so like Gene in their temperaments.)

But it was on us as individuals that Helen's influence showed up the biggest. Es' sculptures acquired an altogether new scope. She dropped her pet mannerisms without a tear and began to take into her work whatever was sound and good. She rapidly developed a style that was classical and yet had in it something that was wholly of the future. Es is getting recognition now and her work is still good, but there was a magic about her "Helenic Period" which she can't recapture. The magic still lives in the pieces she did at that time—particularly in a nude of Helen that has all the serenity and purpose of the best ancient Egyptian work, and something much more. As we watched that piece take form, as we watched the clay grow into Helen under Es' hands, we dimly sensed that in some indescribable way Helen was growing into Es at the same time, and Es into Helen. It was such a beautiful, subtle relationship that even Gene couldn't be jealous.

At the same time Louis gave over his fickle philosophical flirtations and found the field of inquiry for which he'd always been looking—a blend of semantics and introspective psychology designed to chart the chaotic inner world of human experience. Although his present intellectual tactics lack the brilliance they had when Helen was nudging his mind, he still keeps doggedly at the project, which promises to add a whole new range of words to the vocabulary of psychology and perhaps of the English language.

Gene wasn't ripe for creative work, but from being a merely promising student he became a brilliant and very industrious one, rather to the surprise of his professors. Even with the cloud that now overhangs his life and darkens his reputation, he has managed to find worthwhile employment on one of the big nuclear projects.

As for myself, I really began to write. Enough said.

We sometimes used to speculate as to the secret of Helen's effect on us, though we didn't by any means give her all the credit in those days. We had some sort of theory that Helen was a completely "natural" person, a "noble savage" (from the kitchen), a bridge to the world of proletarian reality. Es once said that Helen couldn't have had a Freudian childhood, whatever she meant by that. Louis spoke of Helen's unthinking social courage and Gene of the catalytic effect of beauty. And sometimes we attributed Helen's influence merely to some difference between her life pattern and ours.

Oddly, in these discussions we never referred to that strange, electric experience we'd all had when we first met Helen—that tearing moment when we'd looked back from the doorway. We were always strangely reticent there. And none of us ever voiced the conviction that I'm sure all of us had at times: that our social and psychoanalytic theories weren't worth a hoot when it came to explaining Helen, that she possessed powers of feeling and mind (mostly concealed) that set her utterly apart from every other inhabitant of the planet Earth, that she was like a being from another, far saner and lovelier world.

That conviction isn't unusual, come to think of it. It's the one every man has about the girl he loves. Which brings me to my own secret explanation of Helen's effect on me (though not on the others.)

It was simply this. I loved Helen and I knew Helen loved me. And that was quite enough.

It happened scarcely a month after we'd met. We were staging a little party at Es'. Since I was the one with the car, I was assigned to pick up Helen at Benny's when she got through. On the short drive I passed a house that held unpleasant memories for me. A girl had lived there whom I'd been crazy about and who had turned me down. (No, let's be honest, I turned her down, though I very much wanted her, because of some tragic cowardice, the memory of which always sears me like a hot iron.)

Helen must have guessed something from my expression, for she said softly, "What's the matter, Larry?" and then, when I ignored the question, "Something about a girl?"

SHE WAS so sympathetic about it that I broke down and told her the whole story, sitting in the parked and lightless car in front of Es'. I let myself go and lived through the whole thing again, with all its biting shame. When I was finished I looked up from the steering wheel. The streetlight made a pale aureole around Helen's head and a paler one where the white angora sweater covered her shoulders. The upper part of her face was in darkness, but a bit of light touched her full lips and narrow, almost fennec (or foxlike) chin.

"You poor kid," she said softly, and the next moment we were kissing each other, and a feeling of utter relief and courage and power was budding deep inside me.

A bit later she said to me something that even at the time I realized was very wise.

"Let's keep this between you and me, Larry," she said. "Let's not mention it to the others. Let's not even hint." She paused, and then added, a trifle unhappily, "I'm afraid they wouldn't appreciate it. Sometime, I hope—but not quite yet."

I knew what she meant. That Gene and Louis and even Es were only human—that is, irrational—in their jealousies, and that the knowledge that Helen was my girl would have put a damper on the exciting but almost childlike relationship of the five of us (as the fact of Es' and Gene's love would never have done. Es was a rather cold, awkward girl, and Louis and I seldom grudged poor, angry Gene her affection.)

So when Helen and I dashed in and found the others berating Benny for making Helen work overtime, we agreed that he was an unshaven and heartless louse, and in a little while the party was going strong and we were laughing and talking unconstrainedly. No one could possibly have guessed that a new and very lovely factor had been added to the situation.

After that evening everything was different for me. I had a girl. Helen was (why not say the trite things, they're true) my goddess, my worshipper, my slave, my ruler, my inspiration, my comfort, my refuge—oh, I could write books about what she meant to me.

I guess all my life I will be writing books about that.

I could write pages describing just one of the beautiful moments we had together. I could drown myself in the bitter ghosts of sensations. Rush of sunlight through her hair. Click of her heels on a brick sidewalk. Light of her presence brightening a mean room. Chase of unearthly expressions across her sleeping face.

Yet it was on my mind that Helen's love had the greatest effect. It unfettered my thoughts, gave them passage into a far vaster cosmos.

One minute I'd be beside Helen, our hands touching lightly in the dark, a shaft of moonlight from the dusty window silvering her hair. The next, my mind would be a billion miles up, hovering like an iridescent insect over the million bright worlds of existence.

Or I'd be surmounting walls inside my mind—craggy, dire ramparts that have been there since the days of the cave man.

Or the universe would become a miraculous web, with Time the spider. I couldn't see all of it—no creature could see a trillionth of it in all eternity—but I would have a sense of it all.

Sometimes the icy beauty of those moments would become too great, and I'd feel a sudden chill of terror. Then the scene around me would become a nightmare and I'd half expect Helen's eyes to show a catlike gleam and slit, or her hair to come rustlingly alive, or her arms to writhe bonelessly, or her splendid skin to slough away, revealing some black and antlike form of dread.

Then the moment would pass and everything would be sheer loveliness again, richer for the fleeting terror.

My mind is hobbled once more now, but I still know the taste of the inward freedom that Helen's love brought.

YOU MIGHT think from this that Helen and I had a lot of times alone together. We hadn't—we couldn't have, with the Gang. But we had enough. Helen was clever at arranging things. They never suspected us.

Lord knows there were times I yearned to let the Gang in on our secret. But then I would remember Helen's warning and see the truth of it.

Let's face it. We're all of us a pretty vain and possessive people. As individuals, we cry for attention. We jockey for admiration. We swim or sink according to whether we feel we're being worshipped or merely liked. We demand too much of the person we love. We want them to be a never-failing prop to our ego.

And then if we're lonely and happen to see someone else loved, the greedy child wakes, the savage stirs, the frustrated Puritan clenches his teeth. We seethe, we resent, we hate.

No, I saw that I couldn't tell the others about Helen and myself. Not Louis. Not even Es. And as for Gene, I'm afraid that with his narrow-minded upbringing, he'd have been deeply shocked by what he'd have deduced about our relationship. We were supposed, you know, to be "wild" young people, "bohemians." Actually we were quite straight-laced—Gene especially, the rest of us almost as much.

I knew how I would have felt if Helen had happened to become Louis' or Gene's girl. That says it.

To tell the truth, I felt a great deal of admiration for the Gang, because they could do alone what I was only doing with Helen's love. They were enlarging their minds, becoming creative, working and playing hard—and doing it without my reward. Frankly, I don't know how I could have managed it myself without Helen's love. My admiration for Louis, Es, and Gene was touched with a kind of, awe.

And we really were getting places. We had created a new mind-spot on the world, a sprouting-place for thought that wasn't vain or self-conscious, but concerned wholly with its work and its delights. The Gang was forming itself into a kind of lens for viewing the world, outside and in.

Any group of people can make themselves into that sort of lens, if they really want to. But somehow they seldom get started. They don't have the right inspiration.

We had Helen.

Always, but mostly in unspoken thoughts, we'd come back to the mystery of how she had managed it. She was mysterious, all right. We'd known her some six months now, and we were as much in the dark about her background as when we first met her. She wouldn't tell anything even to me. She'd come from "places." She was a "drifter." She liked "people." She told us all sorts of fascinating incidents, but whether she'd been mixed up in them herself or just heard them at Benny's (she could have made a Trappist jabber) was uncertain.

We sometimes tried to get her to talk about her past. But she dodged our questions easily and we didn't like to press them.

You don't cross-examine Beauty.

You don't demand that a Great Books discussion leader state his convictions.

You don't probe a goddess about her past.

Yet this vagueness about Helen's past caused us a certain uneasiness. She'd drifted to us. She might drift away.

If we hadn't been so involved in our thought-sprouting, we'd have been worried. And if I hadn't been so happy, and everything so smoothly perfect, I'd have done more than occasionally ask Helen to marry me and hear her answer, "Not now, Larry."

Yes, she was mysterious.

And she had her eccentricities.

For one thing, she insisted on working at Benny's although she could have had a dozen better jobs. Benny's was her window on the main street of life, she said.

For another, she'd go off on long hikes in the country, even in the snowiest weather. I met her coming back from one and was worried, tried to be angry. But she only smiled.

Yet, when spring came round again and burgeoned into summer, she would never go swimming with us in our favorite coal pit.

The coal pits are a place where they once strip-mined for the stuff where it came to the surface. Long ago the huge holes were left to fill with water and their edges to grow green with grass and trees. They're swell for swimming.

BUT HELEN would never go to our favorite, which was one of the biggest and yet the least visited—and this year the water was unusually high. We changed to suit her, of course, but because the one she didn't like happened to be near the farmhouse of last August's "rural monster" scare, Louis joshed her.

"Maybe a monster haunts the pool," he said. "Maybe it's a being come from another world on a flying disk."

He happened to say that on a lazy afternoon when we'd been swimming at the new coal pit and were drying on the edge, having cigarettes. Louis' remark started us speculating about creatures from another world coming secretly to visit Earth—their problems, especially how they'd disguise themselves.

"Maybe they'd watch from a distance," Gene said. "Television, supersensitive microphones."

"Or clairvoyance, clairaudience," Es chimed, being rather keen on parapsychology.

"But to really mingle with people..." Helen murmured. She was stretched on her back in white bra and trunks, looking deep into the ranks of marching clouds. Her olive skin tanned to an odd hue that went bewitchingly with her hair. With a sudden and frightening poignancy I was aware of the catlike perfection of her slim body.

"The creature might have some sort of elaborate plastic disguise," Gene began doubtfully.

"It might have a human form to begin with," I ventured. "You know, the idea that Earth folk are decayed interstellar colonists."

"It might take possession of some person here," Louis cut in. "Insinuate its mind or even itself into the human being."

"Or it might grow itself a new body," Helen murmured sleepily.

That was one of the half dozen positive statements she ever made.

Then we got to talking about the motives of such an alien being. Whether it would try to destroy men, or look on us as cattle, or study us, or amuse itself with us, or what not.

Here Helen joined in again, distant-eyed but smiling. "I know you've all laughed at the comic-book idea of some Martian monster lusting after beautiful white women. But has it ever occurred to you that a creature from outside might simply and honestly fall in love with you?"

That was another of Helen's rare positive statements.

The idea was engaging and we tried to get Helen to expand it, but she wouldn't. In fact, she was rather silent the rest of that day.

As the summer began to mount toward its crests of heat and growth, the mystery of Helen began to possess us more often— that, and a certain anxiety about her.

There was a feeling in the air, the sort of uneasiness that cats and dogs get when they are about to lose their owner.

Without exactly knowing it, without a definite word being said, we were afraid we might lose Helen.

Partly it was Helen's own behavior. For once she showed a kind of restlessness, or rather preoccupation. At Benny's she no longer took such an interest in "people."

She seemed to be trying to solve some difficult personal problem, nerve herself to make some big decision.

Once she looked at us and said, "You know, I like you kids terribly." Said it the way a person says it when he knows he may have to lose what he likes.

And then there was the business of the Stranger.

Helen had been talking quite a bit with a strange man, not at Benny's, but walking in the streets, which was unusual. We didn't know who the Stranger was. We hadn't actually seen him face to face. Just heard about him from Benny and glimpsed him once or twice. Yet he worried us.

Understand, our happiness went on, yet faintly veiling it was this new and ominous mist.

THEN ONE night the mist took definite shape. It happened on an occasion of celebration. After a few days during which we'd sensed they'd been quarreling, Es and Gene had suddenly announced that they were getting married. On an immediate impulse we'd all gone to the Blue Moon.

We were having the third round of drinks, and kidding Es because she didn't seem very enthusiastic, almost a bit grumpy— when he came in.

Even before he looked our way, before he drifted up to our table, we knew that this was the Stranger.

He was a rather slender man, fair haired like Helen. Otherwise he didn't look like her, yet there was a sense of kinship. Perhaps it lay in his poise, his wholly casual manner.

As he came up, I could feel myself and the others getting tense, like dogs at the approach of the unknown.

The Stranger stopped by our table and stood looking at Helen as if he knew her. The four of us realized more than ever that we wanted Helen to be ours alone (and especially mine), that we hated to think of her having close ties with anyone else.

What got especially under my skin was the suggestion that there was some kinship between the Stranger and Helen, that behind his proud, remote-eyed face, he was talking to her with his mind.

Gene apparently took the Stranger for one of those unpleasant fellows who strut around bars looking for trouble—and proceeded to act as if he were one of those same fellows himself. He screwed his delicate features into a cheap frown and stood up as tall as he could, which wasn't much. Such tough-guy behavior, always a symptom of frustration and doubts of masculinity, had been foreign to Gene for some months. I felt a pulse of sadness—and almost winced when Gene opened the side of his mouth and began, "Now look here, Joe—"

But Helen laid her hand on his arm. She looked calmly at the Stranger for a few more moments and then she said, "I won't talk to you that way. You must speak English."

If the Stranger was surprised, he didn't show it. He smiled and said softly, with a faint foreign accent, "The ship sails at midnight, Helen."

I got a queer feeling; for our city is two hundred miles from anything you'd call navigable waters.

For a moment I felt what you might call supernatural fear. The bar so tawdry and dim, the line of hunched neurotic shoulders, the plump dice-girl at one end and the tiny writhing television screen at the other. And against that background, Helen and the Stranger, light-haired, olive-skinned, with proud feline features, facing each other like duelists, on guard, opposed, yet sharing some secret knowledge. Like two aristocrats come to a dive to settle a quarrel—like that, and something more. As I say, it frightened me.

"Are you coming, Helen?" the Stranger asked.

And now I was really frightened. It was as if I'd realized for the first time just how terribly much Helen meant to all of us, and to me especially. Not just the loss of her, but the loss of things in me that only she could call into being. I could see the same fear in the faces of the others. A lost look in Gene's eyes, behind the fake gangster frown. Louis' fingers relaxing from his glass and his chunky head turning toward the stranger, slowly with empty gaze, like the turret-guns of a battleship. Es starting to stub out her cigarette and then hesitating, her eyes on Helen—although in Es' case I felt there was another emotion besides fear.

"Coming?" Helen echoed, like someone in a dream.

THE STRANGER waited. Helen's reply had twisted the tension tighter. Now Es did stub out her cigarette with awkward haste, then quickly drew back her hand. I felt suddenly that this had been bound to happen, that Helen must have had her life, her real life, before we had known her, and that the Stranger was part of it; that she had come to us mysteriously and now would leave us as mysteriously. Yes, I felt all of that, although in view of what had happened between Helen and me, I knew I shouldn't have.

"Have you considered everything?" the Stranger asked finally.

"Yes," Helen replied.

"You know that after tonight there'll be no going back," he continued as softly as ever. "You know that you'll be marooned here forever, that you'll have to spend the rest of your life among..." (he looked around at us as if searching for a word) "...among barbarians."

Again Helen laid her hand on Gene's arm, although her glance never left the Stranger's face.

"What is the attraction, Helen?" the Stranger went on. "Have you really tried to analyze it? I know it might be fun for a month, or a year, or even five years. A kind of game, a renewal of youth. But when it's over and you're tired of the game, when you realize that you're alone, completely alone, and that there's no going back ever— Have you thought of that?"

"Yes, I have thought of all that." Helen said, as quietly as the Stranger, but with a tremendous finality. "I won't try to explain it to you, because with all your wisdom and cleverness I don't think you'd quite understand. And I know I'm breaking promises—and more than promises. But I'm not going back. I'm here with my friends, my true and equal friends, and I'm not going back."

And then it came, and I could tell it came to all of us—a great big lift, like a surge of silent music or a glow of invisible light. Helen had at last declared herself. After the faint equivocations and reservations of the spring and summer, she had put herself squarely on our side. We each of us knew that what she had said she meant wholly and forever. She was ours, ours more completely than ever before. Our quasi-goddess, our inspiration, our key to a widening future; the one who always understood, who could open doors in our imaginations and feelings that would otherwise have remained forever shut. She was our Helen now, ours and (as my mind persisted in adding exultingly) especially mine.

And we? We were the Gang again, happy, poised, wise as Heaven and clever as Hell, out to celebrate, having fun with whatever came along.

The whole scene had changed. The frightening aura around the Stranger had vanished completely. He was just another of those hundreds of odd people whom we met when we were with Helen.

He acted almost as if he were conscious of it. He smiled and said quickly, "Very well. I had a feeling you'd decide this way." He started to move off. Then, "Oh, by the way, Helen—"

"Yes ?"

"The others wanted me to say goodbye to you for them."

"Tell them the same and the best of luck."

The Stranger nodded and again started to turn away, when Helen added, "And you?"

The Stranger looked back.

"I'll be seeing you once more before midnight," he said lightly, and almost the next moment, it seemed, was out the door.

We all chuckled. I don't know why. Partly from relief, I suppose, and partly—God help us!—in triumph over the Stranger. One thing I'm sure of: three (and maybe even four) of us felt for a moment happier and more secure in our relationship to Helen than we ever had before. It was the peak. We were together. The Stranger had been vanquished, and all the queer unspoken threats he had brought with him. Helen had declared herself. The future stood open before us, full of creation and achievement, with Helen ready to lead us into it. For a moment everything was perfect. We were mankind, vibrantly alive, triumphantly progressing.

It was, as I say, perfect.

And only human beings know how to wreck perfection.

Only human beings are so vain, so greedy, each wanting everything for himself alone.

It was Gene who did it. Gene who couldn't stand so much happiness and who had to destroy it, from what self-fear, what Puritanical self-torment, what death-wish I don't know. It was Gene, but it might have been any of us…

HIS FACE was flushed. He was smiling, grinning rather, in what I now realize was an oafish and overbearing complacency. He put his hand on Helen's arm in a way none of us had ever touched Helen before, and said, "That was great, dear."

It wasn't so much what he said as the naked possessiveness of the gesture. It was surely that gesture of ownership that made Es explode, that started her talking in a voice terribly bitter, but so low it was some moments before the rest of us realized what she was getting at.

When we did we were thunderstruck.

She was accusing Helen of having stolen Gene's love.

It's hard to make anyone understand the shock we felt. As if someone had accused a goddess of abominations.

Es lit another cigarette with shaking fingers, and finished up.

"I don't want your pity, Helen. I don't want Gene married off to me for the sake of appearances, like some half-discarded mistress. I like you, Helen, but not enough to let you take Gene away from me and then toss him back—or half toss him back. No, I draw the line at that."

And she stopped as if her emotions had choked her.

As I said, the rest of us were thunderstruck. But not Gene. His face got redder still. He slugged down the rest of his drink and looked around at us, obviously getting ready to explode in turn.

Helen had listened to Es with a half-smile and an unhappy half frown, shaking her head from time to time. Now she shot Gene a warning, imploring glance, but he disregarded it.

"No, Helen," he said. "Es is right. I'm glad she spoke. It was a mistake for us ever to hide our feelings. It would have been a ten times worse mistake if I'd kept that crazy promise I made you to marry Es. You go too much by pity, Helen, and pity's no use in managing an affair like this. I don't want to hurt Es, but she'd bet-ter know right now that it's another marriage we're announcing tonight."

I sat there speechless. I just couldn't realize that that drunken, red-faced popinjay was claiming that Helen was his girl, his wife to be.

Es didn't look at him. "You cheap little beast," she whispered.

Gene went white at that, but he kept on smiling.

"Es may not forgive me for this," he said harshly, "but I don't think it's me she's jealous of. What gets under her skin is not so much losing me to Helen as losing Helen to me."

Then I could find words.

But Louis was ahead of me.

He put his hand firmly on Gene's shoulder.

"You're drunk, Gene," he said, "and you're talking like a drunken fool. Helen's my girl."

They started up, both of them, Louis' hand still on Gene's shoulder.

Then, instead of hitting each other, they looked at me.

Because I had risen too.

"But..." I began, and faltered.

Without my saying it, they knew.

Louis' hand dropped away from Gene.

All of us looked at Helen. A cold, terribly hurt, horribly disgusted look.

Helen blushed and looked down. Only much later did I realize it was related to the look she'd given the four of us that first night at Benny's.

"...but I fell in love with all of you," she said softly.

Then we did speak, or rather Gene spoke for us. I hate to admit it, but at the time I felt a hot throb of pleasure at all the unforgivable things he called Helen. I wanted to see the lash laid on, the stones thud.

Finally he called her some names that were a little worse.

Then Helen did the only impulsive thing I ever knew her to do...

She slapped Gene's face. Once. Hard.

THERE ARE only two courses a person can take when he's been rebuked by a goddess, even a fallen goddess. He can grovel and beg forgiveness. Or he can turn apostate and devil-worshipper.

Gene did the latter.

He walked out of the Blue Moon, blundering like a blind drunk.

That broke up the party, and Gus and the other bartender, who'd been about to interfere, returned relievedly to their jobs.

Louis went off to the bar. Es followed him. I went to the far end myself, under the writhing television screen, and ordered a double scotch.

Beyond the dozen intervening pairs of shoulders, I could see that Es was trying to act shameless. She was whispering things to Louis. At the same time, and even more awkwardly, she was flirting with one of the other men. Every once in a while she would laugh shrilly, mirthlessly.

Helen didn't move. She just sat at the table, looking down, the half-smile fixed on her lips. Once Gus approached her, but she shook her head.

I ordered another double scotch. Suddenly my mind began to work furiously on three levels.

On the first I was loathing Helen. I was seeing that all she'd done for us, all the mind-spot, all the house of creativity we'd raised together, had been based on a lie. Helen was unutterably cheap, common.

Mostly, on that level, I was grieving for the terrible wrong I felt she'd done me.

The second level was entirely different. There an icy spider had entered my mind from realms undreamt. There sheer supernatural terror reigned. For there I was adding up all the little hints of strangeness we'd had about Helen. The Stranger's words had touched it off and now a thousand details began to drop into place: the coincidence of her arrival with the flying disc, rural monster, and hypnotism scare; her interest in people, like that of a student from a far land; the impression she gave of possessing concealed powers; her pains never to say anything definite, as if she were on guard against imparting some forbidden knowledge; her long hikes into the country; her aversion for the big and yet seldom-visited coal pit (big and deep enough to float a liner or hide a submarine);

above all, that impression of *unearthliness* she'd at times given us all, even when we were most under her spell.

And now this matter of a ship sailing at midnight. From the Great Plains.

What sort of ship?

On that level my mind shrank from facing the obvious result of its labor. It was too frighteningly incredible, too far from the world of the Blue Moon and Benny's and cheap little waitresses.

The third level was far mistier, but it was there. At least I tell myself it was there. On this third level I was beginning to see Helen in a better light and the rest of us in a worse. I was beginning to see the lovelessness behind our idea of love—and the faithfulness, to the best in us, behind Helen's faithlessness. I was beginning to see how hateful, how like spoiled children, we'd been acting.

Of course, maybe there wasn't any third level in my mind at all. Maybe that only came afterwards. Maybe I'm just trying to flatter myself that I was a little more discerning, a little "bigger" than the others.

Yet I like to think that I turned away from the bar and took a couple of steps toward Helen, that it was only those "second level" fears that slowed me so that I'd only taken those two faltering steps (if I took them) before—

Before Gene walked in.

I remember the clock said eleven thirty.

Gene's face was dead white, and knobby with tension.

His hand was in his pocket.

He never looked at anyone but Helen. They might have been alone. He wavered—or trembled. Then a terrible spasm of energy stiffened him. He started toward the table.

Helen got up and walked toward him, her arms outstretched. In her half smile were all the compassion and fatalism—and love— I can imagine there being in the universe.

Gene pulled a gun out of his pocket and shot Helen six times. Four times in the body, twice in the head.

She hung for a moment, then pitched forward into the blue smoke. It puffed away from her to either side and we saw her lying on her face, one of her outstretched hands touching Gene's shoe.

145

THEN, BEFORE a woman could scream, before Gus and the other chap could jump the bar, the outside door of the Blue Moon opened and the Stranger came in. After that none of us *could* have moved or spoken. We cringed from his eyes like guilty dogs.

It wasn't that he looked anger at us, or hate, or even contempt. That would have been much easier to bear.

No, even as the Stranger passed Gene—Gene, pistol dangling from two fingers, looking down in dumb horror, edging his toe back by terrified inches from Helen's dead hand—even as the Stranger sent Gene a glance, it was the glance a man might give a bull that has gored a child, a pet ape that has torn up his mistress in some inscrutable and pettish animal rage.

And as, without a word, the Stranger picked Helen up in his arms, and carried her silently through the thinning blue smoke into the street, his face bore that same look of tragic regret, of serene acceptance.

That's almost all there is to my story. Gene was arrested, of course, but you can't convict a man for the murder of a woman without real identity, when there is no body to prove a murder had been committed.

For Helen's body was never found. Neither was the Stranger.

Eventually Gene was released and, as I've said, is making a life for himself, despite the cloud over his reputation.

We see him now and then, and try to console him, tell him it might as easily have been Es or Louis or I, that we were all blind, selfish fools together.

And we've each of us got back to our work. The sculptures, the wordstudies, the novels, the nuclear notions are not nearly as brilliant as when Helen was with us. But we keep turning them out. We tell ourselves Helen would like that.

And our minds all work now at the third level—but only by fits and starts, fighting the jungle blindness and selfishness that are closing in again. Still, at our best, we understand Helen and what Helen was trying to do, what she was trying to bring the world even if the world wasn't ready for it. We glimpse that strange passion that made her sacrifice all the stars for four miserable blind-worms.

But mostly we grieve for Helen, together and alone. We know there won't be another Helen for a hundred thousand years, if then. We know that she's gone a lot farther than the dozens or thousands of light-years her body's been taken for burial. We look at Es' statue of Helen, we read one or two of my poems to her. We remember, our minds come half alive and are tortured by the thought of what they might have become if we'd kept Helen. We picture her again sitting in the shadows of Es' studio or sunning herself on the grassy banks after a swim, or smiling at us at Benny's. And we grieve.

For we know you get only one chance at someone like Helen.

We know that because, half an hour after the Stranger carried Helen's body from the Blue Moon, a great meteor went flaming and roaring across the countryside (some say up from the countryside and out toward the stars) and the next day it was discovered that the waters of the coal pit Helen wouldn't swim in, had been splashed, as if by the downward blow of a giant's fist, across the fields for a thousand yards.

THE END

Spaceman On A Spree

By MACK REYNOLDS

What's more important? Man's conquest of space, or one spaceman's life?

CHAPTER ONE

They gave him a gold watch. It was meant to be symbolical, of course. In the old tradition. It was in the way of an antique, being one of the timepieces made generations past in the Alpine area of Eurasia. Its quaintness lay in the fact that it was wound, not electronically by power-radio, but by the actual physical movements of the bearer, a free swinging rotor keeping the mainspring at a constant tension.

They also had a banquet for him, complete with speeches by such bigwigs of the Department of Space Exploration as Academician Lofting Gubelin and Doctor Hans Girard-Perregaux. There was also somebody from the government who spoke, but he was one of those who were pseudo-elected and didn't know much about the field of space travel nor the significance of Seymour Pond's retirement. Si didn't bother to remember his name. He only wondered vaguely why the cloddy had turned up at all.

In common with recipients of gold watches of a score of generations before him, Si Pond would have preferred something a bit more tangible in the way of reward, such as a few shares of Variable Basic to add to his portfolio. But that, he supposed was asking too much.

The fact of the matter was, Si knew that his retiring had set them back. They hadn't figured he had enough shares of Basic to see him through decently. Well, possibly he didn't, given their standards. But Space Pilot Seymour Pond didn't have their standards. He'd had plenty of time to think it over. It was better to retire on a limited crediting, on a confoundedly limited crediting, than to take the two or three more trips in hopes of attaining a higher standard.

He'd had plenty of time to figure it out, there alone in space on the Moon run, there on the Venus or Mars runs. There on the long, long haul to the Jupiter satellites, fearfully checking the symptoms of space cafard, the madness compounded of claustrophobia, monotony, boredom and free fall. Plenty of time. Time to decide that a one room mini-auto-apartment, complete with an autochair and built-in autobar, and with one wall a teevee-screen, was all he needed to find contentment for a mighty long time. Possibly somebody like Doc Girard-Perregaux might be horrified at the idea of living in a mini-auto-apartment...not realizing that to a pilot it was roomy beyond belief compared to the conning tower of a space craft.

No. Even as Si listened to their speeches, accepted the watch and made a halting little talk on his own, he was grinning inwardly. There wasn't anything they could do. He had them now. He had enough Basic to keep him comfortably, by his standards, for the rest of his life. He was never going to subject himself to space cafard again. Just thinking about it, now, set the tic to going at the side of his mouth.

They could count down and blast off, for all he gave a damn.

The gold watch idea had been that of Lofting Gubelin, which was typical, he being in the way of a living anachronism himself. In fact, Academician Gubelin was possibly the only living man on North America who still wore spectacles. His explanation was that a phobia against having his eyes touched prohibited either surgery to remold his eyeballs and cure his myopia, or contact lenses.

That was only an alibi so far as his closest associate, Hans Girard-Perregaux, was concerned. Doctor Girard-Perregaux was convinced Gubelin would have even worn facial hair, had he but a touch more courage. Gubelin longed for yesteryear, a seldom found phenomenon under the Ultrawelfare State.

Slumped in an autochair in the escape room of his Floridian home, Lofting Gubelin scowled at his friend. He said, acidly. "Any more bright schemes, Hans? I presume you now acknowledge that appealing to the cloddy's patriotism, sentiment and desire for public acclaim have miserably failed."

Girard-Perregaux said easily, "I wouldn't call Seymour Pond a cloddy. In his position, I am afraid I would do the same thing he has."

"That's nonsense, Hans. Zoroaster! Either you or I would gladly take Pond's place, were we capable of performing the duties for which he has been trained. There aren't two men on North America—there aren't two men in the world!—who better realize the urgency of continuing our delving into space." Gubelin snapped his fingers. "Like that, either of us would give our lives to prevent man from completely abandoning the road to his destiny."

His friend said drily, "Either of us could have volunteered for pilot training forty years ago, Lofting. We didn't."

"At that time there wasn't such a blistering percentage of funkers throughout this whole blistering Ultrawelfare State! Who could foresee that eventually our whole program would face ending due to lack of courageous young men willing to take chances, willing to face adventure, willing to react to the stimulus of danger in the manner our ancestors did?"

Girard-Perregaux grunted his sarcasm and dialed a glass of iced tea and tequila. He said, "Nevertheless, both you and I conform with the present generation in finding it far more pleasant to follow one's way of life in the comfort of one's home than to be confronted with the unpleasantness of facing nature's dangers in more adventurous pastimes."

Gubelin, half angry at his friend's argument, leaned forward to snap rebuttal, but the other was wagging a finger at him negatively. "Face reality, Lofting. Don't require or expect from Seymour Pond more than is to be found there. He is an average young man. Born in our Ultra welfare State, he was guaranteed his fundamental womb-to-tomb security by being issued that minimum number of Basic shares in our society that allows him an income sufficient to secure the food, clothing, shelter, medical care and education to sustain a low level of subsistence. Percentages were against his ever being drafted into industry. Automation being what it is, only a fraction of the population is ever called up. But Pond was. His industrial aptitude dossier revealed him a possible candidate for space pilot, and it was you yourself who talked him into taking the training...pointing out the more pragmatic advantages such as complete retirement after but six trips, added shares of Basic so that he could enjoy a more comfortable life than most and the fame that would accrue to him as one of the very few who still participate in travel to the planets. Very well. He was sold. Took his training, which, of course, required long years of drudgery to him. Then, performing his duties quite competently, he made his six trips. He is now legally eligible for retirement. He was drafted into the working force reserves, served his time, and is now free from toil for the balance of his life. Why should he listen to our pleas for a few more trips?"

"But has he no spirit of adventure? Has he no feeling for…"

Girard-Perregaux was wagging his finger again, a gesture that, seemingly mild though it was, had an astonishing ability to break off the conversation of one who debated with the easy-seeming, quiet spoken man.

He said, "No, he hasn't. Few there are who have, nowadays. Man has always paid lip service to adventure, hardships and excitement, but in actuality his instincts, like those of any other animal, lead him to the least dangerous path. Today we've reached the point where no one need face danger—ever. There are few who don't take advantage of the fact. Including you and me, Lofting, and including Seymour Pond."

His friend and colleague changed subjects abruptly, impatiently. "Let's leave this blistering jabber about Pond's motivation and get to the point. The man is the only trained space pilot in the world. It will take months, possibly more than a year, to bring another novitiate pilot to the point where he can safely be trusted to take our next explorer craft out. Appropriations for our expeditions have been increasingly hard to come by—even though in our minds, Hans, we are near important breakthroughs, breakthroughs which might possibly so spark the race that a new dream to push man out to the stars will take hold of us. If it is admitted that our organization has degenerated to the point that we haven't a single pilot, then it might well be that the Economic Planning Board, and especially those daddies on Appropriations, will terminate the whole Department of Space Exploration."

"So…" Girard-Perregaux said gently.

"So some way we've got to bring Seymour Pond out of his retirement!"

"Now we are getting to matters." Girard-Perregaux nodded his agreement. Looking over the rim of his glass, his eyes narrowed in thought as his face took on an expression of Machiavellianism. "And do not the ends justify the means?"

Gubelin blinked at him.

The other chuckled. "The trouble with you, Lofting, is that you have failed to bring history to bear on our problem. Haven't you ever read of the sailor and his way of life?"

"Sailor? What in the name of the living Zoroaster has the sailor got to do with it?"

"You must realize, my dear Lofting, that our Si Pond is nothing more than a latter-day sailor, with many of the problems and viewpoints, tendencies and weaknesses of the voyager of the past. Have you never heard of the seaman who dreamed of returning to the village of his birth and buying a chicken farm or some such? All the long months at sea—and sometimes the tramp freighters or whaling craft would be out for years at a stretch before returning to home port—he would talk of his retirement and his dream. And then? Then in port, it would be one short drink with the boys, before taking his accumulated pay and heading home. The one short drink would lead to another. And morning would find him, drunk, rolled, tattooed and possibly sleeping it off in jail. So back to sea he'd have to go."

Gubelin grunted bitterly. "Unfortunately, our present-day sailor can't be separated from his money quite so easily. If he could, I'd personally be willing to lure him down some dark alley, knock him over the head and roll him myself. Just to bring him back to his job again."

He brought his wallet from his pocket, and flicked it open to his universal credit card. "The ultimate means of exchange," he grunted. "Nobody can spend your money, but you, yourself. Nobody can steal · it, nobody can, ah, con you out of it. Just how do you expect to sever our present-day sailor and his accumulated nest egg?"

The other chuckled again. "It is simply a matter of finding more modern methods, my dear chap."

CHAPTER TWO

Si Pond was a great believer in the institution of the spree. Any excuse would do. Back when he had finished basic education at the age of twenty-five and was registered for the labor draft, there hadn't been a chance in a hundred that he'd have the bad luck to have his name pulled. But when it had been, Si had celebrated.

When he had been informed that his physical and mental qualifications were such that he was eligible for the most dangerous occupation in the ultra welfare State and had been pressured into taking training for space pilot, he had celebrated once again. Twenty-two others had taken the training with him, and only he and Rod Cameroon had passed the finals. On this occasion, he and Rod had celebrated together. It had been quite a party. Two weeks later, Rod had burned on a faulty take-off on what should have been a routine Moon run.

Each time Si returned from one of his own runs, he celebrated. A spree, a bust, a bat, a wing-ding, a night on the town. A commemoration of dangers met and passed.

Now it was all over. At the age of thirty he was retired. Law prevented him from ever being called up for contributing to the country's labor needs again. And he most certainly wasn't going to volunteer.

He had taken his schooling much as had his contemporaries. There wasn't any particular reason for trying to excel. You didn't want to get the reputation for being a wise guy, or a cloddy either. Just one of the fellas. You could do the same in life whether you really studied or not. You had your Inalienable Basic stock, didn't you? What else did you need?

It had come as a surprise when he'd been drafted for the labor force.

In the early days of the Ultrawelfare State, they had made a mistake in adapting to the automation of the second industrial revolution. They had attempted to give everyone work by reducing the number of working hours in the day, and the number of working days in the week. It finally became ludicrous when employees of industry were working but two days a week, two hours a day. In fact, it got chaotic. It became obvious that it was more practical to have one worker putting in thirty-five hours a week and getting to know his job well, than it was to have a score of employees, each working a few hours a week and none of them ever really becoming efficient.

The only fair thing was to let the technologically unemployed remain unemployed, with their Inalienable Basic stock as the equivalent of unemployment insurance, while the few workers still needed put in a reasonable number of hours a day, a reasonable number of weeks a year and a reasonable number of years in a life time. When new employees were needed, a draft lottery was held.

All persons registered in the labor force participated. If you were drawn, you must need serve. The dissatisfaction those chosen might feel at their poor luck was offset by the fact that they were granted additional Variable Basic shares, according to the tasks they fulfilled. Such shares could be added to their portfolios, the dividends becoming part of their current credit balance, or could be sold for a lump sum on the market.

Yes, but now it was all over. He had his own little place, his own vacuum-tube vehicle and twice the amount of shares of Basic that most of his fellow citizens could boast. Si Pond had it made. A spree was obviously called for.

He was going to do this one right. This was the big one. He'd accumulated a lot of dollars these past few months and he intended to blow them, or at least a sizeable number of them. His credit card was burning a hole in his pocket, as the expression went. However, he wasn't going to rush into things. This had to be done correctly.

Too many a spree was played by ear. You started off with a few drinks, fell in with some second rate mopsy and usually wound up in a third rate groggery where you spent just as much as though you'd been in the classiest joint in town. Came morning and you had nothing to show for all the dollars that had been spent but a rum-head.

Thus, Si was vaguely aware, it had always been down through the centuries since the Phoenician sailor, back from his year-long trip to the tin mines of Cornwall, blew his hard earned share of the voyage's profits in a matter of days in the wine shops of Tyre. Nobody gets quite so little for his money as that loneliest of all workers, he who must leave his home for distant lands, returning only periodically and usually with the salary of lengthy, weary periods of time to be spent hurriedly in an attempt to achieve the pleasure and happiness so long denied him.

Si was going to do it differently this time.

Nothing but the best. Wine, women, song, food, entertainment. The works. But nothing but the best.

To start off, he dressed with great care in the honorable retirement-rank suit he had so recently purchased. His space pin he attached carefully to the lapel. That was a good beginning, he decided. A bit of prestige didn't hurt you when you went out on the town. In the Ultrawelfare State hardly one person in a hundred actually ever performed anything of value to society. The efforts of most weren't needed. Those few who did contribute were awarded honors, decorations, titles.

Attired satisfactorily, Si double-checked to see that his credit card was in his pocket. As an afterthought, he went over to the auto-apartment's teevee-phone, flicked it on, held the card to the screen and said, "Balance check, please."

In a moment, the teevee-phone's robot-voice reported, "Ten shares of Inalienable Basic. Twelve shares of Variable Basic, current value, four thousand, two hundred and thirty-three dollars and sixty-two cents apiece. Current cash credit, one thousand and eighty-four dollars." The screen went dead.

One thousand and eighty-four dollars. That was plenty. He could safely spend as much as half of it, if the spree got as lively as he hoped it would. His monthly dividends were due in another week or so, and he wouldn't have to worry about current expenses. Yes, indeed, Si Pond was as solvent as he had ever been in his thirty years.

He opened the small, closet-like door which housed his vacuum-tube two-seater, and wedged himself into the small vehicle. He brought down the canopy, dropped the pressurizer and considered the dial. Only one place really made sense. The big city.

He considered for a moment, decided against the boroughs of Baltimore and Boston, and selected Manhattan instead. He had the resources. He might as well do it up brown.

He dialed Manhattan and felt the sinking sensation that presaged his car's dropping to tube level. While it was being taken up by the robot controls, being shuttled here and there preparatory to the shot to his destination, he dialed the vehicle's teevee-phone for information on the hotels of the island of the Hudson. He selected a swank hostelry he'd read about and seen on the teevee casts of society and celebrity gossip reporters, and dialed it on the car's destination dial.

"Nothing too good for ex-Space Pilot Si Pond," he said aloud.

The car hesitated for a moment, that brief hesitation before the shot, and Si took the involuntary breath, from which only heroes could refrain. He sank back slowly into the seat. Moments passed, and the direction of the pressure was reversed.

Manhattan. The shuttling began again, and one or two more traversing sub-shots. Finally, the dash threw a green light and Si opened the canopy and stepped into his hotel room.

A voice said gently, "If the quarters are satisfactory, please present your credit card within ten minutes."

Si took his time. Not that he really needed it. It was by far the most swank suite he had ever seen. One wall was a window of whatever size the guest might desire and Si touched the control that dilated it to the full. His view opened in such wise that he could see both the Empire State Building Museum and the Hudson. Beyond the river stretched the all but endless city which was Greater Metropolis.

He didn't take the time to flick on the menu, next to the auto-dining table, nor to check the endless potables on the auto-bar list. All that, he well knew, would be superlative. Besides, he didn't plan to dine or do much drinking in his suite. He made a mock leer. Not unless he managed to acquire some feminine companionship, that was.

He looked briefly into the swimming pool and bath, then flopped himself happily onto the bed. It wasn't up to the degree of softness he presently desired, and he dialed the thing to the ultimate in that direction so that with a laugh he sank almost out of sight into the mattress.

He came back to his feet, gave his suit a quick patting so that it fell into press and, taking his credit card from his pocket, put it against the teevee-phone screen and pressed the hotel button so that registration could be completed.

For a moment he stood in the center of the floor, in thought. Take it easy, Si Pond; take it all easy, this time. No throwing his dollars around in second-class groggeries, no eating in automated luncheterias. This time, be it the only time in his life, he was going to frolic in the grand manner. No cloddy was Si Pond.

He decided a drink was in order to help him plan his strategy. A drink at the hotel's famous Kudos Room where celebrities were reputed to be a dime a dozen.

He left the suite and stepped into one of the elevators. He said, "Kudos Room."

The auto-elevator murmured politely, "Yes, sir, the Kudos Room."

At the door to the famous rendezvous of the swankiest set, Si paused a moment and looked about. He'd never been in a place like this, either. However, he stifled his first instinct to wonder about what this was going to do to his current credit balance with an inner grin and made his way to the bar.

There was actually a bartender.

Si Pond suppressed his astonishment and said, offhand, attempting an air of easy sophistication, "Slivovitz Sour."

"Yes, sir."

The drinks in the Kudos Room might be concocted by hand, but Si noticed they had the routine teevee-screens built into the bar for payment. He put his credit card on the screen immediately before him when the drink came, and had to quell his desire to dial for a balance check, so as to be able to figure out what the Sour had cost him.

Well, this was something like it. This was the sort of thing he'd dreamed about, out there in the great alone, seated in the confining conning tower of his space craft. He sipped at the drink, finding it up to his highest expectations, and then swiveled slightly on his stool to take a look at the others present.

To his disappointment, there were no recognizable celebrities. None that he placed, at least—top teevee stars, top politicians of the Ultrawelfare State or Sports personalities.

He turned back to his drink and noticed, for the first time, the girl who occupied the stool two down from him. Si Pond blinked. He blinked and then swallowed.

"Zo-ro-aster," he breathed.

She was done in the latest style from Shanghai, even to the point of having cosmetically duplicated the Mongolian fold at the corners of her eyes. Every pore, but *every* pore, was in place. She sat with the easy grace of the Orient, so seldom found in the West.

His stare couldn't be ignored.

She looked at him coldly, turned to the bartender and murmured, "A Far Out Cooler, please, Fredric." Then deliberately added, "I thought the Kudos Room was supposed to be exclusive."

There was nothing the bartender could say to that and he went about building the drink.

Si cleared his throat. "Hey," he said, "how about letting this one be on me?"

Her eyebrows, which had been plucked and penciled to carry out her Oriental motif, rose. "Really!" she said, drawing it out.

The bartender said hurriedly, "I beg your pardon, sir…"

The girl, her voice suddenly subtly changed, said, "Why, isn't that a space pin?"

Si, disconcerted by the sudden reversal, said, "Yeah…sure."

"Good Heavens, you're a spaceman?"

"Sure." He pointed at the lapel pin. "You can't wear one unless you been on at least a Moon run."

She was obviously both taken back and impressed. "Why," she said, "you're Seymour Pond, the Pilot. I tuned in on the banquet they gave you."

Si, carrying his glass, moved over to the stool next to her. "Call me Si," he said. "Everybody calls me Si."

She said, "I'm Natalie. Natalie Paskov. Just Natalie. Imagine meeting Seymour Pond. Just sitting down next to him at a bar. Just like that."

"Si," Si said, gratified. Holy Zoroaster, he'd never seen anything like this rarified pulchritude. Maybe on teevee, of course, one of the current sex symbols, but never in person. "Call me Si," he said again. "I been called Si so long, I don't even know who somebody's talking to if they say Seymour."

"I cried when they gave you that antique watch," she said, her tone such that it was obvious she hadn't quite adjusted as yet to having met him.

Si Pond was surprised. "Cried?" he said. "Well, why? I was kind of bored with the whole thing. But old Doc Gubelin, I used to work under him in the Space Exploration department, he was hot for it."

"*Academician* Gubelin?" she said, "You just call him Doc?"

Si was expansive. "Why, sure. In the Space Department we don't have much time for formality. Everybody's just Si, and Doc, and Jim. Like that. But how come you cried?"

She looked down into the drink the bartender had placed before her, as though avoiding his face. "I...I suppose it was that speech Doctor Girard-Perregaux made. There you stood, so fine and straight in your space-pilot uniform, the veteran of six exploration runs to the planets..."

"Well," Si said modestly, "two of my runs were only to the Moon."

"...and he said all those things about man's conquest of space. And the dream of the stars which man has held so long. And then the fact that you were the last of the space pilots. The last man in the whole world trained to pilot a space craft. And here you were, retiring."

Si grunted. "Yeah. That's all part of the Doc's scheme to get me to take on another three runs. They're afraid the whole department'll be dropped by the Appropriations Committee on this here Economic Planning Board. Even if they can find some other patsy to train for the job, it'd take maybe a year before you could even send him on a Moon hop. So old man Gubelin, and Girard-Perregaux too, they're both trying to pressure me into more trips. Otherwise they got a Space Exploration Department, with all the expense and all, but nobody to pilot their ships. It's kind of funny, in a way. You know what one of those spaceships costs?"

"Funny?" she said. "Why, I don't think it's funny at all."

Si said, "Look, how about another drink?"

Natalie Paskov said, "Oh, I'd love to have a drink with you, Mr…"

"Si," Si said. He motioned to the bartender with a circular twist of the hand indicating their need for two more of the same. "How come you know so much about it? You don't meet many people are interested in space any more. In fact, most people are almost contemptuous, like. Think it's kind of a big boondoggle deal to help use up a lot of materials and all and keep the economy going."

Natalie said earnestly, "Why, I've been a space fan all my life. I've read all about it. Have always known the names of all the space pilots and everything about them, ever since I was a child. I suppose you'd say I have the dream that Doctor Girard-Perregaux spoke about."

Si chuckled. "A real buff, eh? You know, it's kind of funny. I was never much interested in it. And I got a darn sight less interested after my first run and I found out what space cafard was."

She frowned. "I don't believe I know much about that."

Sitting in the Kudos Room with the most beautiful girl to whom he had ever talked, Si could be nonchalant about the subject. "Old Gubelin keeps that angle mostly hushed up and out of the magazine and newspaper articles. Says there's enough adverse publicity about space exploration already. But at this stage of the game when the whole ship's crammed tight with this automatic scientific apparatus and all, there's precious little room in the conning tower and you're the only man aboard. The Doc says later on when ships are bigger and there's a whole flock of people aboard, there won't be any such thing as space cafard, but…" Of a sudden the right side of Si Pond's mouth began to tic and he hurriedly took up his drink and knocked it back.

He cleared his throat. "Let's talk about some other angle. Look, how about something to eat, Natalie? I'm celebrating my retirement, like. You know, out on the town. If you're free…"

She put the tip of a finger to her lips, looking for the moment like a small girl rather than an ultra-sophisticate. "Supposedly, I have an appointment," she said hesitantly.

When the mists rolled out in the morning—if it was still morning—it was to the tune of an insistent hotel chime. Si rolled over on his back and growled, *"Zo-ro-as-ter,* cut that out. What do you want?"

The hotel communicator said softly, "Checking-out time, sir, is at two o'clock."

Si groaned. He couldn't place the last of the evening at all. He didn't remember coming back to the hotel. He couldn't recall where he had separated from, what was her name…Natalie.

He vaguely recalled having some absinthe in some fancy club she had taken him to. What was the gag she'd made? Absinthe makes the heart grow fonder. And then the club where they had the gambling machines. And the mists had rolled in on him. Mountains of the Moon! But that girl could drink. He simply wasn't that used to the stuff. You don't drink in Space School and you most certainly don't drink when in space. His binges had been few and far between.

He said now, "I don't plan on checking out today. Don't bother me." He turned to his pillow.

The hotel communicator said quietly, "Sorry, sir, but your credit balance does not show sufficient to pay your bill for another day."

Si Pond shot up, upright in bed, suddenly cold sober.

His eyes darted about the room, as though he was seeing it for the first time. His clothes, he noted, were thrown over a chair haphazardly. He made his way to them, his face empty, and fished about for his credit card, finding it in a side pocket. He wavered to the teevee-phone and thrust the card against the screen. He demanded, his voice as empty as his expression, "Balance check, please."

In less than a minute the robot-voice told him: "Ten shares of Inalienable Basic. Current cash credit, forty-two dollars and thirty cents." The screen went dead.

He sank back into the chair which held his clothes, paying no attention to them. It couldn't be right. Only yesterday, he'd had twelve shares of Variable Basic, immediately convertible into more than fifty thousand dollars, had he so wished to convert rather than collect dividends indefinitely. Not only had he the twelve shares of Variable Basic, but more than a thousand dollars to his credit.

He banged his fist against his mouth. Conceivably, he might have gone through his thousand dollars. It was possible, though hardly believable. The places he'd gone to with that girl in the Chinese get-up were probably the most expensive in Greater Metropolis. But, however expensive, he couldn't possibly have spent fifty thousand dollars! Not possibly.

He came to his feet again to head for the teevee-screen and demand an audit of the past twenty-four hours from Central Statistics. That'd show it up. Every penny expended. Something was crazy here. Someway that girl had pulled a fast one. She didn't seem the type. But something had happened to his twelve shares of Variable Basic, and he wasn't standing for it. It was his security, his defense against slipping back into the ranks of the cloddies the poor demi-buttocked ranks of the average man, the desperately dull life of those who subsisted on the bounty of the Ultrawelfare State and the proceeds of ten shares of Inalienable Basic.

He dialed Statistics and placed his card against the screen. His voice was strained now, "An audit of all expenditures for the past twenty-four hours."

Then he sat and watched.

His vacuum-tube trip to Manhattan was the first item. Two dollars and fifty cents. Next was his hotel suite. Fifty dollars. Well, he had known it was going to be expensive. A Slivovitz Sour at the Kudos Room, he found, went for three dollars a throw, and the Far out Coolers Natalie drank, four dollars. Absinthe was worse still, going for ten dollars a drink.

He was impatient. All this didn't account for anything like a thousand dollars, not to speak of fifty thousand.

The audit threw an item he didn't understand. A one dollar credit. And then, immediately afterward, a hundred dollar credit. Si scowled.

And then slowly reached out and flicked the set off. For it had all come back to him.

At first he had won. Won so that the other players had crowded around him, watching. Five thousand, ten thousand. Natalie had been jubilant. The others had cheered him on. He'd bet progressively higher, smaller wagers becoming meaningless and thousands being involved on single bets. A five thousand bet on odd had lost, and then another. The kibitzers had gone silent. When he had attempted to place another five thousand bet, the teevee-screen robot-voice had informed him dispassionately that his current cash credit balance was insufficient to cover that amount.

Yes. He could remember now. He had needed no time to decide, had simply snapped, "Sell one share of Variable Basic at current market value."

The other eleven shares had taken the route of the first.

When it was finally all gone and he had looked around, it was to find that Natalie Paskov was gone as well.

Academician Lofting Gubelin, seated in his office, was being pontifical. His old friend Hans Girard-Perregaux had enough other things on his mind to let him get away with it, only half following the monologue.

"I submit," Gubelin orated, "that there is evolution in society. But it is by fits and starts, and by no means a constant thing. Whole civilizations can go dormant, so far as progress is concerned, for millennia at a time."

Girard-Perregaux said mildly, "Isn't that an exaggeration, Lofting?"

"No, by Zoroaster, it is not! Take the Egyptians. Their greatest monuments, such as the pyramids, were constructed in the earlier dynasties. Khufu, or Cheops, built the largest at Giza. He was the founder of the 4th Dynasty, about the year 2900 B.C. Twenty-five dynasties later, and nearly three thousand years, there was no greatly discernable change in the Egyptian culture."

Girard-Perregaux egged him on gently. "The sole example of your theory I can think of, offhand."

"Not at all!" Gubelin glared. "The Mayans are a more recent proof. Their culture goes back to at least 500 B.C. At that time their glyph-writing was already wide-spread and their cities, eventually to number in the hundreds, being built. By the time of Christ they had reached their peak. And they remained there until the coming of the Spaniards, neither gaining nor losing, in terms of evolution of society."

His colleague sighed. "And your point, Lofting?"

"Isn't it blisteringly obvious?" the other demanded. "We're in danger of reaching a similar static condition here and now. The Ultrawelfare State!" He snorted indignation, "The Conformist State or the Status Quo State, is more like it. I tell you, Hans, all progress is being dried up. There is no will to delve into the unknown, no burning fever to explore the unexplored. And this time it isn't a matter of a single area, such as Egypt or Yucatan, but our whole world. If man goes into intellectual coma this time, then all the race slows down, not merely a single element of it."

He rose suddenly from the desk chair he'd been occupying to pace the room. "The race must find a new frontier, a new ocean to cross, a new enemy to fight."

Girard-Perregaux raised his eyebrows. "Don't be a cloddy," Gubelin snapped. "You know what I mean. Not a human enemy, not even an alien intelligence. But something against which we must pit our every wit, our every strength, our strongest determination. Otherwise, we go dull, we wither on the vine."

The other at long last chuckled. "My dear Lofting, you wax absolutely lyrical."

Gubelin suddenly stopped his pacing, returned to his desk and sank back into his chair. He seemed to add a score of years to his age, and his face sagged. "I don't know why I take it out on you, Hans. You're as aware of the situation as I. Man's next frontier is space. First the planets, and then a reaching out to the stars. This is our new frontier, our new ocean to cross."

His old friend was nodding. He brought his full attention to the discussion at last. "And we'll succeed, Lofting. The last trip Pond made gives us ample evidence that we can actually colonize and exploit the Jupiter satellites. Two more runs, at most three, and we can release our findings in such manner that they'll strike the imaginations of every Tom, Dick and Harry like nothing since Columbus made his highly exaggerated reports on his New World."

"Two or three more runs," Gubelin grunted bitterly. "You've heard the rumors. Appropriations is going to lower the boom on us. Unless we can get Pond back into harness, we're sunk. The runs will never be made. I tell you, Hans..."

But Hans Girard-Perregaux was wagging him to silence with a finger. "They'll be made. I've taken steps to see friend Seymour Pond comes dragging back to us."

"But he *hates* space! The funker probably won't consent to come within a mile of the New Albuquerque Spaceport for the rest of his life, the blistering cloddy."

A desk light flicked green, and Girard-Perregaux raised his eyebrows. "Exactly at the psychological moment. If I'm not mistaken, Lofting, that is probably our fallen woman."

"Our what?"

But Doctor Hans Girard-Perregaux had come to his feet and personally opened the door. "Ah, my dear," he said affably.

Natalie Paskov, done today in Bulgarian peasant garb, and as faultless in appearance as she had been in the Kudos Room, walked briskly into the office.

"Assignment carried out," she said crisply.

"Indeed," Girard-Perregaux said approvingly. "So soon?"

Gubelin looked from one to the other. "What in the blistering name of Zoroaster is going on?"

His friend said, "Academician Gubelin, may I present Operative Natalie of Extraordinary Services Incorporated?"

"Extraordinary Services?" Gubelin blurted.

"In this case." Natalie said smoothly, even while taking the chair held for her by Doctor Girard-Perregaux, "a particularly apt name. It was a dirty trick."

"But for a good cause, my dear."

She shrugged. "So I am often told, when sent on these far-out assignments."

Girard-Perregaux, in spite of her words, was beaming at her. "Please report in full," he said, ignoring his colleague's obvious bewilderment.

Natalie Paskov made it brief. "I picked up the subject in the Kudos Room of the Greater Metropolis Hotel, pretending to be a devotee of the space program as an excuse. It soon developed that he had embarked upon a celebration of his retirement. He was incredibly naive, and allowed me to over-indulge him in semi-narcotics as well as alcohol, so that his defensive inhibitions were low. I then took him to a gambling spot where, so dull that he hardly knew what he was doing, he lost his expendable capital."

Gubelin had been staring at her, but now he blurted, "But suppose he had won?"

She shrugged it off. "Hardly, the way I was encouraging him to wager. Each time he won, I urged him to double up. It was only a matter of time until..." she let the sentence dribble away.

Girard-Perregaux rubbed his hands briskly. "Then, in turn, it is but a matter of time until friend Pond comes around again."

"That I wouldn't know," Natalie said disinterestedly. "My job is done. But the poor man seems so utterly opposed to returning to your service that I wouldn't be surprised if he remained in his retirement, living on his Inalienable Basic shares. He seems literally terrified of being subjected to space cafard again."

But Hans Girard-Perregaux wagged a finger negatively at her. "Not after having enjoyed a better way of life for the past decade. A person is able to exist on the Inalienable Basic dividends, but it is almost impossible to bring oneself to it once a fuller life has been enjoyed. No, Seymour Pond will never go back to the dullness of life the way it is lived by nine-tenths of our population."

Natalie came to her feet. "Well, gentlemen, you'll get your bill—a whopping one. I hope your need justifies this bit of dirty work. Frankly, I am considering my resignation from Extraordinary Services, although I'm no more anxious to live on my Inalienable Basic than poor Si Pond is. Good day, gentlemen."

She started toward the door.

The teevee-phone on Gubelin's desk lit up and even as Doctor Girard-Perregaux was saying unctuously to the girl, "Believe me, my dear, the task you have performed, though odious, will serve the whole race," the teevee-phone said:

"Sir, you asked me to keep track of Pilot Seymour Pond. There is a report on the news. He suicided this morning."

THE END

The Spaceman's Van Gogh

By CLIFFORD D. SIMAK

From world to world went Lathrop, seeking the elusive secret of the great painter, Reuben Clay...

THE PLANET was so unimportant and so far out toward the rim that it didn't have a name, but just a code and number as a key to its position. The village had a name, but one that was impossible for a human to pronounce correctly.

It cost a lot to get there. Well, not to get there, exactly, for all one did was *polt* there; but it cost a hunk of cash to have the co-ordinates set up for the *polting*. Because the planet was so far away, the computer had to do a top-notch job, correct to seven decimal points. Otherwise one took the chance of materializing a million miles off destination, in the depths of space; or if you hit the planet, a thousand or so miles up; or worse yet, a couple hundred underneath the surface. Anyone of which would be highly inconvenient, if not positively fatal.

There was no reason in the universe for anyone to go there—except Anson Lathrop. Lathrop had to go there because it was the place where Reuben Clay had died.

So he paid out a pocketful of cash to get himself indoctrinated to the planet's mores and speech, and a bucketful of cash to get his *polting* plotted—a two-way job, to get both there and back.

He arrived there just about midday, not at the village exactly, for even seven decimal points weren't good enough to land him squarely in it—but not more than twenty miles away, as it turned out, and no more than twelve feet off the ground.

He picked himself up and dusted himself off and was thankful for the knapsack that he wore, for he had landed on it and been cushioned from the fall.

THE PLANET, or what he could see of it, was a dismal place. It was a cloudy day and he had trouble making out, so colorless was the land, where the horizon ended and the sky began. The ground was flat, a great plain unrelieved by trees or ridge, and covered here and there by patches of low brush.

He had landed near a path and in this he considered himself lucky, for he remembered from his indoctrination that the planet had no roads and not too many paths.

He hoisted his knapsack firmly into place and started down the path. In a mile or so he came to a signpost, badly weather-beaten, and while he wasn't too sure of the symbols, it seemed to indicate he was headed in the wrong direction. So he turned back, hoping fervently he had read the sign correctly.

He arrived at the village just as dusk was setting in, after a lonely hike during which he met no one except a strange and rather ferocious animal which sat erect to watch him pass, whistling at him all the while as if it were astounded at him.

Nor did he see much more when he reached the village.

The village, as he had known it would, resembled nothing quite so much as one of the prairie dog towns which one could see in the western part of North America, back on his native Earth.

At the edge of the village he encountered plots of cultivated ground with strange crops growing in them; and working among some of these plots in the gathering darkness were little gnome-like figures. When he stopped and called to them, they merely stared at him for a moment and then went back to work.

HE WALKED down the village's single street, which was little more than a well-travelled path, and tried to make some sense out of the entrances to the burrows, each of which was backed by a tumulus of the ground dug up in its excavation. Each mound looked almost exactly like every other mound and no burrow mouth seemed to have anything to distinguish it from any of the others.

Before some of the burrows tiny gnome-like figures played— children, he supposed—but at his approach they scuttled rapidly inside and did not reappear.

He travelled the entire length of the street; and standing there, he saw what he took to be a somewhat larger mound, some little distance off, surmounted by what appeared to be some sort of rude monument, a stubby spire that pointed upward like an accusing finger aimed toward the sky.

And that was a bit surprising, for there had been no mention in his indoctrination—of monuments or of religious structures. Although, he realized, his indoctrination would be necessarily skimpy for a place like this; there was not a great deal known of the planet or its people.

Still, it might not be unreasonable to suppose that these gnomes might possess religion; here and there one still found patches of it. Sometimes it would be indigenous to the planet, and in other cases it would be survival transplantations from the planet Earth or from one of the other several systems where great religions once had flourished.

He turned around and went back down the street again and came to a halt in the middle of the village. No one came out to meet him, so he sat down in the middle of the path and waited. He took a lunch out of his knapsack, ate it, and drank water out of the vacuum bottle that he carried, and wondered why Reuben Clay had picked this dismal place in which to spend his final days.

NOT THAT it would be out of keeping with the man. It was a humble place and Clay had been a humble man, known as the "Spaceman's Van Gogh" at one time. He had lived within himself rather than with the universe which surrounded him. He had not sought glory or acclaim, although he could have claimed them both—at times, indeed, it appeared that he might be running from them. Throughout his entire life there had been the sense of a man who hid away. Of a man who ran from something, or a man who ran after something—a seeking, searching man who never quite caught up with the thing he sought for. Lathrop shook his head. It was hard to know which sort Clay had been—a hunted man or hunter. If hunted, what had it been he feared? And if a hunter, what could it be he sought?

Lathrop heard a light scuffing in the path and turned his head to see that one of the gnome-like creatures was approaching him. The gnome was old, he saw. Its fur was gray and grizzled and when it came closer he saw the other marks of age upon it—the rheumy eyes, the wrinkled skin, the cragged bushiness of its eyebrows, the cramped stiffness of its hands.

It stopped and spoke to him and he puzzled out the language.

"Good seeing to you, sir." Not "sir," of course, but the nearest translation one could make.

"Good hearing," Lathrop said ceremoniously.

"Good sleeping."

"Good eating," Lathrop said.

Finally they both ran out of "goods."

The gnome stood in the path and had another long look at him. Then: "You are like the other one."

"Clay," said Lathrop.

"Younger," said the gnome.

"Younger," Lathrop admitted. "Not much younger."

"Just right," said the gnome, meaning it to be a diplomatic compliment.

"Thank you."

"Not sick."

"Healthy," Lathrop said.

"Clay was sick. Clay…"

Not "died," More like "discontinued" or possibly "ended," but the meaning was clear.

"I know that. I came to talk about him."

"Lived with us," said the gnome. "He (die?) with us."

HOW LONG ago? How did you ask how long? There was, Lathrop realized with something of a shock, no gnome-words for duration or measurement of time. A past, present and future tense, of course, but no word for measurement of either time or space.

"You…" There was no word for *buried*. No word for *grave*.

"You planted him?" asked Lathrop.

He sensed the horror that his question raised. "We…him."

Ate him? Lathrop wondered. Some of the ancient tribes of Earth and on other planets, too, ate their dead, thereby conferring tender honors on them.

But it was not eat.

Burned? Scaffolded? Exposed?

No, it was none of those.

"We...him," the gnome insisted. "It was his wish. We loved him. We could do no less."

Lathrop bowed gratefully. "I am honored that you did."

That seemed to mollify the gnome.

"He was a harmless one," said the gnome. Not exactly "harmless." Kind, perhaps. Uncruel. With certain connotations of soft-wittedness. Which was natural, of course, for in his nonconformity through lack of understanding, any alien must appear slightly soft-witted to another people.

As if he might have known what Lathrop was thinking, the gnome said, "We did not understand him. He had what he called a *brushandpaints*. He made streaks with them."

Streaks?

...*Brushandpaints?* Sure, brush and paints.

STREAKS? Of course. For the people of this planet were colorblind. To them Clay's painting would be streaks.

"He did that here?"

"Yes. It here."

"I wonder. Might I see it?"

"Certainly," said the gnome. "If you follow me."

They crossed the street and approached a burrow's mouth. Stooping, Lathrop followed down the tunnel. Ten or twelve feet down it became a room, a sort of earthen cave.

There was a light of a sort. Not too good a light, a soft, dim light that came from little heaps of glowing material piled in crude clay dishes placed about the burrow.

Foxfire, thought Lathrop. The phosphorescent light of rotting wood.

"There," said the gnome. The painting leaned against one wall of the burrow, an alien square of color in this outlandish place. Under ordinary circumstances, the faint foxfire light would have been too feeble for one to see the painting, but the brush strokes on the canvas seemed to have a faint light of their own, so that the colors stood out like another world glimpsed through a window beyond the foxfire dimness. As Lathrop looked at the propped-up square, the glowing quality seemed to become more pronounced, until the picture was quite clear in all its unfinished detail—and it was not a glow, Lathrop thought; it was a *shiningness*.

AND IT was Clay. The painting, unfinished as it was, could not be mistaken. Even if one had not known that Clay had spent the last days of his life within this village, he still would have known that the work was Clay's. The clean outline was there, the authority of craftsmanship combined with the restrained quality, the masterly understatement, the careful detail and the keen sharp color. But there was something else as well—a certain happiness, a humble happiness that had no hint of triumph.

"He did not finish it," said Lathrop. "He did not have the…(there was no word for time). He (discontinued) before he finished it."

"His *brushandpaints* discontinued. He sat and looked at it."

So that was it. That was how it happened. Clay's paints had given out and there had been no place, no way—perhaps no time—in which he could have gotten more.

So Reuben Clay had sat in this burrow and looked at his last painting, knowing it was the last painting he would ever do, propped there against the wall, and had known the hopelessness of ever finishing the great canvas he had started. Although more than likely Clay had never thought of it as great. His paintings, for him, had never been more than an expression of himself.

To him they had been something that lay inside himself waiting to be transferred into some expression that the universe could see, a sort of artistic communication from Clay to all his fellow creatures.

"Rest yourself," said the gnome. "You are tired."

"Thanks," said Lathrop.

He sat down on the hardpacked floor, with his back against the wall, opposite the painting.

"You knew him," said the gnome.

Lathrop shook his head.

"But you came seeking him."

"I sought word of him."

HOW COULD one, he wondered, explain to the little gnome what he sought in Clay, or why he'd tracked him down when all the universe forgot? How could one explain to these people, who were color-blind and more than likely had no conception of what a painting was—how could one explain the greatness that was Clay's? The technique that lived within his hands, the clean, quick sense of color, the almost unworldly ability to see a certain thing exactly as it was.

To see the truth and to reproduce that truth—not as a single facet of the truth, but the entire truth in its right perspective and its precise color, and with its meaning and its mood pinpointed so precisely that one need but look to know.

That may have been why I sought him, thought Lathrop. That may be why I've spent twenty Earth years and a barrel of money to learn all the facts of him. The monograph I someday will write on him is no more than a faint attempt to rationalize my search for facts—the logic that is needed to justify a thing. But it was the truth, thought Lathrop. That's the final answer of what I sought in Clay—the truth that lay in him and in his painting. Because I, too, at one time worked in truth.

"It is magic," said the gnome, staring at the painting.

"Of a sort," said Lathrop. And that probably had been why, at first; they had accepted Clay, in the expectation that some of his magic might rub off on them. But not entirely, perhaps; certainly not toward the end. For Clay was not the sort of simple, unassuming man these simple creatures would respect and love.

They'd let him live among them, more than likely finally as one of them, probably without the thought of payment for his living space and food. He may have worked a little in the fields and he may have puttered up things, but he would have been essentially their guest, for no alien creature could fit himself economically into such a simple culture.

They had helped him through his final days, and watched him in his dying and when he had finally died they'd done to him a certain act of high respect and honor.

WHAT WAS that word again? He could not remember it. The indoctrination had been inadequate; there were word gaps and blank spaces and blind spots and that was wholly understandable in a place like this.

He saw the gnome was waiting for him to explain the magic, to explain it better than Clay had been able to explain it. Or maybe Clay had not attempted to explain, for they might not have asked him.

The gnome waited and hoped and that was all, for he could not ask. You do not ask another race about the details of their magic.

"It is a (no word for representation, no word for picture)...place that Clay saw. He tried to bring it back to life. He tried to tell you and me what he had seen. He tried to make us see it, too."

"Magic," said the gnome.

Lathrop gave up. It was impossible. To the gnome it was simple magic. So be it—simple magic.

It was a valley with a brook that gurgled somberly and with massive trees and a deep wash of light that was more than sunlight layover all of it. There was no living creature in it and that was typical, for Clay was a landscape artist without the need of people or of other creatures.

A happy place, thought Lathrop, but a solemn happiness. A place to run and laugh, but not to run too swiftly nor to laugh too loudly, for there was a lordly reverence implicit in the composition.

"He saw many places," Lathrop told the gnome. "He put many places on a (no word for canvas or board or plane)...on a flat like that. Many different planets. He tried to catch the (no word for spirit)...the way that each planet looked."

"Magic," said the gnome. "His was powerful magic."

THE GNOME moved to the far wall of the room and poked up a peat-fire in a primitive stove fashioned out of mud. "You are hungry," said the gnome.

"I ate."

"You must eat with us. The others will be coming. It is too dark to work."

"I will eat with you," said Lathrop.

For he must break the bread with them. He must be one of them if he were to carry out his mission. Perhaps not one of them as Clay had been one of them, but at least accepted. No matter what horrendous and disgusting thing should comprise the menu, he must eat with them.

But it was more than likely that the food would not be too bad. Roots and vegetables, for they had gardens. Pickled insects, maybe, and perhaps some alcoholic concoction he'd have to be a little careful with.

But no matter what it was, he would have to eat with them and sleep with them and be as friendly and as thoughtful as Clay had been thoughtful and friendly.

For they'd have things to tell him, data that he'd given up all hope of getting, the story of the final days of Reuben Clay. Perhaps even some clue to the mystifying "lost years," the years when Clay had dropped completely out of sight.

HE SAT quietly, thinking of how the trail had come to an end, out near the edge of the galaxy, not too many light-years from this very place. For year on absorbing year he had followed Clay's trail from star to star, gathering data on the man, talking with those who'd known him, tracking down one by one the paintings he had made. And then the trail had ended. Clay had left a certain planet and no one knew where he'd gone; for years Lathrop had searched for some hint to where he'd gone, and had been close to giving up when he finally had found evidence that Clay had come to this place to die. But the evidence had strongly indicated that he had not come here directly from where the trail had stopped, but had spent several years at some other place. So there was still a gap in the story that he followed—a gap of lost years, how many years there was no way of knowing.

Perhaps here, in this village, he might get a clue to where Clay had spent those years. But, he told himself, it could be no more than a clue. It could not be specific, for these little creatures had no concept of time or otherwhere.

More than likely the painting here in this burrow was in itself a clue. More than likely it was a painting of that unknown place Clay had visited before coming here to die. But if that were so, thought Lathrop, it was a slender hope, for one might spend three lifetimes—or more—combing planet after planet in the vain hope of recognizing the scene Clay had spread upon the canvas.

HE WATCHED the gnome busy at the stove, and there was no sound except the lonely whining of the wind in the chimney and at the tunnel's mouth. Lonely wind and empty moor and the little villages of heaped earth, here at the far edge of the galaxy, out in the rim of the mighty wheel of suns. How much do we know of it, he thought, this thing we call our galaxy, this blob of matter hurled out into the gulf of space by some mighty fist? We do not know the beginning of it nor the end of it nor the reason for its being; we are blind creatures groping in the darkness for realities and the few realities we find we know as a blind man knows the things within his room, knowing them by the sense of touch alone. For in the larger sense we all are as blind as he—all of us together, all the creatures living in the galaxy. And presumptuous and precocious despite our stumbling blindness, for before we know the galaxy we must know ourselves.

We do not understand ourselves; have no idea of the purpose of us. We have tried devices to explain ourselves, materialistic devices and spiritualistic devices and the application of pure logic, which was far from pure. And we have fooled ourselves, thought Lathrop. That is mostly what we've done. We have laughed at things we do not understand, substituting laughter for knowledge, using laughter as a shield against our ignorance, as a drug to still our sense of panic. Once we sought comfort in mysticism, fighting tooth and nail against the explanation of the mysticism, for only so long as it remained mysticism and unexplained could it comfort us. We once subscribed to faith and fought to keep the faith from becoming fact, because in our twisted thinking faith was stronger than the fact.

And are we any better now, he wondered, for having banished faith and mysticism, sending the old faiths and the old religions scurrying into hiding places against the snickers of a galaxy that believes in logic and pins its hope on nothing less than fact. A step, he thought—it is but a step, this advancement to the logic and the fact, this fetish for explaining. Someday, far distant, we may find another fact that will allow us to keep the logic and the fact, but will supply once again the comfort that we lost with faith.

THE GNOME had started cooking and it had a good smell to it. Almost an Earth smell. Maybe, after all, the eating would not be as bad as he had feared.

"You like Clay?" the gnome asked.

"Liked him? Sure, I liked him."

"No. No. You do like he? You make the streaks like he?"

Lathrop shook his head. "I do nothing now, I am (how did you say retired?)...My work is ended. Now I play (play, because there was no other word)."

"Play?!"

"I work no more. I do now as I please. I learn of Clay's life and I (no word for write)...I tell his life in streaks. Not those kinds of streaks. Not the kind of streaks he made. A different kind of streaks."

When he had sat down he'd put his knapsack beside him. Now he drew it to his lap and opened it. He took out the pad of paper and a pencil. "This kind of streaks," he said.

The gnome crossed the room to stand beside him.

Lathrop wrote on his pad: *I was a whitherer. I used facts and logic to learn whither are we going. I was a seeker after truth.*

"Those kinds of streaks," he said. "I have made many streaks of Clay's life."

"Magic," said the gnome.

It was all down, thought Lathrop, all that he had learned of Clay. All but the missing years. All down in page after page of notes, waiting for the writing. Notes telling the strange story of a strange man who had wandered star to star, painting planet after planet, leaving his paintings strewn across the galaxy. A man who had wandered as if he might be seeking something other than new scenes to put upon his canvasses. As if his canvasses were no more than a passing whim, no more than a quaint and convenient device to earn the little money that he needed for food and *polting* plots, the money that enabled him to go on to system after system. Making no effort to retain any of his work, selling every bit of it or even, at times, simply walking off and leaving it behind.

NOT THAT his paintings weren't good. They were—startlingly good. They were given honored places in many galleries, or what passed as galleries, on many different planets.

Clay had stayed for long at no place. He had always hurried on. As if there were a purpose or a plot which drove him from star to star.

And the sum total of the wandering, of the driven purpose, had ended here in this very burrow, no more than a hiding place against the wind and weather.

"Why?" asked the gnome. "Why make the streaks of Clay?"

"Why?" said Lathrop. "Why? I do not know!"

But the answer, not only of Clay's wandering, but of his following in Clay's tracks, might be within his grasp. Finally, after all the years of searching, he might find the answer here.

"Why do you streak?"

And how to answer that?

How had Clay answered? For they must have asked him, too. Not how, because you do not ask the how of magic. But why...that was permissible. Not the secret of the magic, but the purpose of it.

"So we may know," said Lathrop, groping for the words. "So all of us may know, you and I and all the others on other stars may know what kind of being (man?) Clay was."

"He was...(kind?). He was one of us. We loved him. That is all we need to know."

"All you may need," said Lathrop. "But not enough for others."

Although there probably would not be many who would read the monograph once he had written it. Only a pitiful few would take the time to read it, or even care to read it.

HE THOUGHT: Now, finally, I know what I've known all along, but refused to admit I knew; that I'm not doing this for others, but for myself alone. And not for the sake of occupation, not for the sake of keeping busy in retirement, but for some deeper reason and for some greater need. For some factor or some sense, perhaps, that I missed before. For some need I do not even recognize. For some purpose that might astound me if I ever understood it.

The gnome went back to the stove and got on with the meal and Lathrop continued to sit with his back against the wall, realizing now the tiredness that was in him. He'd had a busy day. *Polting* was not difficult, actually seemed easy, but it took a lot out of a man. And, in addition to that, he'd walked twenty miles from his landing place to reach the village.

Polting might be easy, but it had not been easy to come by, for its development had been forced to wait upon the suspension of erroneous belief, had come only with the end of certain superstitions and the false screen of prejudice set up to shield Man against his lack of knowledge. For if a man did not understand a thing, he called it a silly superstition and let it go at that. The human race could disregard a silly superstition and be quite easy in its mind, but it could not disregard a stubborn fact without a sense of guilt.

Shuffling footsteps came down the tunnel and four gnomes emerged into the burrow. They carried crude gardening tools and these they set against the wall, then stood silently in a row to stare at the man sitting on the floor.

The old gnome said: "It is another one like Clay. He will stay with us."

THEY MOVED forward, the four of them, and stood in a semi-circle facing Lathrop. One of them asked the old gnome at the stove: "Will he stay here and die?" And another one said, "He is not close to dying, this one." There was anticipation in them.

"I will not die here," said Lathrop, uneasily.

"We will..." said one of them, repeating that word which told what they had done with Clay when he had died, and he said it almost as if it were a bribe to make the human want to stay and die.

"Perhaps he would not want us to," said another one. "Clay wanted us to do it. He may not feel like Clay."

There was horror in the burrow, a faint, flesh-creeping horror in the words they said and in the way they looked at him with anticipation.

The old gnome went to one corner of the burrow and came back with a bag. He set it down in front of Lathrop and tugged at the string which tied it, while all the others watched. And one could see that they watched with reverence and hope and that the opening of the bag was a great occasion—and that if there could be anything approaching solemnity in their squat bodies, they watched most solemnly.

The string finally came loose and the old gnome tilted the bag and grasped it by its bottom and emptied it upon the earthen floor. There were brushes and many tubes of paint, all but a few squeezed dry and a battered wallet and something else that the old gnome picked up from the floor and handed to the Earthman.

Lathrop stretched out his hand and took it and held it and looked at it and suddenly he knew what they had done to Clay, knew without question that great and final honor.

Laughter gurgled in his throat—not laughter at the humor of it, for there was no humor, but laughter at the twisted values, at the cross-purposes of concepts, at wondering how, and knowing how the gnomes might have arrived at the conclusion which they reached in rendering to Clay the great and final honor.

HE COULD see it even now as it must have happened—how they worked for days carrying the earth to make the mound he'd seen beyond the village, knowing that the end was nearing for this alien friend of theirs; how they must have searched far for timber in this land of little bushes, and having found it, brought it in upon many bended backs, since they did not know the wheel; and how they fitted it together, fumblingly, perhaps, with wooden pegs and laboriously bored-out holes, for they had no metal and they knew no carpentry.

And they did it all for the love that they bore Clay, and all their labor and their time had been as nothing in the glory of this thing they did so lovingly.

He looked at the crucifix and now it seemed that he understood what had seemed so strange of Clay—the eternal searching, the mad, feverish wandering from one star system to another, even in part, the superb artistry that spoke so clearly of a hidden, half guessed truth behind the many truths he'd spoken with his brush.

For Clay had been a survival-member of that strange, gentle sect out of Earth's far antiquity; he had been one of those who, in this world of logic and of fact, had clung to the mysticism and the faith. Although for Clay, perhaps, the naked faith alone had not been enough, even as for him, Anson Lathrop, bare facts at times seemed not enough. And that he had never guessed this truth of Clay was easy to explain—one did not fling one's faith into the gigantic snicker of a Logic universe.

FOR BOTH of them, perhaps, neither fact nor faith could stand alone, but each must have some leavening of the other.

Although that is wrong, Lathrop told himself. I do not need the faith. I worked for years with logic and with fact and that is all one needs. If there is other need, it lies in another as-yet-undiscovered factor; we need not go back to faith.

Strip the faith and the mumbo-jumbo from the fact and you have something you can use. As Man long ago had stripped the disbelief and laughter from the poltergeist and had come up with the principle of *polting*, the fact and principle that moved a man from star to star as easily as in the ancient days he might walk down the street to his favorite bar.

Yet there could be no doubt that for Clay it had not worked that way, that with fact alone he could not have painted as he did, that it took the simple faith and the inner glow of that simple faith to give him the warmth and the dedication to make his paintings what they were.

And it had been the faith that had sent him on his search throughout the galaxy.

Lathrop looked at the painting and saw the simplicity and the dignity, the tenderness and the happiness and the sense of flooding light.

Exactly the kind of light, thought Lathrop, that had been so crudely drawn in the illustrations of those old books he had studied in his course on Earth's comparative religions. There had been, he remembered, one instructor who'd spent some time on the symbolism of the light.

HE DROPPED the crucifix and put out his hand and picked up some of the twisted tubes of oils.

The painting was unfinished, the gnome had said, because Clay had run out of paint, and there was truth in that, for the tubes were flattened and rolled up hard against the caps and one could see the imprint of the fingers that had applied the pressure to squeeze out the last drop of the precious oils.

He fled across the galaxy, thought Lathrop, *and I tracked him down.*

Even after he was dead I went on and tracked him down, sniffing along the cold trail he had left among the stars. And I tracked him because I loved him, not the man himself—for I did not know, nor have any way to know, what kind of man he was—but because I saw within his paintings something that all the critics missed. Something that called out to me. Deny it as I may, it may have been the ancient faith calling out to me. The faith that is missing now. The simple faith that long ago was killed by simple logic.

But he knew Clay now, Lathrop told himself. He knew him by the virtue of the tiny crucifix and by the symbol of the last great canvas and by the crude actuality of the mound that stood at the village end on this third rate planet.

And he knew why it had to be a third rate planet.

For there must be humility—even as in faith there had been humility, as there had never been in logic.

LATHROP COULD shut his eyes and see it—the somber clouds and the vast dreariness of the wastelands, the moors that swept on to foreverness, and the white figure on the cross and the crowd that stood beneath it, staring up at it, marked for all time by a thing they did not understand, a thing they could not understand, but a thing they had done out of utter kindness for one whose faith had touched them.

"Did he ever tell you," he asked the gnomes, "where he had been? Where he came from? Where he had been just before he came here."

They shook their heads at Lathrop. "He did not tell," they said.

Somewhere, thought Lathrop, where the trees grew like those trees in the painting. Where there was peace and dignity and tenderness—and the light.

Man had stripped the husk of superstition from the poltergeist and had found a kernel in the *polting* principle. Man had done the same with anti-gravity, and with telepathy, and many other things but he had not tried to strip the husks from faith to find the hidden kernel. For faith did not submit to investigation. Faith stood sufficient to itself and did not admit of fact.

What was faith and what the goal of faith? In the many tongues of ancient Earth, what had been the goal of those who subscribed to faith? Happy Hunting Ground, Valhalla, Heaven, the Isles of the Blest—how much faith, how much could be fact? One would not know unless he lived by faith alone and no being now, or very few, lived entirely by their faith.

BUT MIGHT there not be, in the last great reckoning of galactic life and, knowledge, another principle which would prove greater than either faith or fact—a principle as yet unknown, but only to be gained by eons of intellectual evolution. Had Clay stumbled on that principle, a man who sought far ahead of time, who ran away from evolutionary knowledge and who, by that very virtue, would have grasped no more than a dim impression of the principle-to-come.

Faith had failed because it had been blinded by the shining glory of itself. Could fact as well have failed by the hard glitter of its being?

But abandoning both faith and fact, armed with a greater tool of discernment, might a man not seek and find the eventual glory and the goal for which life had grasped, knowing and unknowing, from the first faint stir of consciousness upon the myriad solar systems?

Lathrop found the tube of white and unscrewed the cap and squeezed the tube and a bit of oil came out, a tiny drop of oil. He held the tube steady in one hand and, picked up a brush. Carefully he transferred the color to the brush.

He dropped the tube and walked across the burrow to the painting and squatted down and squinted at it in the feeble light, trying to make out the source of the flood of light.

Up in the left hand corner, just above the horizon, although he couldn't be entirely sure that he was right.

He extended the brush, then drew it back.

Yes, that must be it. A man would stand beneath the massive trees and face toward the light.

Careful now, he thought. Very, very careful. Just a faint suggestion, for it was mere symbolism. Just a hint of color. One stroke perpendicular and a shorter one at right angle, closer to the top.

The brush was awkward in his hand.

It touched the canvas and he pulled it back again.

It was a silly thing, he thought. A silly thing and crazy. And, besides, he couldn't do it. He didn't know how to do it. Even at his lightest touch, it would be crude and wrong. It would be desecration.

He let the brush drop from his fingers and watched it roll along the floor.

I tried, he said to Clay.

THE END

No Dark Gallows For Me

By JOHN JAKES

What weird mystery surrounded the House of Gulbrandsen in the dark Venusian wilds? The price of the secret was death!

THEY HUNG you on Venus. The gray skinned natives were old fashioned by Terran standards, and when you committed a Major Offense and they caught you, there was a public execution in the plaza. They made you walk up the long steps to the platform. They put the rope around your neck and their faces might have been cut out of gray stone when they sprung the trap. You dangled and choked and twisted and died on a great black gallows carved from the wood of trees that grew in the steaming jungles.

They hung you for Major Offenses. What the fat man had just proposed was a Major Offense, and yet, I had almost decided to accept his offer.

We sat in the dim bar of the hotel, drinking tall chilly Venusian mak. The fat man massaged his face, "Well, McShane," he said finally, "do we go?"

"Mr. Breen," I answered him slowly, "I've been a professional hunter working out of Venusburg for nearly seven years. But no one's ever asked me to guide them to the House of Gulbrandsen. It just isn't done."

"Well," he murmured again, his little eyes laughing for the hell of it, "I want to do it. I like taking chances. A man in my position has nothing to do but spend his money. It gets damned boring, nothing to do but spend money."

That was it, money. I needed it. I had never wanted much, consciously, because I realized that a man in my position couldn't make a lot. Not too smart, I am, but I found that out long ago. I've always had strength. And weak men are willing to buy strength to guide them and make them glorious hunters.

But business had been bad for the last six months. Cust omers were dropping off. My last one had caught the fever up in swamp country. He died and I never got paid. That was three months back, so I wanted money. Not much; just enough to get off Venus and move to Ganymede. Hunting was picking up there. That's why I even listened to the fat man's offer.

I sat silent for another minute. Thoz, the gray Venusian, polished the bar. Music drifted in from somewhere in the hotel, the crazy weird rhythm of harps and a pair of bongo drums.

"It's hanging if we're caught," I told him.

"Yes," he said, smiling flatly.

"And maybe something worse. Men have gone to the House of Gulbrandsen, and some have come back and not been caught. They say Roger Lorden was one, and that he was power crazy when he walked out of the jungle. He rose to System Imperator. Fontaine came back drunk with the idea of finding beauty in any form. He wrote his poems and died insane, yelling at the wind on a Martian desert." I shrugged. "Those are legends, but the place isn't exactly healthy."

"Yes," repeated Mr. Breen irritatingly, his face hungry. "But think of it. Something new, something exciting, stimulating!" His chubby pink hand clutched the woven table cover and a diamond winked in the hazy light.

"I don't want excitement," I said. "I want money. That's why I even consider…"

"Hello," she said. I looked up. She was warm in her white dress, and not very pretty. Terran, but her face was too wide, her lips too thick, her eyes too dark. Still, she was a problem.

She sat down and touched Breen's sleeve. "Is Mr. McShane going?"

"I don't know, my dear." She'd called me by name, but I'd never seen her before. Evidently the fat man had told her about me. Anyway, he introduced us. Her name was Jan. He didn't say she was his wife, but mistresses were a common thing among the rich men of all the planets.

"If we go," I stated, "only if, we'd have to travel light, in a motor lorry. No native bearers. They couldn't be trusted. They'd run away and shoot off their mouths to the authorities, once they found out where we were really heading."

"Do you know where the House of Gulbrandsen is?" Jan wanted to know.

"Sure. Everyone does."

"And what?"

"A place. That's all."

"You've never gone there?" Surprise.

"No. I've never had a desire to."

"But he does now," Breen put in, giggling. "A desire for a nice fat roll of credits. Correct, eh McShane?"

I LOOKED at Jan; a physical problem, and I liked physical problems, when I could handle them. She seemed easy enough; not like the House of Gulbrandsen.

She pouted with her sticky lips. "Are we going?"

"We..."

"Yes," I announced, "we're going." Rising, I added, "I don't want to talk about it anymore right now. I'll meet you for dinner tonight, if you like."

"Fine," Breen laughed, taking a drink of his mak. I nodded curtly and walked away, feeling the woman's eyes on me all the way.

I said hello to Thoz, the bartender.

He had one customer. Sawtell, the barfly. Sawtell was a fixture in the place; a fixture that guzzled rye, moving from bottle to bottle as other men moved from minute to minute. He had been around the hotel for a long time. Some of the traders said he had once been a college professor. Others related that he had come back from the House of Gulbrandsen, started drinking and never stopped. Anyway, he was a colorless man; nothing more than an ageless walking bottle.

"Hullo, McShane," he shouted from his stool, waving his glass and spilling some of the rye on the sleeve of his dirty whites.

Walking out of the bar and down the broad steep stairway to the hotel lobby, I didn't bother to answer him. I was concentrating on two problems: Jan, and the House of Gulbrandsen. I couldn't decide which was the more important.

FOR SIX days after that, we got ready; renting a big half-track lorry, buying food, clothing, medicine and Steiner Disintegrator weapons. We needed no maps. I knew where to look.

I saw very little of Jan; at dinner the first evening, and a couple of times in the hotel lobby. But always there was Mr. Breen. Fat Mr. Breen, who peered at me once in a while as if he half suspected what I was thinking about the woman. He was not all fat, I'd decided. He, too, had a kind of ruthless strength. It took power to make a fortune in the brawling star-empires, and somehow I knew that he would be strong enough to kill another man, if the occasion arose.

We kept deathly quiet about our destination. The morning of our departure, I walked up the wide stairway into the bar. Thoz was there as always, eternally swiping with his rag.

He looked at me out of his gray stone face. "A hunting trip, Mr. McShane?"

"Yeah, Thoz, a hunting trip. Give me a case of good Terran whisky." Nodding, he vanished through a door at the end of the bar. Someone slapped me on the back. Sawtell, glass of rye in one hand, gazed at me owlishly from bleary eyes.

"Going into the jungle, McShane?"

"That's right." I was getting tired of the questions.

He grinned crookedly. "You're smart, McShane. You'll never go where I went. You'll never go to the House of Gulbrandsen, will you?" He laughed hackingly and downed the rye.

So the stories were true. He had come back. I kept my eyes on the shiny top of the bar as I replied, "No…no of course not."

I must have said it wrong. He set down his glass and murmured, "You know, I think maybe you would go. I think maybe…"

His eyes widened and his scrawny blue-veined hands clutched at me. "Don't ever go, McShane. Don't ever go, or you'll lose your immortal soul!"

Throwing off his hand, I shot back, "Stop talking like a goddam TriDimensional. You ought to be writing their tear-jerkers for them."

Thoz returned silently, hefting the case of liquor. I paid for it and headed out of the bar. Sawtell tagged behind, babbling, "You'll lose your soul. McShane…I know…"

I think I said, "Go to hell," as I walked away lugging the heavy case. Now that I think back, it sounded as if Sawtell was almost...sobbing...

OUT IN THE street, Jan and Mr. Breen were waiting in the parked lorry. The equipment was loaded and the motor turned over quietly. Handing up the case of whisky, I climbed into the driver's seat. Breen was wearing his usual expensive and sweat-stained whites, which he'd have to change for an anti-disease suit once we hit the jungle. Jan was already wearing hers, a tight-fitting rubberized black garment.

Perspiration beaded around her mouth as she pulled on her cigarette. "Scared?"

"Why should I be? I'm getting paid."

"Certainly," Breen chuckled, "getting paid. Perhaps in more than money." Jan looked straight ahead.

I jammed my foot on the accelerator, shifted into hyper-low, and the lorry started to roll.

Right then I should have turned back. I know that now. I should have gotten out, but there was the woman, and the money to get to Ganymede, and the stories of the House of Gulbrandsen that were probably, in reality, only the confused dreams of men like Sawtell. We rumbled through the gray streets, past the gray people who hung you for a Major Offense such as we were setting out to commit. I should have gotten out.

But I didn't.

*   *   *

Have you ever seen a picture of the jungles, up country from Venusburg? Most atlases have them, and they show the thick dark vegetation, the strange forms of plant life. And yet, they lie.

They don't show the fog that hangs like an endless shroud. They don't show the leeches and the thousands of filthy little insects that stick to your skin and suck your blood. They don't show the monstrous animal-things that creep through the endless twilight. And they don't show the heat.

Above all, the heat. It blankets you and makes you weak. It tears and grates and shreds your nerves. It makes something dark rise from the hidden corners of the mind.

The House of Gulbrandsen was seventy miles from Venusburg. We made forty of those miles the first day. There were roads, if you want to call them that, up to ten miles of the place.

We made camp in a glade, and set up the air-conditioned tents. One for Breen and Jan, one for me, and a third for cooking and washing. In the everlasting twilight, we ate our supper.

No one said much. The other two were tired and irritable from the day's ride. Breen looked pale and even a little sick. I offered him an inoculation tablet against the fever that stalked the jungle, but he didn't want it in any manner or form.

"Don't need tablet," he gargled, stuffing a piece of bread into his pink mouth. "Feel fine…fine. Eat, drink and be merry." He laughed and spluttered.

"Oh for God's sake shut up," Jan snapped, rising from the little table.

AFTER SUPPER they vanished into their tent. I sat in mine, smoking and listening to the creechcreech of the insects. I tried to sleep, but even in the icy coolness of the air-conditioning, I couldn't. The twilight had deepened into semi-blackness when I went outside. Striking a match to another cigarette, I climbed up to the front seat of the lorry.

Something moved beside me. My hand grabbed for the knife at my belt, but I stopped.

"Hello, McShane," she was saying. Her cigarette winked like a little orange star in the fetid night.

"What's the trouble? Couldn't sleep?"

"No." Her voice was harsh, intense. "The thought of tomorrow…seeing someplace new and dangerous. I couldn't stop thinking about it. In that way, I'm like him." She motioned with the cigarette at the fat man's tent.

"You're not like him in any other way," I told her.

"No, I'm not. I'm like you, McShane. I've never had beauty. But there are other things more important to men than bodily beauty. Modes of conduct…" She laughed bitterly. "Breen bought those things, like he's buying your knowledge of this country. I hate it, really. I wish...I always wish I could be buying and selling people like he does." She stopped, the thought dying away.

And suddenly, without any kind of dramatic awakening, the thought seeped into my brain. Yes, that would be fine. To have money that could control people. To...I cut off my thoughts. There was no sane and legal way for me to reach that faraway goal. I had to be satisfied with selling my strength, and being practical. Get to Ganymede; that was all that mattered.

I started to reply, and bumped into her mouth, moist and warm on mine. Her arms went around my neck holding tightly. A moment later, she whispered in a damp little voice, "We're both being bought, but we can forget for a while..."

As I kissed her again, a voice shot through the gloom, "Lovely, lovely!"

There was a light in my eyes, bathing the two of us in a white glow. The voice behind the light was Breen's. It sounded weak.

"Get down, will you, McShane? We've got to discuss this." He laughed, and I thought I heard him retch.

"Turn that light away," I told him. Jan sat quietly beside me. Breen did as I asked, and I stood up, ready to jump to the ground.

I saw that he had a small Steiner Disintegrator in his fist, aimed at my belly. He was swaying to and fro, his face unhealthy, his eyes full of hatred.

I jumped wide, purposely. My feet struck his arms and the gun went sloshing into the mud. I slugged him once and he collapsed.

As I was bending over him, Jan climbed down. Breen's skin was blotchy and pale. It's the fever," I said after a moment. "He didn't put on the anti-disease suit soon enough. We'd better go back to Venusburg in the morning."

"I'm going on," she bit out. "He's always been able to buy everything, but here's one thing he couldn't buy...safe passage to the House of Gulbrandsen, whatever it is. He wanted to see it. Well, I'm going to have the satisfaction of having been there, when all his money only got him half way."

"You're sure?" I asked her.

"Yes. You can go back."

She knew, cleverly, that I wouldn't let her wander off in the jungles alone. Death could come quickly…

"I'll go. We can leave him in the tent and set up a Repulse Barrier around it so that no animals can reach him." I lifted the flabby body, dragging it toward one of the shelters.

As I ducked through the flap, I heard Jan say, "I'll be waiting in your tent, McShane."

She was waiting all right.

WE STARTED out next morning in the lorry, leaving Breen unconscious behind an unbreakable wall of force. Twenty miles we traveled through the jungle; twenty miles without a word. I kept my hands on the wheel and my eyes straight ahead on the muddy road. Jan smoked nervously, fierce exultation on her face.

The road ended ten miles short of the place. We abandoned the halftrack and made our way on foot, chopping and hacking with bush swords, slapping the insects, and sweating.

At last I pointed up ahead and announced, "There." It was an open tract of ground, perhaps a hundred yards across, cleared of all vegetation. The bare strip stretched off out of sight in either direction, forming a circle of open land that surrounded the House of Gulbrandsen.

Jan rushed to the edge of the trees and started across the open space. I grabbed her arm and pulled her back. "Wait! I told you it was hanging if we were caught!"

She laughed sharply. "Caught? There's no one within ten miles of this godforsaken place."

"No humans," I corrected, motioning to the right where the clearing curved away. A black box-like thing, some six feet square, was trundling toward us around the bend in the circle.

"There's the guard. It's a spotting device with a televisor lens hooked to a receiving set in Venusburg." I indicated a round aperture in the front of the thing. "There are three of those, powered by atomics. That clearing circles the House of Gul-brandsen, and those three boxes move around the clearing at regular intervals. They never run down, and if their lens picks up any human life crossing the path, a picture is relayed to Venusburg and a patrol flier is sent out to pick up the offenders."

"But it can be avoided?" she asked eagerly.

"Sure. The Venusians themselves don't know what's beyond that clearing. And those machines are inefficient. They only spot in front of themselves, but the native police rely on the boxes, plus fear of the place, to keep people out. Get down!" I pulled her to the ground beside me, and crouched behind a pale blue fern as we watched the black box roll by.

Jumping up, I yelled, "Let's go. We haven't got much time. Run...and run fast!"

We ran. The first box was almost out of sight, but to the right, where the first had come from, came another. Its eye cell was not quite on us as it trundled around the bend. We pounded across the open strip and I shoved Jan forward to the ground, taking a dive myself. Lying flat, we watched the box wheel by. Its lens remained dark, a sign that we had not been detected.

As we rose cautiously, Jan grimaced and asked, for the second time this trip, "You scared?"

"Let's get going."

The area inside the circle was jungle; no more horrible than the outside, no less. We tramped for a minute or so, and then, abruptly, we broke through the trees.

There, in the center of a second clearing, stood the legendary House of Gulbrandsen!

I was almost disappointed. It was a massive stone place, much like the squat temples of Desert Mars. There was a dark doorway carved through the stone. And that was all.

"So this is the place where men go out of their minds," Jan said hollowly. "Good God."

We walked up the slight hill to the building. It was so simple when I look back. So damned innocently simple...and so deadly.

Cautiously I stuck my head in the door. Blackness. The room couldn't have been very large. I found a piece of plant fiber on the ground and set fire to it. Thrusting it ahead, we walked in.

The guttering torch gave a little light. On one wall was something that looked like a machine. Panels, dials, strange calibrations; I didn't understand any of it. We advanced, the torch throwing a circle of yellow before us.

Jan screamed thinly.

OUT OF THE darkness loomed the figure of a man, seated cross legged on a shelf of stone. He wore a tattered robe, and he looked, how many years old in the knowledge of mankind? His face was a mesh of wrinkles, his hair long and dirty. He held his hand folded quietly in his lap, and his eyes seemed to be the only living things in that whole dim universe. Those eyes burned; burned with the brightness of unborn worlds, with the light of hellish rituals, with the glow of dying suns. They were infinitely old, infinitely wise and infinitely cruel.

Standing there with Jan clinging to me, I only sensed those things. I turned to drag her from that place of the old man of hell when he spoke, dryly, croakingly. His voice was that of one who detests life.

"Welcome to the House of Gulbrandsen. I trust that your true wants shall be satisfied." That was all he said. Jan whimpered softly behind me.

And then, I realized that something was emanating from that machine on the wall. Something that swept into my mind, over and through it. Something so terrible that even now I cannot describe it, can only see its devilish results.

That machine seemed to probe my mind, as I instinctively knew it was probing Jan's. It stripped away the layers of consciousness, one by tearing one, until it reached the root of all being. It tore and flayed, making me ashamed and sick, as if I had been suddenly standing at the altar of a church, stark naked before the congregation. That was how the machine humiliated. The thing…raped…our minds.

And as quickly as it had begun, it was over. I felt oddly different. Free. Powerful.

That old man smiled, the torchlight crawling along his wrinkled face in canyons of obscene humor. He raised one wry hand. "Farewell."

Unable to move, I stood there with the torch heavy in my hand. From somewhere, a gust of stale, rank wind rushed through the stone building. The torch flared and vanished. The old man, too, was gone. The spell broken, I whirled, seized Jan and dragged her toward the square of gray light that was the door.

We kept on running, to the circular clearing, where we dodged by the trundling black boxes, and on. I don't see how, but I think we must have run or stumbled the ten miles back to the lorry.

The next thing I remembered, we were jolting along the road back to the camp.

"How do you feel?" I said to her.

"Wonderful, McShane. I don't know why, but I feel wonderful. Was there…something…inside your mind, too?" I nodded.

After a moment, she spoke resolutely, "I think I'm through with Breen. I'm through with being bought and sold."

"So am I," I said; I didn't know why then, but I do now, and today those words are the beginning of the real horror from the House of Gulbrandsen.

I thought for a while as the lorry bounced along. An idea was forming, slowly, darkly, within my mind. Still staring ahead, I asked her, "Who gets the money if Breen dies?"

"I do," she said, and her voice whispered with death.

That night we dragged Breen, screaming with fear and the fever, from his tent. We tied him on the ground behind the lorry. He kept screaming as I shot the lever into reverse gear, and the half-track backed up slowly and ground him to a bloody mess on the rear treads.

We took what was left of his body back to Venusburg, and told the native police that he had been horribly mangled and killed in a hunting accident. There were a few of the grisly remains in a canvas bag, and that seemed to satisfy the Venusians. I remember standing there before them, opening the bag and staring down calmly at the red horror within it, and not feeling sorry.

Jan and I split up after that, but only for a while. Breen had a will, and Jan would get the money, but I couldn't see her until after the deal was carried through. So I've been waiting here in the hotel while she cleared things up.

And this morning, I learned. And now I know why the road will wind through death and cruelty, and why there is nothing that can be done…

I was sitting in a dim corner of the bar, drinking mak. Thoz was there, still polishing. Sawtell came lurching over and sat down.

"I haven't seen you since you got back," he mumbled. I didn't answer.

"How was the hunting?"

"No good."

"I heard about the accident."

"So?"

"So," he replied, gulping some of his rye and wiping the sleeve of his coat across his mouth, "you want to hear a story?" His eyes watched me, alert.

"What about?"

"Well, you see, a long time ago I was a professor of Chemistry at the University of Venus, over in Cloud City."

I couldn't help laughing. "A professor? You've been hitched to that damned bottle all your life."

HE LIFTED one shoulder. "I said this was only a story. It's about a friend of mine, another professor over there; a brilliant man. His field was the brain. My friend knew that the subconscious mind of man would control man's actions, if the conscious were not stronger, and full of conditioned responses like conforming to society, developed from birth right on down. My friend also knew that the subconscious mind was inherently bad, and that it was this deep ego that caused sudden outbreaks of cruelty, and obscenity, and evil."

"This isn't very interesting," I told him, sipping the mak. He ignored me and took another drink to make the story flow more freely.

"My friend had a wife and three children. They were in Cloud City at the time of the People's Uprising. You know about that?" Seeing me nod wearily, he went on, "His family was slaughtered by the revolutionists; butchered to death. But my friend got away. As I said, he was a brilliant man, and like most brilliant men, he bordered a bit on madness. When his family was wiped out, he ran away into the jungle and never came back. I went in to see him, once. He had built an instrument which could reshape man's brain, because he hated everyone, Terran and Venusian alike. He hated humanity." Sawtell was grinning drunkenly, and a nagging fear began to bite at me.

"This machine he housed in a building, and he is there with it today. Whenever a human being walks into the building, the machine begins to function. My friend will die someday, but his machine will never run down. It'll liberate the subconscious mind of all who approach it, making them prey to its drivings. It will wipe away all the mental blocks in conscious thinking."

"Is that place..." I choked.

"My friend's name was Dr. Erik Gulbrandsen. You know the name of the place. He hated life after Cloud City, and he made himself god there in the jungle, changing the life of anyone who happened to come there. I don't know his motivations, really, but a madman's motivations are hard for so-called sane people to understand. I only know I went to see him. Years ago, I had trouble with liquor. Bad trouble. But I got over it. Then, when I went in to see if I could help Erik, the machine fixed me. I got what I wanted, whether I really wanted it or not. So here I sit. A sopped rag full of cheap rye..."

I remembered the legends. Roger Lorden came out, hungry for power. He fought and chiseled and bribed and murdered his way up to System Imperator. Fontaine had an overwhelming desire to find beauty, and he followed it, thought it drove him out of his mind. And McShane...McShane...?

Sawtell was looking into his glass, looking sorry for himself. "I told you, McShane, your immortal soul is what you lost. I wonder what you got in return..."

"Get away from me, goddam you!" I yelled. Thoz looked over at us and went back to his bar rag.

Sawtell staggered up from the table, blubbering to himself. He reeled toward the door of the bar at the top of the steep wide steps. Teetering there, he looked back, and gestured with his glass. "Your soul, McShane, your soul..." Crying, slobbering drunk, he started out and down the stairs, vanishing beyond the door frame. I sat staring at the table, the impact of what I had learned welling up in me. Dimly, I heard a woman cry shrilly from the lobby.

Thoz went out and came in again. He glanced in my direction and said, "Sawtell stumbled down the stairs. Neck broken."

I looked at my mak glass, sick. Picking it up, I weighed it in my hand and then smashed it on the table top. My hand got cut...

SO THAT'S the way it is. You can see how it works out. Jan and I had wanted to be able to buy and sell people. Before the House of Gulbrandsen, that had been a dream that the rationalization of our conscious minds smashed before it even found words. But now the walls were ripped down. We had gone after what we wanted when we killed Breen. After all, the mind is the only thing that ever stops any of us from obeying the impulses to evil that live in every one of us.

I'm not a lucky man. If I was, I'd have been caught back there by those trundling machines. I'd be hanging on one of the big black gallows in the plaza, with no trouble. Jan is coming to the hotel in an hour. She's got free rein with Breen's money, and we're heading back for Terra, to buy and sell other people and make them dance with the fat red millions.

We've got the money-hunger, and it will drive us. We'll be together just so long, and then one of us will want it all. I'll kill her, or she'll kill me, whichever one it starts eating on first.

Erik Gulbrandsen sits in the stone building up in the jungle, keeping watch over his machine, waiting for others.

He's taken care of us. I hope he's satisfied.

THE END

If you've enjoyed this book, you will not want to miss these terrific titles...

ARMCHAIR SCI-FI & HORROR DOUBLE NOVELS, $12.95 each

D-121   **THE GENIUS BEASTS** by Frederik Pohl
       THIS WORLD IS TABOO by Murray Leinster

D-122   **THE COSMIC LOOTERS** by Edmond Hamilton
       WANDL THE INVADER by Ray Cummings

D-123   **ROBOT MEN OF BUBBLE CITY** by Rog Phillips
       DRAGON ARMY by William Morrison

D-124   **LAND BEYOND THE LENS** by S. J. Byrne
       DIPLOMAT-AT-ARMS by Keith Laumer

D-125   **VOYAGE OF THE ASTEROID, THE** by Laurence Manning
       REVOLT OF THE OUTWORLDS by Milton Lesser

D-126   **OUTLAW IN THE SKY** by Chester S. Geier
       LEGACY FROM MARS by Raymond Z. Gallun

D-127   **THE GREAT FLYING SAUCER INVASION** by Geoff St. Reynard
       THE BIG TIME by Fritz Leiber

D-128   **MIRAGE FOR PLANET X** by Stanley Mullen
       POLICE YOUR PLANET by Lester del Rey

D-129   **THE BRAIN SINNER** by Alan E. Nourse
       DEATH FROM THE SKIES by A. Hyatt Verrill

D-130   **CRY CHAOS** by Dwight V. Swain
       THE DOOR THROUGH SPACE By Marion Zimmer Bradley

ARMCHAIR SCIENCE FICTION CLASSICS, $12.95 each

C-55   **UNDER THE TRIPLE SUNS**
       by Stanton A. Coblentz (single) 1950s, Fantasy Press

C-56   **STONE FROM THE GREEN STAR**
       by Jack Williamson, Amazing 10 & 11/31, (cleared by Eli)

C-57   **ALIEN MINDS**
       by E. Everett Evans

ARMCHAIR SCI-FI & HORROR GEMS SERIES, $12.95 each

G-13   **SCIENCE FICTION GEMS, Vol. Seven**
       Jack Vance and others

G-14   **HORROR GEMS, Vol. Seven**
       Robert Bloch and others

If you've enjoyed this book, you will not want to miss these terrific titles…

ARMCHAIR SCI-FI & HORROR DOUBLE NOVELS, $12.95 each

D-131 **COSMIC KILL** by Robert Silverberg
BEYOND THE END OF SPACE by John W. Campbell

D-132 **THE DARK OTHER** by Stanley Weinbaum)
WITCH OF THE DEMON SEAS by Poul Anderson

D-133 **PLANET OF THE SMALL MEN** by Murray Leinster
MASTERS OF SPACE by E. E. "Doc" Smith & E. Everett Evans

D-134 **BEFORE THE ASTEROIDS** by Harl Vincent
SIXTH GLACIER, THE by Marius

D-135 **AFTER WORLD'S END** by Jack Williamson
THE FLOATING ROBOT by David Wright O'Brien

D-136 **NINE WORLDS WEST** by Paul W. Fairman
FRONTIERS BEYOND THE SUN by Rog Phillips

D-137 **THE COSMIC KINGS** by Edmond Hamilton
LONE STAR PLANET by H. Beam Piper & John J. McGuire

D-138 **BEYOND THE DARKNESS** by S. J. Byrne
THE FIRELESS AGE by David H. Keller, M. D.

D-139 **FLAME JEWEL OF THE ANCIENTS** by Edwin L. Graber
THE PIRATE PLANET by Charles W. Diffin

D-140 **ADDRESS: CENTAURI** by F. L. Wallace
IF THESE BE GODS by Algis Budrys

ARMCHAIR SCIENCE FICTION & HORROR CLASSICS, $12.95 each

C-58 **THE WITCHING NIGHT**
by Leslie Waller

C-59 **SEARCH THE SKY**
by Frederick Pohl and C. M. Kornbluth

C-60 **INTRIGUE ON THE UPPER LEVEL**
by Thomas Temple Hoyne

ARMCHAIR SCI-FI & HORROR GEMS SERIES, $12.95 each

G-15 **SCIENCE FICTION GEMS, Vol. Eight**
Keith Laumer and others

G-16 **HORROR GEMS, Vol. Eight**
Algernon Blackwood and others

Made in the USA
Coppell, TX
04 February 2025

45431591R00121